The Moment My Life Changed

Jill Schafer Godbersen

Jill Godbersen

ISBN: 1-4515-6797-9
ISBN-13: 9781451567977

There are things that we don't want to happen,
But have to accept,
Things we don't want to know
But have to learn,
And people we can't live without
But have to let go.

—Author Unknown

Prologue

I'm lying on my death bed. Literally, I am lying on the bed that I will die on in a matter of days or possibly weeks. It's a strange feeling, really, to just lie here and wait for death to overcome me. I'm getting impatient. Just take me now, death.

I'm ninety-one years old, and if I must be completely honest, I've been waiting fifty-one years for death to take me. I lived a wonderful first forty years of life, and then my journey took a wrong turn. I'm not scared to die. On the contrary, really. I can't wait to see what's on the other side. I've dreamt about it for decades.

"Anna, good morning. How are you feeling today? It's time to take your vitals."

The young RN has been sweet to me these past weeks. I know she pities me. She checks my blood pressure and listens to my heart.

She rubs my feet and combs my hair. I feel embarrassed when I imagine that it will be her that finds me asleep forever in this bed, with a puddle of urine and worse around my body.

Charlton Hospice House has been good to me. I've only been here for few weeks, but my doctor doesn't think I'll be here much longer. After suffering a stroke a month ago, I've never been the same. After the stroke I came down with pneumonia. When I left the hospital they took me to Hospice. I thought it would be terrible. I always assumed it would be a dark and dingy place where everyone is just waiting for you to die.

That's not been the case at all. Hospice is bright, cheerful, and not much different than a hospital or nursing home. We just all know that once you check in, you're *never* checking out.

My breathing is labored and my heart literally hurts. Every breath is an effort and I just hope to die while I'm sleeping, peacefully. I hope I don't have pain when I go. I've had nightmares about how my life will end. I've dreamt about drowning, a fiery car crash, a fall down the steps. My dreams have been littered with drama and fear regarding my death. But the truth is, I'll probably go out without much notice.

I shuffle around my wing of the Hospice House three times a day, and it's too much work. I prefer to lie in my bed and dream of better days. And of what I have to look forward to on the other side.

I've outlived my husbands, my children, my parents, and my sisters. Most of my friends have died. There really isn't anyone left that I care about greatly. Oh, a few friends, but they're in no better condition than myself. I rarely have visitors here anymore. The obligatory visits from my attorney, banker, and insurance agent really don't count.

I really look forward to bed time. Then I can dream and remember. The people that I loved are forever etched in my mind, and it won't be long now for our reunion. Will they know who I am? I will be so old now. What if they don't love me like I've loved them all these years?

My story is a sad one, and one that I am not embarrassed to tell now. It has taken me fifty-one years of heartache, humiliation, and loss to finally accept my life story. I am free now, at last. I have forgiven those that needed forgiveness. I have prayed for their souls and learned to love again. I still struggle with forgiving myself, though. *That* has been the biggest struggle of my life.

Part 1
The Façade of my Perfect Life

1

I have heard it said that we will all know precisely that one moment in life that forever changed your world. That you could look back over your life and pin point the exact moment that changed the outcome of your life so obviously and so noticeably. I didn't really believe that, to be honest.

Until it happened to me.

Until the phone call came. When the news reached my ears, my world turned upside down.

That was my defining moment. I will never forget it, unfortunately.

The news of the incident ripped my heart in two, and it left me scarred for eternity.

That one moment in time was the catalyst for change in my perfect world.

Friendship isn't a big thing—
It's a million little things.

—Author Unknown

2
Before

I remember when I thought my life was perfect. When things just couldn't possibly get any better.

I remember lying on my favorite chaise lounge chair at our back yard pool. It is a hot summer Iowa day. The temperature sign hanging on the pool house says ninety-one degrees. The sky is bright blue, with absolutely no clouds. I have sweat running down my neck and between my breasts, from my scalp down into my ears, and I can feel it puddling in my belly button.

My best friend, Tammie, is telling me about her latest shopping trip to East View Mall with her two year old. She 'misplaced' Anthony for about an hour at the mall. I almost pee my swimming suit, I am laughing so hard.

Thankfully we both have frozen strawberry margaritas in hand to chill the effects of the unspoken reality of what could have happened. A Clinique Cosmetic Specialist finally found

Anthony hiding in her storage cabinet, behind the makeup and moisturizers.

I look over my sunglasses to our kids in the pool. Our kids are the best of friends, and I don't know what I would do without Tammie in my life.

Splash! Tammie and I get water sprayed on us from the kids' cannon balls. It actually feels good to get a little relief from this heat, but we give our obligatory squeals pretending not to like it to please the kids.

I met Tammie when Paul and I moved to Gannon, Iowa. We didn't know a soul in this small community, and Tammie and I gravitated towards one another immediately. I met her in the doctor's office, of all places. My first pregnancy ended in a miscarriage at fourteen weeks, and I was devastated. Paul and I were so ready to have a baby.

I was sitting in Dr. Foster's waiting room, impatiently waiting to talk to him about why I miscarried. A pretty young woman with long dark hair comes in and sits next to me. She didn't look so chipper either. We're both perusing through Parents magazines when she starts to small talk with me. She ends up telling me that she just miscarried the day before, on September twenty-nine. I surprise myself and confide that I miscarried yesterday as well. From that day forward it was as though we were meant to share our lives together.

And here we are, ten years later. Still the best of friends, sharing the ups and downs of our lives together. I am closer to Tammie than I am to my own sisters right now. I tell her everything. From my worst thoughts about my husband to my dreams of finishing that novel I began a year ago. Tammie's three kids, Gretchen, who is eight, Carli who is five, and baby Anthony at two, are part of our extended family. We share holidays with them and celebrate life's achievements together.

As I watch our kids play together, I am just so very content. My oldest, Connor, now eight, has literally grown up with Gretchen from the day he was born. Connor and Gretchen couldn't be more night and day if we tried to make them so. Gretchen is beautiful like her mother. Thick, dark, hair and dark, brown eyes. Beautiful olive skin that gets so tan in these Iowa summers. She is cute as can be in her little orange and pink striped bikini.

Connor, on the other hand, is her exact opposite. His white hair gets even whiter in the summer, if that's possible. His blue eyes and sun burnt nose shine in the afternoon sun. They head off to second grade together this fall, where I'm hoping they'll be in the same class. They are both skinny at age eight and so happy. I wonder if some day they will be boyfriend and girlfriend. Tammie and I secretly wish for that, but we'll have to see. For now they are best friends. They push each other off the diving board, giggling as they come up for air.

My middle child, Ryan, at age six, will be in first grade this fall. Ryan and Carli are best buds as well, and they are small replicas of their older siblings. Ryan could pass for Connor's twin and Carli is just a little mini Gretchen. The two middle children are floating together on a raft in the middle of the pool, playing with their Star Wars action figures on top of the raft.

My youngest, five year old Cassy, is playing by herself on the pool steps, sitting in just far enough to be wet up to her chest. She is talking to herself, playing with two dolls. You can tell she is from the Dawson family. She has her brothers' white hair and blue eyes.

So, as our kids cavort around in the pool, Tammie and I flip over onto our stomachs to get an even tan. She finishes her story about the mall incident, and makes me promise not to tell her husband, Jack. He would be furious if he knew, and I know she is right. I run inside to make one more pitcher of margaritas for the afternoon. I don't want this day to end. There will be many more of these this summer. I love my life. God has blessed me with many riches.

3

Before

My fortieth birthday is in a couple of weeks. I told Paul I didn't want jewelry, didn't want flowers, didn't want any more sexy negligees. All I really wanted was a weekend with him. Without the kids. Two blissful days with just him. We spend so much time as a family. We have put our family first for eight years now.

I miss him. I miss being with just Paul. We're never alone. I wouldn't trade my kids for anything, but their presence has definitely changed our relationship.

Paul says he will see what he can do. He wants to surprise me. Cool—I love his surprises. I never know quite what to expect with him.

I've been walking on cloud nine for a month. Just anticipating this time with my husband. Not necessarily a big romantic weekend or anything, but just a weekend. I daydream about what we will do. I see us sleeping in like we used to before we had kids. Casually getting up after a morning love fest and making coffee, reading the newspaper, making eggs, bacon and toast. Watching a little TV.

Maybe we'll sneak out to the golf course and play a quick nine holes, maybe even eighteen. We'll have a beer and mini tacos at the club. We'll go home, snuggle on the couch, and then go out for a casual dinner at Nick's Pub, our local eatery. Nothing major, not an expensive weekend. Just simple, easy, and comfortable. What we used to do most weekends before kids.

I think that maybe I should feel guilty for dreaming about a weekend without my kids, but I don't. My kids are my life, and I wouldn't know what to do without them. But doesn't everyone deserve a little time off every now and then? It's not as though I want to ship them away for a year. Just two days. I've spent the past eight years having my days revolve around the school's schedule, dance classes, guitar lessons, church night, soccer games, ball practices, piano lessons, tae kwon do, etc. I'm so damn excited to have Paul all to myself for two days of adult bliss!

It's Friday, March eighth today. My birthday isn't for sixteen more days, on March twenty-fourth. I'm still praying that Paul can pull my request off. I'm starting to worry that maybe it won't happen.

I hear the dog barking, which means someone has just pulled into our driveway. I look out the dining room window, and see my parents coming to the door. What are they doing here?

They live two hours away, in Mason, and they always call before they show up. I throw open the door and my parents are yelling, "Surprise! Happy early birthday!" After hugs and kisses, I figure it out. Paul has pulled it off.

"We're taking the kids to our house for the weekend," Mom explains. Paul did it! Bless his heart. I'm so excited. "He called a few weeks ago and wanted to grant you your 40th birthday wish. So here we are!"

"I'll run up and get the kids' suitcases packed. The bus will be here in half an hour with the kids. They will be so tickled to go with you guys. Is this a surprise for them too?" I ask.

"The kids know nothing. Paul didn't trust them to keep it a secret from you," Dad says. I'm throwing clothes and pajamas and tooth brushes and socks and underwear into their suitcases.

"This is so great," I yell down to my parents. "I really hope you don't mind doing this."

"We had nothing planned for this weekend anyway, so you know we'd love nothing better than to have our three angels for two whole days," Dad replies.

"Your father wants to take the kids to the new glow-in-the-dark mini-golf course at the mall," Mom adds. "I'm sure we'll go to the park if it's warm enough outside. We'll have a great time. Don't you worry at all."

"You're the best, Mom. I don't know how to thank you both. Please make the kids mind, and don't hesitate to call if they're being naughty. I think I hear the bus."

"Grandma! Grandpa! What are you doing here?" yells Cassy as she runs into my Mom's arms. "How long are you staying here?"

"Actually, you three get to come with us to Mason for the weekend. How about that?" says Dad.

"Awesome. Can we bring our video games?" asks Ryan.

"Of course you can. I've already packed your bags and they're in Grandma and Grandpa's car already. Take anything else you want," I offer.

"Mom, are you coming with us?" Cassy wonders.

"No. This is your father's birthday present to me. A weekend alone with him. So you three kids get to have a special time with your Grandma and Grandpa."

"Cool!" expresses Connor, already out the door and heading to my parents' car.

Everything is happening so quickly. I really didn't think it would be *this* weekend. But I'll take it. Paul got me good. Could I be any luckier?

After hugs and kisses, the kids buckle up in their booster seats, I tell Mom and Dad a few final notes about bed time that I know won't get honored anyway. The kids are so excited to go. I blow kisses as the car heads out of the driveway.

Aaahhhhh. Alone. So this is how it feels. My shoulders already begin to soften. It is Friday at four o'clock, and I have the whole weekend ahead of me. Just my darling husband and me. I hear my cell phone ringing as I open the door to the house.

"Are you alone yet?" asks Paul when I pick up the phone.

"Have I mentioned lately that I love you?" I say.

"I thought you might be surprised. I called your parents weeks ago and begged them to keep this a secret. I knew it would be tough for your Mom not to spill it to you."

"I was hoping you could pull it off, you amazing, handsome, sexy man, who is all mine. Now I get you all to myself for two and a half days. Hhmm, wonder what we'll find to do?" I tease.

"I'm all yours for the weekend. I'll be home by 6:00, and I thought I'd take you out for dinner tonight. Nothing fancy, just you and me at Nick's Pub. What do you say?"

"I say, 'now I remember why I married you.' You're the best. I'll be ready. And say..."

"Yes?" Paul asks.

"I love you. You spoil me. I'm not sure I deserve you. But I love you just the same."

"I know. Happy birthday, sweetheart. I love you too. See you tonight."

I hop in the shower, shave my legs, as the growth is actually furry. Paul deserves smooth legs tonight after all his work to make me so happy. I put on a new outfit, blue jeans and a tight black top. Simple gold jewelry, all from Paul over the years. I blow my hair dry, add a little make up and open my favorite bottle of wine. I'll just have one glass before Paul gets home. If I die now, I die content, I think.

4
Before

I hear Paul come home. He comes into the living room and plops down beside me on the loveseat with the wine glass I left for him on the counter.

"Cheers to my favorite wife," he toasts as he comes over and kisses me deeply on the lips. This is going to be one good weekend. I already have naughty thoughts racing through my naughty mind.

"Happy?" he asks, settling in next to me. He grabs my hand and caresses the top of it.

"Honestly, I don't think I could be any happier right now. This may sound gushy, but I am *so* in love with you. Thank you for doing this for me. It's all I truly wanted. Just to have one weekend alone with you. No kids. No schedule. Just you and me. Is it awful to wish for that?"

"No. And I'm thankful for a weekend together too, honey. It may seem selfish, but we need this. I miss you too. The kids will have a great time with your parents, and they'll be back before you know it. Now quit worrying about them and your conscience. You're not neglecting them. You're a great mom, and you know it. Now have one more glass of wine. I want to get you good and drunk so I can take advantage of you tonight, my dear."

God, I love this man. Paul has gotten more good looking with age. His jaw line has hardened, and his few wrinkles make him look wise. His body has softened just slightly, but he is as handsome as he was twenty years ago.

We go out to Nick's Pub, and to my surprise again, Paul has called my best girl friends and their husbands to meet us there. We're at a table of twelve in the back, laughing, joking, toasting and eating. I sneak a look across the table at Paul, and he winks at me. His signal for, "Wait 'til later, baby."

Tammie raps her knife against her wine glass and stands up.

"I'd like to embarrass Anna for just one moment."

She clears her throat, and I know she is choking up. We have been through a lot together, she and I. We know each other's secrets, some even our husbands don't know about. I love her like my sister.

"I'd like to make a toast to Anna. To my friend and confidant. We all love you, respect you, and wish for you the best fortieth birthday. Now everyone continue drinking before I cry."

I get out of my seat and go give Tammie a hug.

"You know I love you, too." I'm beginning to feel drunk. My slight buzz has turned into a bigger buzz, I realize as I attempt to get out of my chair.

I'm floating on life right now. I love my husband, I have great friends, and I really just can't stop smiling for the life of me. I haven't eaten much off my plate. The wine tastes just fine, thank you.

We spend two more hours at Nick's, eating, drinking, and reminiscing. My girlfriends give me naughty over-the-hill gifts. I laugh so hard I tinkle just a bit in my panties. At this point I realize I should stop drinking. It's eleven o' clock and Paul asks me if I am ready to go home.

"Yes, let's get out of here. I want you all to myself for the rest of the night now," I tell him.

We say our good byes and I thank everyone for coming. Again, I am reminded that my husband orchestrated this dinner...all by himself! How many husbands could or would do that for their wives? I watch him give Tammie a hug good bye and shake her husband, Jack's, hand. We four go way back. I can't remember my life in Gannon without them in it. We miscarried together, had babies together, sent our kids off to school together. Our lives blur into one.

On the car ride home, I begin to feel tired.

"Too much to drink, old lady?" Paul asks.

"Way too much for this old lady. But it was worth every drop. Thank you for tonight. You are the best," I tell him, feeling my belly warm with wine.

As we walk into the house, it is an odd feeling to hear nothing. No kids yelling "Mom" or backpacks slapping the counter. No fighting, or cupboard doors slamming. No refrigerator door opening and closing. Nothing. Just silence.

I feel a warm body around me. Paul comes up from behind me and wraps both arms around me, kissing the back of my neck. He knows this always gets me warmed up. I sigh, sinking into his strong arms. He smells so good. His skin is hot. He pulls me upstairs. Past the kids' bedrooms, stepping over the toys left in the hallway.

We stumble onto our bed, entwined as two people can be. When was the last time I really kissed this man, I think. It's been too long. His lips are heavenly. He brushes his lips against my neck and I shudder. We help each other undress, and I only glance at the bedroom door once, and remember that the kids are gone. Oh, for the love of God. What this man can do to me.

5

Before

When Paul and I moved to Gannon we rented a small, red brick, ranch style house on Sixth Street for a few years. It wasn't the house of our dreams, but there wasn't anything available at that time that we fell in love with. After two years in Gannon, Paul announced to me that he could spend the rest of his life here. I hadn't really even thought that far ahead, to be honest.

But when Paul Dawson gets something in his head, there is no stopping him. He wanted to make our life here, and he was ready to build our dream home in Gannon. I wasn't thrilled about the thought of all the work that building a home would require. But once Paul talked to a contractor and got the ball rolling, the project took on a life of its own. We had just had Connor, and we decided not to use birth control after his birth. We were ready to get our family going. We needed a bigger home to accommodate all of our kids, Paul reminded me.

We found a few acres of land at the edge of town that appeared to offer privacy and yet was still close to town. After many home tours and leafing through floor plan books, Paul and I found a plan that we thought our family would grow into. We built a two-story white brick, with a walk out basement. We left plenty of room in the back yard for an eventual pool.

So the house began going up, and Paul was at the site every day to talk with the contractors and make sure things were going smoothly. I found out I was expecting baby number two during the construction, and Paul was so thrilled. We would be filling up this big house sooner than expected.

The day finally came for the big move. After eighteen long months it was completed, thank God. I was more excited than I thought I would be. With two kids at home, the small space of our rental had been closing in on me. The new home was huge. I was overwhelmed with all of the space.

I soon found out after we moved that once again, I was pregnant with baby number three. I was getting very tired, physically and emotionally. Paul was so thrilled! He wanted six kids, he kept telling me. I thought he was crazy, and that perhaps I should leave him home with two small children for a weekend just so he could see what my life was like on a daily basis. But I know he just loved our family and wanted it to keep growing.

Paul was living his dream, really. I envied him some days. He had a banking career that he thrived at, that he was successful at, and he could see as his future. He knew where he was going and what he wanted. I rarely had a vision past a few months. But I knew I was lucky. I had a wonderful husband, two beautiful kids and one on the way, and good friends around me.

6

The Moment

I hear a noise. I think it is Paul's alarm and I hit him on his back, my signal for "Turn your alarm off, please." Paul doesn't move, and I realize it is not his alarm. Rather, the phone keeps ringing and ringing. Oh, my head is not feeling well. I haven't had this much to drink in awhile. I have no idea why the answering machine hasn't picked up yet.

I roll over and look at my alarm clock. 3:12 a.m. The phone won't stop ringing. I sit up, and grab the phone. I am fuzzy, but I push the "talk" button.

"Hello. Dawsons," I struggle out.

"Hello. May I please speak with Mr. or Mrs. Dawson."

"This is Anna Dawson. Who is this?"

"Mrs. Dawson, this is the Iowa State Patrol. I apologize for waking you, Maam, but there's been an accident."

My fog clears quickly at this.

"An accident? What kind of accident?" I look over at Paul and he is snoring loudly on his side of the bed, oblivious to this phone call. I kick at his back, but get no movement from him.

"I'm sorry to tell you that there has been an automobile accident with an Iowa vehicle license number AKF842. The vehicle is a 2008 blue Chevy Tahoe."

My brain is spinning at this point. I don't really know what this man is trying to tell me. Someone was in an accident? Why is he calling me? My parents have a blue Tahoe but I have no idea what their license plate number is.

"Maam, are you there? Maam?"

"Yes, I'm here. I'm sorry, I'm just very confused. It's 3:00 a.m. and you are frightening me. What are you trying to tell me?"

"I do apologize for the late night call, Mrs. Dawson. But we have reason to believe that your children were involved in this automobile accident. We need you to report to Mercy Hospital in Mason, Iowa, as soon as possible, Mrs. Dawson."

My children? Has this man lost his mind? My children are in Mason with my parents. Oh my God. It hits me hard and I yell, "Paul! Wake up, Paul!" He sits up groggily and says, "What?"

I'm yelling into the phone now. "Please just tell me where my children are and we'll be there as soon as possible. Are they all right? Was anyone hurt?"

"Mrs. Dawson, I don't have any answers for you right now. I was instructed to inform you that you need to come to Mercy Hospital in Mason as soon as you can. Your children and parents were involved in an automobile accident at approximately 9:00 p.m. last night and they are all being treated at Mercy Hospital in Mason."

The State Trooper gives me his phone number and the number for Mercy. I turn on the lights, scribble down the phone numbers, and feel myself move in slow motion. I put the phone back in its dock, and I look at Paul. He is sitting up in bed, and doesn't have a clue as to what just happened.

"Who in the hell called at 3:00 a.m.? It better be good. Did Tammie have a fight with Jack again? She has got to learn not to call here at all hours of the night, Anna."

I must be in shock. I know what I have to tell Paul, but I don't want to. I just want to curl up next to him in our warm bed and go back to sleep. I want to celebrate my birthday with my husband. My hangover has already begun. My head is pounding, my mouth is dry, and I feel as though I could vomit at any moment.

"Paul, that was the Iowa State Patrol. Mom and Dad and the kids were in a car accident and…"

"What the hell? Where?"

"I'm not sure," I say. "But we need to get to Mercy Hospital in Mason as soon as we can."

Paul is out of bed before I am. He is running, pulling on clothes and heading into the bathroom. I am stuck on the bed. My body feels so heavy. I really can't breathe at the moment. My chest feels like it has bricks on it.

"Anna, let's go! Come on! Why are you just sitting there? We need to get moving fast! It's a two hour drive to Mason."

I feel myself start to cry. I feel the tears fall down my cheeks. I am shaking. No one in my family has ever been in a car accident. I don't remember any kind of accident, ever. This doesn't happen to my family. I read about these things in the paper, but they don't happen to me.

Paul comes right up to me and shakes me by the shoulders. "Anna, get dressed! What is wrong with you? We need to go NOW!"

He is already running out of the bedroom. I slowly get up and go into the bathroom. I look in the mirror and see myself. My makeup is smeared all over my face. My black mascara is running down my cheeks. My hair is tousled. I go to the bathroom and then pull on my favorite weekend sweats. I can hear Paul down in the kitchen. He's grabbing some Ibuprofen from the cupboard and a Diet Coke out of the frig. I hear his keys jingling.

I hope I'm dreaming. Paul yells at me again to hurry up. It hits me that this is not a dream. I am still shaking as I head downstairs. We get into his Volvo and I look at Paul. His face is flushed. His eyes are wide.

"Tell me everything the State Patrol told you on the phone," he says.

"They just said the kids and mom and dad were involved in a car accident at 9:00 p.m. last night and that they were all at Mercy Hospital in Mason. They said to get to the hospital as fast as we could. That's all I remember."

"Is everyone ok? Did he say what happened?"

"Paul, I've told you everything already! The man didn't give me much information. I was out of it when I answered the phone. He said he didn't know much, anyway. Oh God, Paul. I'm so scared."

I'm really crying now. I just can't believe this is happening. How in the hell did this happen? I just saw my parents and kids eleven hours ago, and everyone was fine. My parents have taken our kids with them to their home many times over the years. My parents are only in their mid-60's, and they both still drive fine. I need to know what happened.

There is no one on the road at this time of night, and I notice that Paul is driving really, really fast.

"Please slow down, honey. We don't need to get in an accident, too."

"Well, dammit, Anna, we need to get to Mercy fast. We have no idea what condition our kids are in. They've been in an accident and we've been out partying. Just great. Why don't you call that number for the hospital that the State Trooper gave you. See if the hospital can tell us anything."

I call the number for the hospital. I tell them what I know and ask if they know the condition of our kids. The nurse at admitting tells me that she can only verify that they were admitted. She can't tell me their condition because she does not have that information. I thank her and hang up. She says they will give us more information when we get to the hospital.

"The kids are at the hospital, Paul. That's all they will tell us."

"Shit. Wasn't your dad looking? He was probably distracted by one of the kids. I told you his driving was getting poor, Anna. And what in the hell were they doing out driving around at 9:00 at night? They should have had the kids home getting ready for bed."

"Quit blaming my parents! We have no idea what happened. Or how it happened. Just drive safely and we'll be at the hospital soon." I want to be mad at Paul, but really I'm terrified to admit that I'm feeling a horrible amount of guilt myself. I'm beginning to freak out.

"Oh Paul, what if one of the kids is really hurt? I'd never stop blaming myself. This is all my fault. I insisted that the kids go away for the weekend, and now look at what happened."

I don't know how Paul can understand what I'm saying because I'm crying so hard while I'm trying to talk. I begin to gag. I roll down my window and vomit outside in the wind. Some of it sprays back at my face. I'm freezing, I'm shaking, and my head still hurts really badly.

I roll the window back up and wipe off my face with my shirt sleeve. The odor makes me gag again. How can this be happening? I open the glove compartment and take out two of Paul's Ibuprofen.

"Anna, this is no one's fault. It happened. We don't even know that anyone is hurt. Just relax. You're making yourself sick." No shit, Paul. Ya think?

I try to call my sisters, Courtney and Abby, at their homes, but when I get their recorded messages, I remember that they are both gone for the weekend. I call them on their cell phones and leave messages to call me as soon as they can.

Paul is always the calm one. It's what makes him good in business. I am too emotional. I think with my heart. And where my kids are concerned, well, I'm a mom. First and foremost, my number one job in life is to make sure that my kids are safe. I failed. How will they ever forgive me? How will I ever forgive myself?

I stare blankly ahead at the road for the two hour drive. Paul and I barely speak. Music is on the radio, but I don't really hear it. It is dark and cold out. How did the kids feel when they were in the accident? Scared to death, I'm certain. It's March in Iowa, and it's no more than thirty degrees out. What have I done to my family?

7

Before

I admit it. My life is pretty darn near perfect. I hate to say it out loud, for fear of jinxing it, but it's true. I have led a blessed life to date. My sisters want to hate me for it, but they can't. They're my sisters. They're supposed to love me no matter what.

I have everything I've ever dreamed of. A husband who is wonderful. Really, he is. Paul is great. He adores me, and I adore him. Our marriage is great. We have three awesome kids. I truly couldn't be happier at this moment. My whole life has been pretty easy. There are days when I wonder why. Why has God blessed me so? I try to be a good person and do the right thing. But I'm certainly not perfect. I make mistakes and I have issues. But nothing major, or so I think. I do wonder some days when the ceiling will come crashing down. My whole life can't just be one big happy occasion, can it?

My mother thinks it's just my attitude. I've always been optimistic, positive. I see the bright side of every situation. My cup is half full. I just don't know any other way to live, I guess. But what if my life really isn't that wonderful? Maybe I just think it is. Either way, I'm content and happy and thankful, so I'll take it.

***

I truly never thought I would end up living in a small town in Iowa. I spent the first eighteen years of my life in a small, rural Iowa town, always dreaming of big city life after college. Never say never, I guess. Now I wouldn't trade my simple life for the flashy lights of the big city, ever. I am completely content living in Gannon, Iowa, population 10,000. We are two hours away from the biggest town in Iowa, Des Moines. So if we want Broadway shows or good shopping, we just make a weekend out of it.

I like knowing my kids' friends and their parents. I like it that I will hear what my kids are doing, both good and bad, downtown at the coffee shop. Gannon is small enough that it is a community of friends, and yet big enough that it isn't a total fish bowl experience.

Gannon sits in the flat, rural north central area of Iowa. You drive north out of Des Moines and slowly the towns fade away to corn fields and bean fields. You pass through many small towns, all littered with their respective churches, schools, main streets, and a smattering of homes.

Gannon has been fortunate. There has been industry here to keep the town alive. A few family businesses have survived for generations, keeping the town stocked in jobs and prosperity. With a business degree from Iowa State University, there are days when I yearn to use my knowledge and experience here. As a stay at home mom, I can feel like I'm just the maid and chef some days.

But since Paul has done well in banking here in Gannon, thankfully I haven't had to work, yet anyway. Our plan is that Paul and I will raise Connor, Ryan, and Cassy here in Gannon through their high school years. After that I wouldn't mind traveling during the cold Iowa winter months. But Gannon will always be our home. We have made our friends here and we don't plan on leaving.

8
After

We approach Mason and the city lights light up the night sky. It is 5:30 a.m. and there still isn't much movement around outside. Only a few other straggler cars are out. We drive right to Mercy Hospital. Paul drives into the parking garage and gets a good spot on level two. We both rush out of the car, run towards the garage staircase, and continue racing down the steps. The lights inside the hospital shine brightly this early in the morning. I wonder what Dad will say about the accident. I just pray that everyone is fine and that we can take them all home with us right now.

I'm envisioning some bruises, scratches, band aids, bumps. Possibly a broken arm. The kids always buckle up, so I know nothing terrible could have happened. Paul is talking with the lady at the Admitting Desk, and she is typing on her computer. I don't hear what they are saying, but I see their mouths moving. I look around at the inside of the hospital. It is decorated in purple and green coordinates. It looks as though it has been updated recently.

"Let's go, Anna," Paul says as he heads for the double doors just ahead of us. I follow him.

"A doctor is waiting for us at the 4th floor Waiting Room. He wants to talk to us before we can see any of the kids, or your parents," Paul explains.

The elevator takes forever on a night when no one else appears to be around. What in the hell is taking so long? Finally we hear a ding, and the doors open. Paul and I walk in together and he pushes number four on the wall. We go up ever so slowly three floors. When the doors open, a few nurses look up from their desks at the nurse's station. They all look away quickly. I'm sure they are all very busy, with three young children and two older people as patients this evening.

To our right is a large sign over a door, "4th Floor Waiting Room." I see two doctors inside, sitting on chairs, holding their heads. They both look so very tired. I'm guessing they are my heroes. Here are the doctors I need to hug and thank for taking care of my babies. For making everything all better.

The big doctor with glasses and black hair sees Paul and I approaching through the window in the door. He says something to the other doctor, and they both stand up. The look they exchange between one another makes me freeze on the spot. They are not smiling. They look horribly sad. I'm sure we have the wrong doctors.

"Mr. and Mrs. Dawson?" asks the big doctor with glasses, as Paul and I walk through the door. "Hello, I'm Dr. Forson, and this is Dr. Andreesen. Won't you please have a seat?" He gestures to the chairs across from him.

"We'd really just like to go see our kids as soon as possible, Doctor. We've driven two hours to get here and we're very shaken up by this accident. Can you tell us what happened? How are our kids?" I ask.

That look is exchanged once again between Dr. Forson and Dr. Andreesen. I'm shaking openly now. My mouth has gone dry and I feel myself needing to gag again. Paul and I both sit down slowly into chairs, and he grabs my hand and squeezes it too tightly.

"Mr. and Mrs. Dawson, your three children and your parents were involved in an automobile accident at approximately 9:00 p.m. last evening just three miles outside of Mason on county road M59. From what the Iowa State Patrol gathers, the car your family was in hit a semi truck head-on at the crest of a hill. The accident was severe, and all passengers were taken by ambulance to Mercy at approximately 9:15 p.m."

I am in a zone. I have been in this zone before. My vision is impaired, my hearing is gone, and I feel numb. I couldn't stand up right now if I had to. Everything around me has gone colorless. The only other times I remember being in this zone were when I gave birth to Connor and just before I passed out at church when I was pregnant with Ryan.

During my delivery of Connor I lost too much blood and almost lost Connor. When I was pregnant with Ryan I got light headed at church one morning and passed out. I hit the floor hard, and knocked out my two front teeth. I only know that being in the zone is not good. Nothing positive happens to me when I am in the zone.

"We want to give you all the information we know before you can see your family, okay Mr. and Mrs. Dawson?" Dr. Andreesen asks. "We want you to understand what happened last night, so that you don't have so many questions later. It's important that you listen carefully now so you fully understand the situation."

Paul sinks back in his chair and sighs deeply. He is obviously frustrated and wants this conversation to speed up. I want to run out of this room right now. I want to turn the clock back to yesterday and forget that I ever asked for my kids to be gone for a weekend. How could I have ever thought that having them out of my house for a weekend would be a good thing? All I want to do at this moment and forever more is hold them tight and never let them out of my sight again.

Dr. Forson sighs deeply and begins again. "Witnesses at the accident scene called 911 immediately. One witness saw the accident occur directly in front of him. The response time was amazing. Almost a record. An ambulance was on site within seven minutes of the accident, and left the scene eight minutes later. We want to highlight that effort by the emergency personnel. They did an outstanding job."

Dr. Forson stops and wipes the sweat from his forehead. He is nervous and wringing his hands. He looks too old for this to be his first time talking to parents after an accident, I think. He must have had a long day.

"When your family was brought here to Mercy Hospital we had a full staff ready to handle the situation. Every nurse and doctor available did exactly what they were trained to do."

Paul is squeezing my hand too tight. I try to pull it away, and I look at him. There are tears running down his cheeks. He is as white as a ghost. I have never seen him like this before. He is always the strong one. *Get a grip Paul*, I think. The doctors are almost finished with their nice little story here, and then we can go see our kids. Be patient. I wonder if the kids are all in the same room, or if they separated them? I hope they're together. That will make it easier for Paul and I to see everyone at once.

"Your father, who was driving, Mrs. Dawson, suffered severe internal damages. There was nothing we could do to save him. I'm so sorry."

"What? What are you saying? That my father *died*?" I explode.

I look from Doctor Forson to Doctor Andreesen to Paul. Paul's head is hung low. So low that I cannot see his eyes. Both doctors are just staring at us.

"Yes, we're so very sorry to tell you that your father did die earlier this morning. The damage to his heart was irreversible," explains Dr. Forson.

My heart is racing too fast. My stomach is in a knot. I'm just stunned. I don't know what to say. Dad died? How can this be?

"What about my Mom and our kids?" I yell, as I stand up and stare pointedly at the doctors. "Please just hurry up and tell us how everyone is, dammit!" I'm upset now. Dad is dead and these doctors are so damn slow with their story. Get to the point. We are wasting precious time. Paul and I could be hugging our kids right now.

Dr. Forson continues, "Your mother had a chance, Mrs. Dawson, but her internal injuries caught up to her as well. She just didn't make it, either. I'm so very, very sorry."

Mom *and* Dad both died? You have got to be kidding me. I just gave them both hugs fourteen hours ago. I'm not crying. I'm just staring straight ahead, looking through the doctors. Paul is still silent and weeping in his hands. This is all so surreal, I think. My perfect life. My blessed existence. This has got to be a dream.

"There's more, Mr. and Mrs. Dawson. And there's no easy way to tell you any of this. May we just say that it appeared that you had a wonderful family," says Dr. Forson.

Had? I *had* a wonderful family? No, excuse me. I *have* a wonderful family. And don't even think for one second that that is going to change. My family is my life. Without my family I have no life. I have no reason to live. So please don't even bother suggesting to me that I *had* a wonderful family.

I am too stunned to speak at first. Paul is openly sobbing, so he is of no help to me.

"What exactly is it that you are trying to tell us, doctors?" I ask evenly, looking them both directly in the eyes, as my wimp of a husband continues to cry beside me.

"Your three children were buckled in the back seat of the vehicle as they were supposed to be. But unfortunately, the sudden impact of the head-on crash caused the vehicle to be crushed. Emergency personnel had to use the jaws of life to retrieve all passengers from the vehicle. In accidents such as these, many times the trauma to the chest and head is just too great. Your children didn't suffer, Mr. and Mrs. Dawson. They were gone before their arrival at the hospital."

Doctors Forson and Andreesen both sigh and stand up. I stare at them and feel my heart quicken. My head is throbbing, and I can't comprehend this horrific news. I feel sick and overwhelmed by the news.

"We will leave you two alone for a little while to let all of this sink in. If we can answer any more of your questions, we will be happy to. We will need someone to identify the bodies. It does not have to be you. An Iowa State Patrol Officer can also help in answering any questions you may have about the accident. The crash was a high impact collision, and much trauma was done to their bodies. We also have a grief counselor available per your request. She will arrive in about half an hour. Again, please accept our condolences for your losses. We truly wish that things would have turned out differently."

The doctors attempt to take our hands, but neither Paul nor I make an effort to raise a finger in their direction. Dr. Forson gives a reserved squeeze to my shoulder as he heads out the door.

I know I am in shock. I heard what the doctors just told us. That every one of our babies is dead. That my parents are dead. They all just died in a terrible car accident. I just don't believe them. Perhaps they have the wrong bodies? How do they know it's not a case of mistaken identity?

"Anna, they're gone," Paul mutters as he grabs onto me, giving me a big bear hug.

They're gone? I just don't understand it. Why would God allow such a horrible thing to happen to innocent people? Paul sobs into my shoulder. I caress his neck and hair. How strange for him to be the one that is losing it. He is our strong one. I am the emotional wreck. But apparently I have no emotions. I just learned that my children and parents have all died, and I am just staring straight ahead.

My cell phone rings, and I grab my phone out of my coat pocket. I see that it is Courtney calling. I try to gather myself together and prepare myself for this conversation.

Courtney does not take the news well, as expected. She is hysterical, and I can't understand what she is saying to me. She is in Cancun on vacation, and she is insisting that she will be on the first flight out of there today.

I try calling Abby again on her cell phone. I know she is in Minneapolis at a dance competition with her daughter Brooke. I get a hold of Abby this time, and I am crying before she even answers the phone. I tell her the terrible news, and she can't believe it either. The whole thing is so unexpected, and Abby is sobbing just like I am now. Abby was always closest to Mom, and I know this is going to be very hard on her.

I take a deep breath. I know what we need to do. "I need to see my babies, Paul. Let's go ask the doctors to take us to them. Maybe it's all been a horrible mistake."

Paul looks like a ghost. His face is pasty white, and he has dark circles under his eyes. I can see the scar above his right eyebrow from when he fell off the swings when he was a kid.

"I'm not sure you want to do that, Anna. I don't think we want to remember our children this way."

"Paul, don't you get it? It might not be them! It might be a horrible mix up, and our kids and my parents are home in bed sleeping at this moment."

I pull out my cell phone and hit the speed dial for my parents' house. After four rings, their message comes on. I say, "Hi Mom and Dad. It's me, Anna. Just calling to check on the kids. I know it's early. Just hope everything is all right. Call me when you all wake up."

Paul stares at me with a bewildered look on his face. "Anna, they're gone. They won't be calling you back. You have got to accept this. *Right now.* You cannot continue to deny what happened."

I'm shaking again. God, I hate it when I do that. It destroys the strong image I so badly want to project.

"I just want to see our kids, Paul. If it's them, then we'll know the truth. If not, then we'll know this has all been a bad mistake." I stand up, attempt to wipe out the wrinkles on my shirt, and feel my legs wobble as I walk.

Paul and I approach the nurse's station hand in hand. We get a look of pity from the nurse seated at the desk. Her name tag reads Margaret.

"Can I help you?" she so pleasantly asks.

I feel myself wanting to be a bitch so badly. "We're Mr. and Mrs. Dawson. The parents of Connor, Ryan, and Cassy Dawson. They were brought in here earlier. We would like to see them, please," I politely say.

Nurse Margaret looks at us sadly, "I'll need to get Dr. Forson's permission to grant that request. One moment, please." Paul can't quit wiping at his eyes.

Margaret turns away from us, picks up the phone, and we hear her mumbling into the phone. She shakes her head up and down, and I hear her say, "I understand. But that is what they are requesting."

She puts the phone down, and turns back towards us. "Dr. Forson will meet you at the elevator and take you down to the morgue. Although he does not recommend this."

"It's all right, Margaret," I say. "This whole mess will be cleared up in just a few minutes. There has been a big misunderstanding." Margaret glances at Paul for a moment and turns away.

Dr. Forson comes strolling down the hall towards us. His hands are in his pockets, and he looks very, very tired. Paul is wiping his eyes, pulling his hands through his hair. I am clenching my favorite brown purse really, really tightly by the handles.

But what *if* the people brought into the hospital aren't who they think they are? What if these three children and two adults aren't my babies and my parents? It is possible.

Paul and I follow Dr. Forson into the elevator and we go down to the basement. When the elevator door opens, all I can see is a white, sterile hallway. We continue to follow Dr. Forson in silence. Paul grabs onto my arm. No one speaks. The atmosphere is very tense and I'm ready to explode with emotion and anger.

Dr. Forson takes a clipboard off a wall rack and glances at it briefly. "We will get the bodies out and come get you in a few minutes when we're ready. Please wait here in the hall." We sit down on cold, hard, steel chairs to wait.

In what seems like only a few seconds later, Dr. Forson opens the door nearby and gestures us into the room. There are five slabs pulled out of what looks like giant refrigerator doors. Each slab has a body lying on it with a white sheet covering the body.

I catch my breath, and my hand goes up to my mouth. My God, please tell me these are not my babies. They cannot be. I know my babies are with my parents right at this moment. Probably sleeping on their living room floor. Their phone is probably not working, that's why they aren't answering my calls. I know there is a logical explanation for this misunderstanding.

"Are you ready?" I hear Dr. Forson say, although his voice sounds muffled to me. Paul and I both slowly nod our heads "yes." We are standing closest to one of the larger bodies. Dr. Forson pulls down the white sheet over the body, and I see brown hair. The skin has a bluish tint to it. There is much bruising to the face and she has cuts all over her neck and face, but I can tell instantly that it is my mother. I feel dizzy, and I sense that I am falling.

I open my eyes and I am lying on the floor, looking up at Paul. The floor is hard and cold beneath me. The side of my head hurts.

"Are you ok, Anna?" Paul asks. "You fainted when you saw your mom. It is your mom, honey." He is caressing my hand, kneeling down beside me. "And I looked at the other bodies. They are our babies and your dad. I am so, so sorry."

I glare at Paul. I need him to be wrong, just this once. But his eyes are filled with tears, just waiting to fall down his cheeks.

His lips are quivering, and his nose is running. I have never, ever, seen him look this awful.

"I want to see them," I say. Paul helps me up. I have a goose egg bump on my right temple. God, it hurts. I must have hit a table or the floor when I fainted.

Dr. Forson motions me over to another table. He pulls back the sheet and again I see brown hair. I come around and stand close to this body. It is my dad. He has a lot of cuts and gouges on his face and neck. His skin is bluish too. I feel myself gagging and Paul pulls a trash can over to me. I lean over it and retch. I feel around in my purse for a Kleenex to wipe the vomit strands off my lips and chin. It stinks, and I am embarrassed.

I give each of my parents a kiss on the forehead. Their skin is cold and hard. It doesn't feel like a real person at all. I am suddenly, once again, overcome by emotions. My parents are dead. They loved me like no other parents ever could. They gave up so many things so I could advance further in life. I loved them dearly, and now they are gone. Tragically gone. This is so wrong.

I walk over to the other three tables. I look up at Paul, and his face is ashen. He looks horrible, like he's physically in pain, which I don't doubt that he is. Dr. Forson walks to the back of the room, giving Paul and I some privacy to do this by ourselves. I am visibly shaking. My hands are so cold and sweaty at the same time. I feel perspiration on my neck, and it is cold. Goosebumps pop out on my neck and arms. I slowly lift back the white sheet on the first little body.

Paul and I both lose it simultaneously. Although she looks very different, we can tell that the mangled body is our baby girl, Cassy. We both drop to our knees and take her in our arms. I am wailing and Paul is sobbing.

"No, no! This can't be, Paul!" I say. Snot is running into my mouth, my tears are hot and they are stinging my eyes. I want to pick up this tiny little body and take her upstairs so Dr. Forson can fix her. I look back at Dr. Forson, and he is wiping his eyes. He looks down from my glare.

"Why, why? Why would God take our baby girl from us? This is so not fair, Paul!" I just lay my head on her chest for a moment, but I quickly raise up. The feeling freaks me out. Her body is so cold. It is not my Cassy here. She looks awful.

I quickly pull the sheet back over my angel's head and move to the next little body. I am more prepared for this one. I know it will be one of our boys. It is Connor, our oldest son. Paul rips the last sheet off the next little body and it is Ryan. The boys don't appear to have much trauma to their faces, but their chests are a deep purple color. That must be where the internal damage occurred, I think.

I feel myself begin to retch again and I run to that stinky trash can. I barely make it, and this time I really vomit up everything that was in my stomach. It hurts my throat to vomit this hard. I am loud and I am crying, and my long hair is getting some puke in it. I am pissed off by this. Where the hell is Paul? Why isn't he beside me holding my hair back while I puke?

I wipe my face yet again and turn around to see where Paul is. He is praying. He is whispering, but I can hear what he is saying. He is asking God to watch over our family. He is saying that they are good kids and to please take care of them, that we will see them again someday.

"Paul, I want to go now," I say, louder than I mean to. I turn around too quickly and feel myself get dizzy again. I slow down and rest my hand on a table. Paul comes up behind me and puts his arm around my waist. We walk out of this horrible room and sit back down into the hallway chairs again. We can hear Dr. Forson pushing the slabs back into their cases, and the doors shut loudly. Our babies are lying on hard, stone slabs in refrigerators.

I don't remember much after that for the rest of the day. I know Paul and I go back upstairs. Paul signs some papers before we leave the hospital. I hear Paul being told that the bodies will be driven to Gannon tomorrow to prepare for the funerals. I vaguely hear Paul talking to people, but I don't understand what he is saying. I feel as though I am in a dream-like state. I stare straight ahead and my vision gets cloudy.

I am so, so tired. I don't ever remember feeling this tired. I just want to lie down and go to sleep. Maybe when I wake up this terrible nightmare will be over. Paul stops at a Pharmacy near the hospital, as Dr. Forson had given him a prescription to fill for sleeping pills that either of us can use if we need to. We drive back home in silence. There is nothing to say. What can we possibly say to one another? I sleep for most of the ride home.

9

Before

I haven't moved far geographically since birth. I grew up in Mason, Iowa, just two hours east of Gannon. My parents, David and Susan Dennison, still live in my childhood home. Dad was the Vice President of the Utilities Company until his retirement two years ago. Mom worked as a pharmacist throughout our childhood, working part time when we were younger and then going full time when we were in middle school. My two younger sisters and I pretty much lived typical, small town lives. We really had a very conservative life experience. I actually think we were pretty sheltered growing up. I just remember a nice, easy childhood.

We lived in the same two story, white home with green shutters throughout our childhood. It was within three blocks of all the schools in Mason, so we could walk to school each day with our friends. We had the liberty of riding our bicycles all over town, as a town of two thousand people didn't encompass that much territory anyway. You literally almost knew everybody in town. I especially liked the swimming pool, golf course, and park in town. You could ride your bike to any of those places and find someone there to hang out with. With no cell phones back then, you just left a note for Mom telling her where you were going and when you would be home. She would start calling my friends' homes if I wasn't home when I said I would be.

I remember marching in the Memorial Day parade each year. First as the middle school drum majorette and then in high school with the flag corp. Summers were the best. On weekends we went to nearby Lake Channing where mom and dad had bought a small cottage. Goofing around at the lake was wonderful. Swimming, fishing, playing mini-golf, shuffle board, playing in the sand, or at the pin-ball shack...decisions, decisions for a ten year old.

There weren't all of the organized kids' activities back then. Now they start almost every sport in kindergarten. But back then you didn't really begin organized sports until middle school. You got to be a kid for a lot longer. I don't ever remember being bored during my childhood. There was always something to do or someone to play with. If not, we organized our own neighborhood back yard game of flashlight tag at night or a game of kick the can. There were plenty of kids our age in the neighborhood to gather up for a good game of wiffle ball or kick ball.

Although I don't strive to exactly replicate my childhood for my own kids, in some ways I want to. I want my kids to play outside in the snow, sled down the hills, make snow forts and snow angels. I want them to build tree houses and run through the sprinklers in the summer. I love to look out on the back deck and watch my kids eat their freezy pops in July. I don't mind them playing their video games as well, but in moderation.

So when Paul was offered the Bank Presidency position at First National Bank in Gannon, it didn't take us long to fall in love with this smaller, quaint community. Paul grew up in a small Iowa town as well, Fresno. Gannon is bigger and has more opportunities than many real small towns. So here we are...lifers, we call ourselves, in Gannon forever.

Death leaves a heartache no one can heal,
Love leaves a memory no one can steal.

—From a headstone in Ireland

10

After

When we get home, I immediately go up to bed. It is eleven in the morning and I am physically and emotionally drained. I take a sleeping pill, as I want to sleep forever. Paul comes into our bedroom and I hear him open the shades. The light is so damn bright.

"Stop it, Paul!" I yell at him. "I need to sleep, dammit. Leave me alone." I am so tired.

He sits down on the side of the bed. I feel his arm on my hip, and I roll over farther away from him so it slips off.

"Anna, we have to talk. Please sit up so we can talk. We have to discuss the funeral arrangements. Please, honey. I know you don't want to do this, but we have to do this. The funerals are on Monday. I know you want the memorial services to be beautiful."

"I'm not going, Paul. You can go by yourself for all I care. There is no way I am getting out of this bed. I am exhausted. Just leave me alone."

I pull the covers up over my head and turn over farther away from him. I hear him sigh, and he sits there for a few more minutes. He finally pats my butt, and then he walks out of the room. I close my eyes and pray for sleep.

***

I get out of bed only to go to the bathroom. My clock says 4:52 a.m. and it is pitch dark outside. Paul is sleeping in the bed too. I see in the bathroom on the counter that Paul has laid the funeral service programs for me to obviously find. I refuse to look at them. I won't even pick them up. I use the bathroom and then I go back to bed. I smell something gross, and I think it might be me, but I really don't care if it is. I'm still wearing the same clothes from the day before at the morgue. I probably have a little puke on them. Oh well, like anyone really cares if I stink.

In my sleep I can dream. I dream about when I gave birth to all three of my kids. I dream about how they smelled, how their hair felt, how they snuggled into me when I rocked them to sleep. I can dream about anything I want when I sleep, and it makes me so happy. It's when I wake up that I'm mad. The good dreams stop then, and the nightmares begin. I prefer sleep.

There is a loud ringing noise and I want it to stop. It continues and continues and it is waking me from my good dreams. I roll over and let the ringing go on until it stops.

I hear someone in my bedroom and I know it is not Paul. Someone is shaking me and calling my name. I know that voice. Who is it? Who dares to wake me from my good dreams? I might hurt the person who is taking me away from my good dreams.

"Anna, Anna. Honey, are you awake?" It is Tammie's voice. I figure this out before I open my eyes. I try to sit up in bed, but my whole body is sore, and I feel as though I haven't slept in days. I pull the covers down under my chin, and look at Tammie until my eyes adjust to the darkened room.

"Hey, there. How are you feeling? You have a lot of people worried about you, you know."

Tammie is trying not to cry, but I know her too well. I can hear the emotion in her voice. I sit up as quickly as I can, and I put my arms around her. I sob loudly, and she cries too. I smell that awful smell again.

I pull away from her and ask, "Do I stink?" knowing that my best friend will tell me the truth.

"Something awful. Let me help you into the shower. Paul is so worried about you, Anna. The funeral services are tomorrow morning and he's worried that you won't be well enough to go. You really need to get out of bed, get showered, and come downstairs with me. Please."

My reality hits me smack in the face. I sob again, harder this time. My stomach muscles ache from all of the sobbing.

"Tammie, you have no idea what it has been like. My world has crashed. My parents have died. My three babies are dead. I saw them in the morgue! I can't even believe this has happened to us. I don't want to get out of bed. My heart is broken into pieces."

"I don't begin to know what you are going through, and I won't pretend to. I am so sorry. I can't believe any of this, either, Anna." Tammie hesitates, and I know she has more to say.

"Apparently the doctor at the hospital gave you some sleeping pills before you and Paul left the hospital, Anna. I guess you were not in a good state, and he thought it would be best for you to just rest for awhile. But you have got to shake it off now, and get prepared for the funerals. You do not want to miss this, or you will regret it for the rest of your life, Anna. You need to stop taking the sleeping pills."

"I just don't think I can do it, Tammie. I can't bear the thought of the whole town staring at me in church. I know the looks of pity that family members get from people. I just can't bear to do it."

"I will be there with you, Anna. You will not be doing this alone. Paul needs you there with him. His parents are here, the rest of your families are all in town staying at the Highland Hotel. Your sisters are here too. You have got to get up, get showered, and help Paul. He cannot go through this without you."

Inside I know she's right. But I just want to sleep for a little while longer. "I'll get in the shower in a couple of hours, Tammie. I promise. I'll sleep for a little bit longer, and then I *will* get up."

Tammie just looks at me while I cover myself back up, lay back down, and close my eyes. I hear her breathing. I'm hoping she will just go away.

"Anna, the funerals are at 10:00 tomorrow morning. It's 5:00 p.m. right now. You don't have a whole lot of time to prepare for the morning. I will go downstairs and help Paul the best I can. But I will be here tomorrow morning to drag your butt out of bed, get you in the shower, and go with you to the church. Got it? You are not getting out of it. I'm so sorry, honey. We've been friends forever, and I can't even imagine the pain you are in right now, but I do know that you will want to be at the church tomorrow."

I feel myself getting really pissed. How dare she boss me around.

"You're right. You don't have a clue what I'm going through right now. If you're such a good friend, then please just leave me the hell alone," I say through clenched teeth. I don't ever remember talking like that to Tammie.

She stands up immediately and walks out of my bedroom. Thank God. She has no idea how I feel. I take two more of the little white pills on my bedside table, take a sip of water, and go back to my dreaming.

Last year Paul and I took the kids to Sanibel Island for a summer vacation. In my dream we are lying on the beach, watching the kids splash around in the ocean. Their white hair and tan bodies are glistening in the sun. The kids are catching little starfish and just having the time of their lives. I roll over on the beach chair and smile at Paul. I tell him I love him. He pretends to be sleeping, so I kick him in the shin. He laughs and rolls over closer to me. I am so happy here. Life is beautiful in my dreams.

11

Before

I am so thankful to be blessed with two sisters who I can also count as two best friends. Courtney and Abby are one and two years younger than me, so the three of us grew up very close in age. At times we were good friends and hung out a lot together, but we also went through our spurts in childhood where we were too competitive and didn't get along so well. We never recycled each other's boyfriends, which I think helped our relationship. And we fortunately didn't have to compete for the same spots on school teams. We each did our own thing and supported one another. And once we all went away to college, we became even closer.

People say we all three look alike, but of course we don't think so. I think because we are generally about the same size, five foot seven, medium build with dark blonde hair (light blonde when we were younger, but now we have to pay for the highlights), that people think we're similar. But our faces are all very different, and so we don't see the 'Dennison look' that others find so similar in us.

Growing up we were very good girls. If we did sneak a beer, we were discreet about it and didn't get caught. We hung out with nice kids and didn't get in trouble. There was a definite unwritten rule in our family that with dad's position at the utility company, it was expected we be role models. And really that mold fit us quite well. We were a church going family that obeyed rules and fit in the community just fine. But once we all three got out of Dennison and away to college, we all let loose a bit.

I remember feeling very free at college. I didn't need to be 'daddy's good little girl' anymore. And I had a need to be naughty just because I could. I could be anonymous at Iowa State and no one really knew who I was, or cared. It was such a relief.

Courtney, Abby, and I have all shared that we each perhaps experimented to the extreme once in awhile when at college. But thankfully nothing bad happened. It wasn't anything more than alcohol and sex, but for good girls even those two vices can be dangerous. I think we had guardian angels watching over us during our college years.

Abby had a propensity for drinking too much alcohol and puking. I was with her during a few of these rampages, and it was never pretty. Man, could she put down the booze. She has always been able to out drink me. Of course she generally pukes it back up too.

Courtney was on the swim team at The University of Iowa, so I think she was the most responsible one of us three. Although she still knew how to have a good time on the weekends. And Courtney had some wild swim team friends. They introduced us both into smoking pot one weekend at Iowa. Boy, how we laughed! Thankfully none of us could remember things real clearly the next morning.

After college Abby took a teaching job in Minnesota and married a farmer up there. Courtney lives in Des Moines and works as an accountant for Principal Financial, Corp. She has been concentrating on her career, but has been seeing someone for a couple of years now. We all don't get to see one another as much as we would like, but we do manage a few get-togethers throughout the year. We can still pull a two hour phone call with each other, no problem. So I love my sisters, and I'm so glad they are still a big part of my life. They go through my ups and downs with me, and I with them.

12
After

I know I am at the church, nestled in between Paul and my sis-ter Abby. But it's like it's foggy all around me. Time is moving so slowly, and I can't hear very well. I'm watching the priest at the front of the church. We stand, sit, kneel, sit again. I see the five coffins at the front of the church. So many people around me are blowing their noses, wiping their eyes. I feel like a bystander, someone who is watching a bad movie.

Paul grabs my arm a little roughly and we walk down the aisle of the church together. The same church that we baptized our three children in. So many people are staring at me. They are crying and I am not. I glance to my left and then to my right. I see Paul's boss, my children's teachers, my friends from Book Club, and people I've never seen before in my life. They all look so sad.

We get into a black limousine and I slump against the back seat. I close my eyes and immediately feel myself drift off to sleep. I hear Paul talking, telling me to wake up and get ready to go to the cemetery. He just doesn't understand how fatigued I am. If he only understood, he would just let me go home and get into bed. The limousine stops, and Paul and his family all get out of the car. I don't open my eyes, and I plan to just sit here. Someone yanks on my arm, pulling me out of the car. It is so frigging cold out here, and so bright. Turn off the lights, please.

Thankfully we walk only a few short steps to a tent. We sit down on freezing cold metal chairs. It is really cold for March in Iowa right now. People are standing around us, and as usual, everyone is just staring at me. How I wish they would all stop looking at me. Father Daniel says some prayers, and then people begin walking over to Paul and I. They take my hands in theirs, or hug me, and tell me how sorry they are. They say they know my babies are in heaven right now. That they are in a better place. That they are happy with God. That I am not to worry.

Apparently they have never buried their children and parents before.

I can't help but stare at the five coffins waiting to be lowered down into the cold, frozen ground. It is impossible for me to believe that my children are in these coffins, dead. Within the hour, they will be buried under the ground. I will never see or hold them again. How does one's life go downhill so very quickly? One day you believe you are living the American dream, and literally the next day you are living the American nightmare.

Paul wants to go back to the limo now. It is frigging freezing cold out here. But I have a need to see the coffins go down into the ground. I want to see the dirt put on top of them. Do the coffins withstand worms and bugs? Will the coffins ever erode? What is the guarantee that my babies' bodies will never be exposed to dirt, water, and mud down there? No one answers my questions. Paul just looks at me with horror on his face.

***

Back in the warmth of the limousine, Paul announces that now we are going back to the church for lunch. That people will want to greet us there. I tell him there is no way in hell I'm going back to the church. I am worn out and I am going home. He stares at me, and for the first time that I can ever remember, he looks disgusted with me.

I see his lips turn in, and his cold eyes stare at me. He half stands up and walks bent over to the front of the limousine. I see him talk to the driver for a minute, pointing which way to turn.

Paul comes back to me and says that he will be home after the funeral lunch. Then he turns his head away from me and just looks out the window. Everyone else in the limo has stopped talking. I hear some quiet sobs, and no one will look at me when I try to catch their eyes. So now *I'm* a bitch?

The car comes to a stop in front of our house. I help myself out, and walk alone up to our front door. I get the key out of my purse and open the front door. It is so heavy. I have never noticed that before. It is a big door. I turn to wave to Paul, but the car is already gone. The house is so quiet and still. When the kids were toddlers, I used to dream about this day. The house was always a disaster area, toys were scattered everywhere, the floor was full of crumbs, and I felt like a failure as a housekeeper.

Now my house is impeccable. It is decorated, it is furnished, it is complete. It is void of life. It is silent; there is no movement. There is no heart left in this house. It has stopped pumping. It is lifeless.

I walk to the back of the house and hang my coat up in the back closet. I put my purse away in the closet, and slip my black heels off. I walk past the hall mirror and I then go back. I stop and look at myself. I look terrible. Who is this woman? I have huge, dark circles under my eyes. My face is pasty white. And I even put makeup on this morning. Well, Tammie put most of it on. My hair looks horrible, all strewn about. No wonder everyone stared at me this morning. They were laughing at me. I look like a zombie. Even my black sweater and dress are wrinkled and disheveled. I am embarrassed that I was out in public looking like this. I looked like a freak at my own kids' funerals.

I pause in the kitchen. Where did all of this food come from? There are plates and plates of cookies, bars, cakes, and more desserts than I have ever seen at a bake sale. I lift open one lid and start to take a bite of the chocolate covered brownie. But then I smell it, and it makes me gag. I drop the brownie. I go to the refrigerator hoping for a Diet Coke, and the food in there makes my eyes pop open. Tupperware containers galore are stacked all over inside the refrigerator. I have no idea what's inside of them, but I know I won't be able to eat any of it. My stomach makes a sound, and I think it is growling. But I'm not hungry. The mere thought of putting anything in my mouth makes me want to throw up.

I just stand in the kitchen and look toward the living room. The kids used to run home from school, throw their back packs in the laundry room, and then run in the living room and turn on TV. They immediately wanted a snack. Ryan always wanted to watch Sponge Bob, Connor wanted to watch Zach and Cody, and Cassy would come into the kitchen and ask to turn on Mickey Mouse Clubhouse. I can see it all happening as plain as day.

"I need a snack, Mom," Cassy would say.

"How about popcorn?"

"Yeah! Can I pour the cheese on top?" She then would proceed to show me what was in her backpack and tell me about her day at school. I thought she would have a tough time at kindergarten this year. But she adjusted just fine.

It took me longer to adjust to the change. I missed picking her up from preschool every day. I missed our girls' lunch dates together. She seemed to be just fine. I longed for the days when we would stay in our pajamas until noon, playing Hi Ho Cherry O! and Sorry! again and again. I longed for the days when we would put in *Sleeping Beauty* and snuggle up together on the couch munching on licorice together.

I hear the furnace kick in. Wow. The house is really quiet. The kids' school pictures are on the mantel. I walk over to look at them. It hits me then. Hard. My kids are dead. I saw them in the morgue. They died in a car accident with my parents. My parents and my three kids have died. Their funerals were this morning. We buried them in the ground at the cemetery this morning.

My eyes fill up with tears and spill over onto my cheeks. The tears run down my face and into my dress. I wipe away at my neck. The grief grabs at my heart. I am overcome by this wave of sadness. I set their school pictures back on the mantel and I walk upstairs.

Someone has cleaned my house. The carpet has been recently vacuumed, I smell cleaning products. Everything is too perfect. It is so difficult to walk up the thirteen steps to the upstairs floor. My feet are so heavy. Every step is a challenge, and I pause to rest midway up the staircase. I hang onto the banister and pull myself up each last step.

When I walk by Cassy's room, I have to go in. Her room has never been this organized. Someone, perhaps Tammie, has picked up every last little doll and figurine and set everything just so on her shelves and dresser top. Her closet is too perfect. Who would do this to me? Who would *dare* to come into my little girl's room and mess with her things?

I am hurt and upset that anyone would think that it would be ok to trespass here. I go over to the wall shelves and I take half of the dolls and stuffed animals off. I throw some on Cassy's bed, and some I just toss around the room. There, that's better. That's how it should look.

God, I will never see my angel girl again. I will never hug her, never tuck her into bed at night. I will never help her pick out her clothes for school again. I will never run her bath water and wash her long blonde hair. I will never lay down with her at night and tell her how much I love her.

This sucks. This really sucks. I pull down her pink bedspread and I get into her twin bed. The sheets are cold, but I can smell her in here. I grab her pillow and pull it to my face. My tears are soaking the pillow case, and snot is running out of my nose. I don't care. I am so beyond grief, and maybe entering insanity. I know my babies are dead, but I can't possibly deal with it.

I close my eyes and dream. I remember how Cassy loved to play with her Barbie dolls. She probably has thirty Barbies, and she always wanted another one. She asked me daily to play Barbies with her. How many times did I tell her I couldn't right now? How many times did I tell her I would in just a few minutes, and then I never did?

I want every one of those moments back. I will play with her every single time she asks. I will forget about doing the laundry for half an hour. I will sit on the living room floor and dress up our Barbies and pretend that we are going to the dance. If you give me the chance, God, I will do it right this time. I promise.

Please, God, just let me have one more chance with them.

13

Before

My parents are the best. Seriously, all my friends throughout high school and college always commented that I had the coolest parents. And they were right. Mom and dad were not over involved in my life, and not under involved. Just the right amount. They supported me through everything I ever did, even when they probably knew it wasn't the best idea. But they let me figure things out on my own and they have always been my biggest fans. I think because they both were first generation college students, they really wanted their kids to have more opportunities to succeed. They expected us to do well in school and to go to college.

Dad was perhaps a bit over protective of his three daughters when we were dating in high school, but I guess I can't blame him now that I have a daughter too. He told me a couple of times that he didn't want me to date particular guys. It made me mad at the time, but I always agreed with his choices. *I* just wanted to be the one to make the decision, not have him *tell* me who I could date.

Dad was a hands-on parent. His personality was such that he always asked daily what was going on in school and wanted me to tell him details. Mom didn't ask as much, so I probably didn't tell her as much. I was into sports, so dad and I had that common ground. Mom supported me in my sporting endeavors, but you knew it wasn't her thing.

But after I got married I began to have more in common with my mom, and we became closer then. When I was pregnant, oh my word, mom was frothing at the mouth. Now we shared the same interests! She loved babies and had all kinds of advice for me as a new mom. I have relied on my mother as my first call for any baby advice over the years, and both she and my dad love my kids as much as I do. So I can brag about how wonderful my kids are to my parents without feeling an ounce of guilt. They are wonderful grandparents as well as parents. My high school and college friends were right—I really did luck out in the parent category.

The relationship I have with my parents is respectful, supportive, and loving. I learned from them how to love unconditionally and how to forgive. I think that I don't have feelings of insecurity because I've always known that they were there for me at all times, and under all circumstances. I want to be a parent to my kids like my parents were to me.

14
After

Someone is pushing me, calling my name. "Anna, Anna, wake up, honey." I turn over and about fall out of Cassy's bed.

It is Paul and he looks awful. He has big, dark circles under his eyes, too. His necktie is pulled loose, and he spilled something yellow on his white shirt. I'll have to spray that before I wash it.

He sits on the bed next to me. "What are you doing in here?" he asks. I look around Cassy's room, and I feel my throat tighten.

"I don't want it to be real, Paul. I don't want this nightmare to be really happening. I'm so mad, and I'm so horribly sad. My heart hurts all the time. I'm so very tired, and I can hardly move my body. I'm sorry I'm acting like a baby, but I want to pretend that none of this really happened. I want my babies back." Again, I cry and wipe my nose.

Paul looks at me and then he pulls me into his embrace. He holds me for a long time, stroking my hair. I sniffle into his shirt, getting it wet. Can I possibly cry anymore?

"Listen, baby, we need to talk. I know the past three days have been a living hell. I'm so sorry that all of this has happened to us. But you have to deal with it, Anna. Our kids and your parents died in a horrible car accident. We buried them this morning. It is a terrible tragedy, but it did happen. And it's going to take both of us a long time to get over it, ok? I don't know exactly how we even begin to go about dealing with it, either. But I do know that we just have to take one day at a time, and keep on living."

Paul has always been so darn smart. He did very well in school, but he's even smarter about life. He just knows what to say and what to do in every situation.

I know Paul will grieve the correct way. Paul will go about the mourning process in the textbook manner. He will deal with it, get through it, and come out on the other side. He will be sad, and he will never be the same again, but he will be ok. Because Paul is strong, and he is a good man.

I, on the other hand, am weak. I have always been weak. When the going gets too tough, I quit. I don't really want to do things that challenge me. I like things to come easy to me. I cave quite easily, really. I know that Paul's confidence and perseverance attracted me to him from the very beginning.

His confidence was enlightening. He believed we could do anything. Even when he failed, it was no big deal to him. He just moved on and tackled another project. Without him, I would have lost my confidence.

But I'm struggling to understand how we can keep on living given our current circumstances. Even Paul should be dragged down into the utmost depths of despair on this given challenge. Our three kids were killed. How do we begin to keep on living now? Paul and I are both forty. I don't want more kids now.

"Paul, I know that I need to deal with this. But I may need more time than you, ok? We deal with things differently, and I don't even know how to begin to accept this loss. The kids were my life. You have your career that you go to every day. The kids were my career. My life revolved around their daily activities. My daily schedule depended on their daily schedule. You have another life, but I do not. So now what kind of life do I have? I have nothing. You still have your career. You still get to go to the bank every day. What in the world am I going to do every day now?"

I had him and he knew it. He knew that all I ever wanted out of life was to be a mom and a wife. My focus in life was our family, our house, our life together. Sure, I helped at school, and served on various committees in the community, but my priority was raising our kids. I loved being a mom. That's who I was. Now who am I? I'm no longer a mom. I no longer have any kids. They were taken away from me three days ago. I no longer have a purpose in life.

"What is my reason to get up tomorrow morning, Paul?" I'm yelling now. And I am mad. Not really at him, but I'm mad.

"You tell me, why do I need to wake up tomorrow? What should I do tomorrow? Where should I go? I have nothing to get up for! I have no reason to wake up, do I? My kids and my parents are dead! You tell me how I should "deal" with this little issue, Paul, and then we'll both be happy."

"Anna, you do have reasons to wake up tomorrow. First of all, you do have family left. You have me. I need you. I am your husband, and I need you to be here with me. Your sisters are here, your many friends, and we all need you. Don't even think about backing out on me now. We are in this together. I don't have all the answers for you right now. I don't know how to tell you to move forward, because I don't know how to do it either." He's getting really worked up and I know I started this.

"There isn't a workshop that I've attended called 'How to survive after your kids are killed in a car accident.' But I do know that I love you, that I need you, and that we will get through this together. You cannot retreat into your own misery right now."

He's right, and I know it. But it doesn't make things any easier. I can't believe how awful I feel. I just want to never wake up. Paul stands up, and pulls down Cassy's pink bedspread so I can get out of her bed. We walk into our bedroom and change out of our funeral clothes.

"I told the office that I wouldn't be in the rest of the week, Anna. I plan to stay right here with you. We need each other right now. My family wanted to come over to our house after the church lunch, but I told them that you and I just needed to be alone. Everyone was asking about you at the church. But they all understand that this is just too much to comprehend right now. Everyone cares about you and loves you, Anna. You are going to have many people trying to help you through this difficult time."

It's only two o'clock in the afternoon, but Paul and I get in bed and turn on the TV. We cuddle and watch Dr. Phil, Oprah, and Jeopardy. I fall asleep at some point, and when I open my eyes next, it is dark outside. The clock says nine o'clock, and Paul is not in bed with me anymore. I get up and go to the bathroom. My stomach hurts, and I realize that I don't think I've eaten for a few days. I go downstairs and see Paul in his study, working on his computer. I don't want to talk to him.

I eat a little leftover hamburger casserole from the refrigerator. It is bland and tasteless, but my stomach doesn't hurt anymore. There is a large pile of envelopes lying on the counter. I pick up a few and they all say, "Paul and Anna Dawson."

I open the first one and it is a card from one of Paul's co-workers. In it is a fifty dollar bill. He writes that he hopes we accept his condolences and that he knows our children and my parents are in a better place. I look at the large pile of cards and it is too much for me to open anymore.

I look around the house, but there is nothing for me to do. And plus I'm beat. I go back to bed.

15

Before

One of the happiest times of my life was when Paul and I were engaged. We were young, living in Des Moines, and had our futures ahead of us. We didn't know where we'd end up, and we were content to take our lives one day at a time. We had a nine month engagement, and I loved every minute of it. I loved calling Paul my fiancé. I enjoyed telling the story to people of how Paul proposed to me. I basked in showing off my ring and telling people about our wedding plans.

We decided to get married in Des Moines, much to my mother's dismay. She thought we should get married in Mason. But Mason was no longer my home.

We had been going to a smaller Catholic church periodically in Des Moines, St. Paul's. It was a beautiful, newer, more modern Catholic church. They had a children's choir on Sunday mornings at the late mass. The young priest, Father Ross, was so likeable. He understood people of our generation.

Paul didn't care much for the wedding planning, typical of most men. I would tell him about my ideas, the reservations I made, and he just said, "Great, honey. That sounds wonderful."

I found a simple gown at Shaffer's Bridal in downtown Des Moines that was on clearance. I had Courtney, Abby, and two college girlfriends stand up with me, Caitlin and Lauren. We chose straight, black dresses for them. I had red roses for the flowers, and my Aunt Madeline took care of the music.

Paul was breathtaking on our wedding day. We got married on June twelfth, and it was a perfect early summer wedding, seventy-five degrees and breezy. Paul looked so very handsome in his black tux. He had three of his college friends and one high school friend stand up with him. The whole wedding ceremony was simple, yet refined, and we had a blast at the reception afterwards at the Hartford Hotel, downtown Des Moines. The day was just grand.

I was so proud to be Paul's wife. I loved him very much, and I was so excited about our new married life together. My mom cried, but I think they were tears of joy for me. You could never tell for sure with her. I saw the lump in my dad's throat. I was honored that he could walk me down the aisle and hand me over to Paul.

At twenty-five, I still felt young, but I knew I was making the right choice by marrying Paul. And I've never, ever regretted that decision. I know one of the best decisions in my life I made was to marry Paul Dawson.

We went to St. Kitt's on our honeymoon. I had never been to a Caribbean island, and I wanted to spend a relaxing week with Paul somewhere hot and at the ocean. We had an ideal honeymoon. Two young lovers in love with the idea of marriage, not knowing the truth yet. That sometimes even the best laid plans go awry. That sometimes all the love in the world can't keep you happy. That sometimes life deals you a crappy hand, and you need to leave the table or go broke.

Our honeymoon was magical. Paul and I were so in love. We talked endlessly that week about our dreams for our future together. We didn't know where we'd end up geographically, with Paul's banking career. He could be transferred almost anywhere in the country. And that was fine with us. But we loved Iowa. We had no problem if we never left Iowa. It meant family and security.

We talked about having a family some day. We knew we wanted a few kids, whatever that meant. But we wanted to enjoy married life without kids for a few years first. I told Paul that if possible though, someday I'd love to be a stay at home mom. If it was possible financially, I wanted to give our kids my undivided attention. My mother provided a solid foundation for my sisters and I when we were young, and I wanted to do the same for our kids. Paul didn't care either way. He just wanted me to be happy.

After our time on St. Kitt's, it was back to Iowa and to the reality of careers and a young marriage. We didn't see each other a lot those first few years of marriage, really. We both worked long hours, trying to work our way up the corporate ladder of life. Weekends were our haven together. We enjoyed life in Des Moines with all of the bars and restaurants and the entertainment. We had good friends and life was great. I never would have dreamt in my wildest dreams how our life would have changed in the next ten years.

16
After

Paul tells me that Courtney called and said that she, Abby, and I are supposed to meet with mom and dad's attorney tomorrow in Mason to go over their wills. I call Courtney back and I tell her that I can't do it. I just can't make it to the meeting. I know they'll be fine without me.

I get a call from Courtney a few days later, after their meeting with the attorney from Bradford Brothers Attorneys at Law. Mom and dad left the three of us girls with a substantial amount of money, four hundred thousand dollars each. Wow. I am really surprised. I knew they had done well, and saved a lot. But this is more than I imagined. I'm brought to tears by their generosity and kindness once again.

Courtney says she can take care of selling mom and dad's home if that's ok with me. We need to clean out their house sometime soon, go through everything and we can all take what we want. I can't even comprehend this task right now. I tell Courtney that if she and Abby want to do it, that's fine with me. They can give me whatever they want. I just can't do it. She understands. She will take care of everything.

Other things may change us,
But we start and end with the family.

—Anthony Brandt

17

Before

Paul and I met in college at Iowa State University. I was a Business major and Paul was a Finance major. We had Microeconomics together with Professor Wilson. I hated the class. It absolutely bored me to death. This cute guy always sat near me. Never right by me, but near enough that I always saw him. After a month in the class, he started talking to me briefly. He would ask if I knew what chapter we were supposed to have read for that day. He would ask if he could borrow my notes from the last lecture.

Then we ran into each other at an Iowa State Cyclone basketball game at Hilton Coliseum one Saturday afternoon. He was sitting two rows behind me in the student section. We all ended up at the same bar after the game to brag about the Cyclone's win over Missouri. I think I fell for him that day. He was polite, yet fun. He was handsome, yet normal. He asked me if I wanted to go to a movie the next night, and we ended up dating the next two years of college.

So many couples don't make it through the college years together. It can be hard to have a steady boyfriend or girlfriend and still be wild and have fun. Paul and I had a good balance. We spent time together, but not too much. We both enjoyed our outside friendships and allowed each other that time. We both wanted to do well in college, so we studied a lot together, too. I think we both fell hard for each other, and didn't want to ruin a good thing.

We came from similar backgrounds, which helped our relationship. I grew up in Mason, Iowa, just two hours from Iowa State. My parents still lived in Mason and I was close to them. Paul grew up in southern Iowa, in Fresno. We both had simple, down to earth Iowa values. We both wanted to get college degrees and raise a family. We just seemed to fit easily into one another's life goals and futures.

Right before graduation, Paul was offered a job with a bank in Des Moines. He wanted to take it, but he asked me if I would move to Des Moines with him. He wanted us to be together. So we moved to Des Moines together, and I ended up finding a job in Human Resources at an accounting firm. Paul moved up in the banking world quickly. After eight years in Des Moines, he was offered the bank Presidency position at First National Bank in Gannon, Iowa. It was a smaller community, but Paul felt like this was a big opportunity for him.

We visited Gannon and immediately fell in love with the community. We knew we would raise our family here and be in Gannon for awhile. So here we are. Paul has helped his bank grow immensely and he has become a state leader in the banking industry. I am so proud of him.

I worked at Taylor Accounting Firm in Gannon for three years and then became pregnant. After Connor was born I decided to stay home. There have been days when I've missed the challenge of my own career. I enjoyed the adult conversations and the accomplishments that came with my chosen profession. But after my kids were born, I really was too busy to think about an additional career outside of my kids. Paul travels enough that it would have been difficult to juggle child care when he was out of town anyway.

So overall, I have been content to be a mom. I honestly never saw myself as a stay at home mom. I was always a career woman. But once you have three little kids, you realize that being a mommy is a full time job. My hat is off to moms who work outside the home full time as well. They are amazing people.

18
After

In my heart, I know I am struggling. I just don't want to deal with it. Or maybe I don't know *how* to deal with it right now. The pain is so overwhelming. Just being awake is too painful for me to bear. I prefer to be holed up in my bed, sleeping.

It is too much of an effort to keep my eyes open anymore. I think I might have cancer or something. I have never felt this physically awful before in my life. It is an effort to turn the TV on while I'm lying in bed. It is an effort to sit up in bed and turn on my lamp. The effort it takes me to get out of bed and go to the bathroom about kills me. Literally, I can't even breathe well now. It's as though I'm gasping for air when I walk.

I'm embarrassed to go see Dr. Foster about my condition. How much can Paul endure? He's had the loss of his kids, and then to deal with my serious medical situation? I think it's better if I just stay in bed and get through it on my own. I just need to sleep.

I know I only shower about once a week now. I can smell myself when I'm sleeping. At first it made me sick to my stomach, but now I'm used to it. It's the smell of sick people. I've noticed that Paul sleeps very far away from me in bed. He hasn't touched me in weeks. I know I disgust him. But guess what? He can go to hell. He isn't sick like I am, so he has no idea how horrible it is for me.

Tammie keeps leaving messages on my phone. She is really starting to irritate me. Can't she take the hint that I have no desire to talk to her? What can she possibly say that would brighten my day?

"Hey, I know you're kids are dead, but let's do lunch anyway?" She's probably not going to make me feel better.

I wake up during my nap and realize I have to go to the bathroom really badly. But oh, the thought of the energy it will take me to get up, walk to the bathroom, and walk back to bed again gives me a headache. I just physically can't do it.

While I'm debating whether or not I should get up and go, I feel warm liquid around my legs. I can't imagine where it is coming from. I lift up the covers and there is a big wet spot all around my butt. Oh my God, I think I've wet the bed. The pressure on my abdomen is gone now. I feel much better. I pull up my legs and kick my underwear off, leaving them down under the wet sheets. I am too tired to get up, so I roll over to a dry area on the bed and go back to sleep.

***

The bed wetting incident should have clued me in to how far down I had gone. But it didn't. In fact, it seemed to make a little sense to me. Why get up and go to all that work to go to the bathroom?

That night when Paul came to bed, he tried to move me over to my own side of the bed. When that didn't work, he went over to my side of the bed, pulled back the covers, and yelled, "Anna, what in the world happened here? You wet the bed? It reeks! This is insane."

He stormed out of the room. I don't know if he slept in one of the kids' beds that night or on the couch. I vaguely remember hearing him in the shower the next morning, but I was too tired to get up and talk to him.

Later that morning, I heard someone downstairs in the kitchen. I wondered why Paul was home from work. Maybe he was sick, or he just couldn't deal with things today. Maybe he just wanted to lie in bed like me all day. That would be nice. We could sleep together. We could both have good dreams together about the kids.

Tammie walks into my bedroom. I had the local news on.

"Anna, hi! Paul called and asked me to come by to check on you today. He's worried about you, sweetie. We're all actually pretty worried about you. You won't answer the phone, you won't answer the door bell, and Paul says you have been in bed for over a month now. I love you, and I'm here to help you. Please talk to me, Anna."

Paul must have told her about the wet bed, because she is already preparing the washing machine. She comes over to the bed and begins raking the sheets off. I sit up and move over so she can remove all the sheets and blankets. The smell hits me then.

Man, that does reek. Did I do that? I should be embarrassed. I have never wet the bed before. Not as an adult, anyway. But I don't really care. When you're as worn out as I am, why would you care?

I want to talk to Tammie. She is my best friend. I know she cares about me and she loves me no matter what. But I just don't even know where to begin. How do I tell her that I want to die? How do I tell her that I've been thinking about ways to kill myself? She will tell Paul, I know she will.

I don't want her to think badly of me. I know I'll feel better soon. This too shall pass, Father Daniel said so. It's just a phase I'm going through. I just buried my children and parents, for God's sake. Give me a little time to mourn.

"Tammie, thank you," I mutter.

She walks back over to me and gives me a big hug. "Girlfriend, you smell pretty funky. Let's get you into the shower."

For the second time in a month, my best friend helps me shower. She helps me wash my hair, and soaps me all over. She dries me off. She helps me get dressed. I show her where extra linens are, but she says the mattress needs to air out for awhile, with all the urine that soaked it wet. She tries to laugh at this, but I'm not in the mood for laughs right now.

She holds my hand and we walk downstairs. She has a pot of coffee on, my favorite, French vanilla. I sit at the kitchen table and stare out at the backyard. The yard where I would watch the kids play for hours in the summer. They loved that old sandbox that Paul built for them. Connor pushed Cassy on the swings every day last summer. The trampoline sits there empty, just begging for kids to jump on it. Do I keep all that stuff? Do I give it away to a family who wants it? What do I *do* with all of the kids' stuff now?

Tammie comes over to the table and sits down next to me. I try to muscle up a smile for her, but it is a weak effort. I am so thankful she is here with me at this moment. She's not pushing me to talk. She's not judging me. She's not telling me what I should be doing. She's just being my friend. Or so I thought.

"Anna, I think you are depressed. I want to have Dr. Hansen prescribe some anti-depressants for you. Dr. Hansen is a psychiatrist that I know, and I know that she can help you. Would you be ok with that?" Tammie quietly asks, looking at me with hesitation but kindness.

"Why do you think I'm depressed?" I ask, feeling myself becoming defensive immediately.

"Oh, sweetheart. You haven't come out of your room in a month. You have lost at least ten pounds. You have dark circles under your eyes. You don't bathe, and your personal hygiene has all but disappeared. And sweetie, you wet the bed yesterday, and you kept sleeping in it. A normal person does not do that," Tammie says, as she squeezes my shoulder, trying to soften the blow.

"Normal? Oh, I get it. You're here to tell me I'm crazy, aren't you?"

I try to shrug her hand off my shoulder. I don't want her pity.

"Did Paul put you up to this? He won't even talk to me, you know. He just avoids me and looks at me in disgust, Tammie. Did he tell you that? What kind of a husband does that to his grieving wife?" I really don't want to be having this conversation right now.

"Anna, Paul loves you and only wants to help you. We both believe medication will help you get through this. Don't you want to get better? Or do you really want to spend the rest of your life holed up in your house, peeing in the bed, and have me come over every day to help you shower?"

She says this with a smile, trying to be funny. But now I am embarrassed. Maybe she's right. I can't quite seem to shake this funky mood I'm in. But I don't know how 'normal' people whose kids died are supposed to act. Maybe this is normal for people in my situation, I think.

I sigh. I feel defeated and irritated.

"If Dr. Hansen thinks I should take some medication to get me through this, then fine. But only if she thinks so. Tell her I'm just so damned tired all of the time. Tell her it's like there's a forty pound weight on my chest and I struggle to sit up in bed. It's that difficult, Tammie. Every movement is hard. And my head hurts all the time. Just tell her all that and see what she thinks."

"Great. I'll call Dr. Hansen and tell her what you just said. You need to see that there is life after the accident. You do need to go on with your life."

"We'll see, Tammie. Right now I am tired again, so I'm going to lie down and dream. In my dreams I hear Connor, Ryan, and Cassy talk, Tammie. When I close my eyes I am happy. I see them! My thoughts are only happy when I lie down and dream, and remember the past. I'm not sure I want to be awake anymore, Tammie. It's a nightmare when I'm awake. I don't expect you to understand it. You can go home to Jack and your kids. I have nothing anymore. My life is a living hell, Tammie."

She looks at me sadly. I think she understands. I know that she knows my pain. She may not fully feel it, but she knows I am hurting and she respects it. She doesn't dismiss it, like so many well intentioned people do after a loved one's death.

You can clutch the past so tightly to your chest
That it leaves your arms too full
To embrace the present.

—Jan Glidewell

19

After

According to my wall calendar, it has been six weeks since the accident. It feels more like two years. I have only left the house to go to the funerals. I rarely leave my bedroom. I wander downstairs during the day when Paul is gone to see if there is any food that I can force down. The plates of food continue to come in.

I hear the doorbell ring at least twice a day, but I ignore it. People just leave their casserole dishes on the front porch and Paul brings them in at night. He comes home every night at six o'clock. I struggle to talk with Paul. He has kind of given up trying himself. I don't blame him. I have only showered twice in the past two weeks, so I am smelly again. My hair is extremely greasy. I just don't have the energy that it would take to tackle a big project like showering.

The phone hasn't rung in a few days. I'm sure people just stopped trying. I wouldn't answer it anyway, and I haven't checked the voice mails or returned any calls. What would I possibly have to say to people? Yes, I am hurting. Yes, I feel terrible and no, I don't feel like going out for lunch with you. I never did get to that psychiatrist that Tammie recommended to me.

My cousin Jessica stopped by the other evening. Paul came in the bedroom and asked if I wanted to come out and talk to her. Is he frigging nuts? He knows we don't care for one another. I have never liked Jessica. She has always been critical of me, she competes with me, and she has never had anything good to say about me.

The rest of the family always said she was just envious of me, that's why she behaved that way towards me. I don't really care why she has always been a bitch to me, I just know that she is the absolute *last* person that I want to see right now. I know she has come here to celebrate my loss. Inside she is so happy that I have lost everything that ever meant anything to me.

Thinking about Jessica gives me a little energy boost. I haul my butt out of bed and walk out into the upstairs hall. I can hear Paul talking to Jessica in the living room. I yell down, "Get her the hell out of my house. She is the last frigging person I want to ever talk to. And Paul, make sure she never sets foot in my house again."

I feel a little better after that. I go back into my bedroom, slamming the door shut loudly. Although Jessica lives an hour from us, over the years it has felt like she was way too close. She is just one of those critical people that constantly complains and evaluates everything. She complains about the school system, she criticizes the church, the teachers, you name it. Nothing is ever good enough for Jessica. But then she was from a big city, and mentions daily that 'that's not how they do it in Kansas City.' All of my family and friends that know her think she's a priss, and I have given up defending her, even though she's family.

I expect Paul to come upstairs and lecture me for how I treated Jessica. He doesn't come up, though, and I go to sleep. When I awake in the morning, he has already left for work. I feel kind of bad, but not badly enough to tell Paul that I am sorry. He is back to his life as he knew it before the kids died. He seems to be able to transition back to a 'normal' life just fine. He gets to go into work and take his mind off of the nightmare. What do I get to do? Sit in this house and think about all that I have lost.

20

Before

In my dream I am at Gannon's public swimming pool with the kids. Connor is probably four, Ryan is three, and Cassy is two. We are there with Tammie and her kids. It is a really hot, great summer day. Tammie and I are sitting near the baby pool, busy talking and watching the kids. It is a perfect day. I go to stand in the deepest end of the baby pool, about two feet deep, where Connor wants me to watch him run and jump in about a hundred times.

I'm busy listening to Tammie talk about her jerk of a boss when I glance down and see Ryan floating face down in the water. I grab him and pull him up. His eyes are closed and he is limp. I lay him down on the pool side and watch as Tammie blows into his mouth and pumps his chest. I am frozen.

I watch my baby and I am dizzy and I think I'm going to faint. Finally, Ryan spits water out of his mouth and sits up gagging and crying. I grab him and hug him. Tammie hugs me and we both have a moment of 'what the hell just happened here.' Ryan gets out of my arms and goes back to splashing in the water. Tammie and I sit on the edge of the pool, drained from emotion and scared about what could have happened.

"I am a terrible parent. My son could have drowned right under my own eyes, a foot away from me, Tammie. What kind of a mother would let that happen to her own child?"

"Anna, there are six moms in this pool, and no one saw it. We were right here. It happens. You can't watch your kids one hundred percent of the time. He's fine. That won't be the worst scare you have with your kids, unfortunately."

She had no idea how right she would be.

21

After

I feel guilty because although my parents died too, I'm not feeling as much pain for them. I loved them dearly. They were awesome parents. But they were in their mid sixties, and let's face it, they were going to die sometime way before my kids. They were *supposed* to die before their grandkids, anyway. I feel bad for even thinking this way. But my kids were not supposed to die for a very long time. They were supposed to die *after* me. I feel as if I should be mourning my parents' death more.

But all I can think about is *my* family. When I got married and had kids, *my* family took precedence over my extended family, as is the norm, I believe. I am so deeply heartbroken by my loss. I feel so badly for Paul and I. But Paul has moved on. I know he misses his kids as much as I do, but his life seems to have just taken a detour, and now he's back on track. My life seems to have fallen over the edge of a cliff, and I am left wounded on a ledge, and no one knows I'm down here crying for help.

I go online and look up 'depression.' The on-line dictionary tells me that depression is "low spirits, gloominess; dejection; sadness; an emotional condition, either neurotic or psychotic, characterized by feelings of hopelessness, or inadequacy."

I don't like what I read. But Tammie is probably right. I think I am depressed. And my thoughts are starting to bother me. I haven't shared them with anyone, for fear that they'll lock me up on a psych ward somewhere.

I do think about ending my life. I obsess over the thought. I need something that would happen really quickly, as I am a coward and I don't like pain. And I don't want it to fail. I don't want to wake up after the 'accident' and be paralyzed. Then I would be pitiful. My heart, soul, *and* body would be wounded. That would be too much to accept.

I picked up my big carving knife the other day and thought about what it would feel like to just drive it through my heart. Or my neck. I don't think I could use a knife, though, in reality. I think you'd need to be really strong. And again, I can't afford a mistake. If I'm going to kill myself, I need it to work the first time.

We don't have a tall enough building in Gannon, but I could drive to Des Moines and jump from a really tall building. I'm not sure how I would get to the rooftop though, or to a window to jump out of. They make it look so easy in the movies.

Part of me knows that these thoughts are not ok. But I am *not* ok. I think it is normal for someone in my situation to have these thoughts. Until you're there, don't judge me.

22
After

My head is throbbing and I feel nauseous. I just can't seem to shake the grogginess I feel constantly. I have no energy. My eyelids are too heavy to hold open. I have the TV on in my bedroom almost twenty-four hours a day, but I can't seem to watch it for longer than thirty minutes at a time. Paul leaves food on a tray by my bed in the morning and at night. Sometimes I peck at it a little. I mostly just drink water and munch on crackers.

I've been questioning my existence. I feel so sad all of the time. It's hard for me to admit this, but I continue to brainstorm ways that I could put myself out of my misery. I know that Paul has hunting guns down in the basement in the gun safe. But I can't remember where he keeps the combination to the safe. He told me once years ago. And I really don't know where he keeps the bullets for the guns, and I have never even loaded a gun. So that may not be a realistic option for me.

I only have a few sleeping pills left in the container right now, but I could wait until it is refilled and then swallow the whole bottle. But how many pills does it take to go to sleep forever? I certainly don't want my effort to fail.

A rope is not an option either. I need to do it quickly and without thinking about the pain or consequences. A car accident is a possibility. A quick, sudden swerve would be instantaneous.

But that's what happened to my family. And do I want Paul to go through another death again? I could be with my babies again in heaven. But then again, I was raised to believe that if you commit suicide you can't go to heaven.

How awful would that be, to kill myself to be with my kids and then I wouldn't even get to be with them. Kind of defeats the purpose. Man, how I want them back. I just want my life back. I want to be happy again. But I have serious doubts that it will ever happen.

23

Before

Once when I was at college, late at night a bunch of us girls were walking back to our dorm. We had been out at an Iowa State hockey match. It was after midnight and pitch dark outside. As we were walking past the ten story dorm, all of a sudden we heard what sounded like glass breaking. We all turned around toward the dorm and we expected to see glass on the ground. But since it was dark outside, we couldn't see much at all. We started to walk toward the noise, but then some guys from our dorm floor yelled at us to hurry up for their floor party. We ran ahead, forgetting all about the strange noise.

The next morning we heard that a college student had jumped from the tenth floor of the dorm last night and died. I asked where exactly this happened. We were told that he was found about twelve fifteen early this morning right outside where we thought we heard glass breaking. We all looked at one another and I shuddered. The noise we heard was the young man's bones breaking. I haven't forgotten that noise in twenty years. And he didn't even scream on the way down.

What could be so bad at eighteen that you feel the need to kill yourself? And what pushes you to jump off a ten story building? Do you regret it as soon as you feel yourself free falling? Or is the freedom exhilarating? Do you hurt when you hit the ground? Or is death immediate? I would hate to lay there alive in pain for even a few seconds, knowing what you just did. But would it be worse to not die? What if the paramedics saved you? What if you woke up and realized your effort was in vain? Would you be upset or relieved?

Twenty years ago I could not imagine what would make someone even consider taking their own life. When life is good, it never occurs to you that life won't always be good. Today I know the difference. When life is bad, it never occurs to you that life can be good again.

24
After

I realize that I really haven't even seen Paul in days. I go to sleep before him and get up after him. I don't know that he's even sleeping in our bed. And it should bother me more that I really don't care.

My attitude is horrible these days. How many days in a row have I been holed up in my bedroom? I don't know. Maybe two months? I seriously have not even left my bedroom in so long, that I can't remember the last thing I've done outside of this room.

I'm dreaming of happy things, and I feel someone shaking me. I slowly open one eye and Tammie is in my face.

"Hi there, sleepy head. Paul let me in. Hope you don't mind."

Of course I mind. How dare she just barge into my private sleeping quarters.

"Anna, it smells awful in this room. When was the last time you took a shower?" She invades my privacy and now she insults me as well? A great best friend she has turned out to be.

"What do you want, Tammie? I'm really not feeling too great right now. So if you've come to offend me, you can leave now."

"I'm not leaving until I get you out of this bed and into the shower." She quickly pulls back my covers and makes a face.

I smell it right away too. I absolutely reek. I have never smelled body odor this putrid before, and it is all mine.

"Paul is so worried about you. He asked if I would come and talk to you. I don't want to make you mad. I'm truly just trying to help. You know I'm not going to leave you alone. We've been best friends for too long. I know you are hurting so badly. Please let me try to help."

Tammie looks sincere. Should I tell her the truth? I think she knows the truth already. It has gotten really, really bad. I am pitiful. And I don't know what to do.

She slowly pulls me out of bed and into the bathroom. She undresses me like a child. I don't look at her. I am too embarrassed. She turns on the water for the shower and pushes me in, again. The warm water feels so good. But I have no energy to wash myself. Tammie is in the shower with me, with her t-shirt and jeans on. She is washing my hair, and she takes the bar of soap around my body. Everything smells so much better now. I am crying in the shower, and so is Tammie. What am I going to do with my pathetic life?

After Tammie helps me get dressed, she walks me downstairs. We sit in the living room together. She gets us each a Diet Coke. I expect her to lecture me. I expect her to tell me I need to pull out of my funk. But we just talk. About nothing. She tells me what's been going on in Gannon lately. She tells me what her kids have been up to. She is attempting to make my life normal again. I am so thankful for her friendship. She knows I am in deep, deep pain and she knows that it might take me a long time to come out from under it. But I know she will be by my side the entire time.

25

Before

When Connor was born I nursed him for one month. He was colicky and such a high maintenance baby. After a month of nursing we figured out that I was not producing much milk at all. The poor child was probably starving! I switched over to formula and he just puked it up all the time. I tried soy formula and that worked a little better, but not much.

I think when it's your first child you don't know what to expect, so you think this must be normal. But I remember being so worn out from spending the day with him. As a newborn, he needed to be held all the time. I couldn't put him in his swing or the bouncy seat or on the floor with his mobile for more than ten minutes. Then he would cry and it was hard to settle him down.

I listened to other mothers with babies about the same age as Connor. I was ashamed to admit that he wasn't a good baby like their babies. The other moms made it sound so easy, so fun to be a mom. I really struggled. I wondered what I was doing wrong. I loved him so much, and I truly wanted to be a great mom.

But motherhood was harder than I imagined. This little crying and pooping machine ruled my life. I had to plan when the best time to go to the grocery store with him would be. When his naps would be, when his feeding times would be for the day. He was fussy all the time and it was hard to be out in public with a crying baby.

Paul was traveling a lot during this time, so I felt all alone in my struggles. I told Paul about it, but he didn't really understand. And so many people thought that I was so fortunate to be able to stay at home with my baby. So many moms have to work today and don't get this special bonding time with their baby.

Some days I would have paid someone to let me work for them, just to get out of the house. But it's not politically correct to admit that. I could tell Tammie, and she wouldn't judge me. But anyone else would look at me like I was an unfit mother.

I loved Connor with all my heart. I had always wanted to be a mommy, and I had dreamt of this time in my life for years. Now that it was here, it wasn't quite as I had imagined.

When I discovered I was pregnant again, I couldn't believe it. I initially freaked out. I couldn't handle one baby, let alone think about having another one! But truly I was thrilled, and Paul was so happy to hear the news. It stressed me out just thinking about how I was going to handle two babies. But slowly Connor became less fussy, and much more of a joy to me.

Connor was born with a full head of brown hair, which turned blond quickly, chubby cheeks and bright blue eyes. Everyone said he looked like Paul from the day he was born. He was such a momma's boy. He always needed to be near me, and did not enjoy having a sitter, ever.

Even as a toddler he was a remarkable little thing. People would comment that he spoke maturely for his age. I never saw it, but I didn't have anything to compare it with. Years later I understood.

They say your first born child will always be special to you because they were your first one. Connor will always hold a place in my heart with the many firsts he brought to my life. Feeling him kick in my tummy when I was six months pregnant is a feeling I can still remember. Having my water break at home at three a.m. a week before his due date is etched in my mind. Going into labor and pushing for two hours on September fourteen is a day I will never forget. Dr. Foster had to use forceps to remove him from the birth canal. I will always remember that pain.

And then he was here—my sweet Connor Paul Dawson. We didn't know if we were having a boy or a girl, and it was so much fun to hear the doctor say, "It's a boy."

They handed him to me when he was fresh out of the womb, laid him on my chest and I just cried my eyes out. Our son! What a miracle birth is. This little baby is half of Paul and half of me. It's almost too much to wrap your mind around. Genetically it is crazy.

Connor didn't get to be in the spotlight for very long. From the first day we brought Ryan home, Connor was mesmerized by his baby brother. He always wanted to be on my lap, too, when I was feeding or rocking Ryan. He gave his little brother many slobbery kisses and too many tight hugs. I don't remember Connor being jealous; he just wanted to be in on the action as well.

It wasn't long before the two little boys were always together. Once Ryan could crawl, he followed Connor everywhere. And Connor was thrilled to have a playmate. To this day, they are usually seen together no matter what they are doing. They can definitely fight and torment each other, as most brothers enjoy doing. But they truly love each other and look after one another.

My Connor always wanted to be five years older than he was. He enjoyed hanging around older boys, and for some reason they always let him tag along. He wasn't shy, so he had no problem conversing with anyone. Connor would get asked to join older boys in a round of golf, in a game at the swimming pool, or to play basketball at the fitness center.

Everywhere we went, people all knew Connor. People Paul and I didn't even know. We would ask Connor who that was, and much of the time he would tell us just a first name and that he knows him from school.

Connor had a firm loyalty to his family at a young age. He wanted to know the stories of Paul and I and our parents, and our grandparents. He needed to understand where he came from and what the bigger picture was. At age seven, he told Paul and I that he wanted to go to college like Paul and then come and work with him at First National Bank. He wanted to do everything his dad did. Connor looked up to Paul and admired him unconditionally. We couldn't have been more proud of him as a person, let alone a little boy.

26
After

I think I sleep on and off for the next few days. Paul attempts to get me up and out of bed at times. He suggests that we go for a walk, for a drive, out to eat, rent a movie, anything I want to do. I don't want to do anything, I tell him. I am doing exactly what I want to do. I am resting.

Paul walks in the bedroom and closes the door. I am half awake with the TV on. He says we need to talk. He says he is worried about me, and that he is concerned that I am depressed. He says that Father Daniel was happy to come over to talk with me. Could I please sit up so Father Daniel can come in and talk to me?

He brought the priest over to my house? He thinks I'm depressed and now he wants me to talk to our priest? Who does Paul think he is? Is he out to completely humiliate me? I just stare at him, and he knows I'm pissed.

"Anna, why don't you get up first and comb your hair, brush your teeth, and maybe put on some clean clothes. You will probably feel better if Father Daniel doesn't see you like this."

Of all the nerve.

"No, I'm fine, Paul. If you want Father Daniel to come in and talk to me, then by all means, have Father Daniel come in and talk to me. I have nothing to hide," I spit at him.

Paul hesitates, and then looks back at me as he walks towards the bedroom door. I hear him talking behind the door, and then it opens and he and Father Daniel walk in. Father is in a black suit with his white collar. He has a look of pity on his face, which I hate. It is so condescending. I wish everyone would stop looking at me like that.

"Hello, Anna. How are you?" says Father Daniel. He walks over and sits down on the edge of my bed.

"I've been better, actually."

"Paul asked me to talk to you. He's worried about you, Anna. He loves you very much, you know. You two have been through a lot lately, more than most people go through in a lifetime. I want you to know that I'm here for you. Your God is here for you. If you talk to Him and let Him help you, I think you'll feel better."

He appears so nice. He appears to mean well. I've known Father Daniel for years. He baptized our babies, heard Connor's first confession. I should be able to trust this man.

"I'm just so sad, Father. I don't know how to explain it, except that I am sad all of the time. There is a black cloud hanging over my head, and it is pulling me down daily, all the time, every minute of every day. I just can't seem to get out of this funk."

"You should not feel bad for feeling the way you do, Anna. It is normal. But I am here to tell you that most people who have experienced tragedy in their life say there were a couple of things that helped them move on. The first thing is faith. I know you have faith in God, so let Him help you. The second thing is counseling. Talking to a professional can help immensely, if you let it. Do not shut out everyone in your life. You need Paul, and he needs you right now. Let him know what you are feeling, what you are thinking. You might be embarrassed for him to know your deepest feelings, but exposing yourself to him will only bring you two closer."

I know he's right. "Thanks, Father. I will think about it. I truly appreciate your visit today. I will call you if I need to talk again."

I dismiss him with my eyes. I scrunch down in bed, pull the covers closer to my neck and hit the TV clicker. As I stare blankly at the TV screen, Father sighs and stands up. He puts his hand on my knee, and bends his head downward.

"Father in heaven, please look down on your child, Anna, and be with her right now. She needs your love now more than ever before, Father. We know her family is with you, enjoying peace and life in your garden. Bless Anna and make her strong. In your holy name, we pray, Amen."

I whisper, "Thanks" as Father Daniel quietly walks out of my bedroom into the hall. He closes the door. I thought I would feel humiliated, but really, I don't. I think Father meant well. And he prayed for me! Maybe God will hear his plea and have mercy on me. I know I need help.

27

Before

Ryan's entry into this world will always be etched into my mind as well. Paul and I found out in an ultrasound that we were expecting another boy. Initially I was a little disappointed that I didn't get my girl yet, but also thrilled with the thought of another precious boy.

The second pregnancy was even more difficult at age thirty-three with a baby at home. I remember being very nauseous and lying on the couch while Connor played on the floor, watching yet another Baby Einstein movie. There were quite a few mornings where I felt I was a horrible mother. When you're sick, it is very difficult to take care of others very well.

I had strong contractions two weeks before Ryan's due date, and sure enough, they landed me in the hospital in labor. I expected my water to break like it did with Connor, so I wasn't as sure that I was in labor this time.

I waited too long to figure it out. By the time I couldn't walk or talk very well anymore, I was grumpy and yelling at Paul to hurry up and get me to the hospital.

Thankfully, I didn't have to push for two hours this time again, but Ryan's birth was not much easier or painless in my book. It hurts like hell no matter what. But he was born without issue as well and we were so thrilled to have our two little men.

Ryan was born bald as a billiard ball. He had long, skinny fingers and toes. His bright blue eyes were no surprise, and when he did finally begin to grow hair you could hardly tell because it was so white.

Ryan was a true gift from God. He had listened to my prayers of having an easier baby this time around. And Ryan was such an easy baby to have! I couldn't believe the difference from Connor. Ryan ate and slept, and didn't cry unless he was hungry or had a dirty diaper. The difference was amazing.

Ryan grew up trying to do everything that Connor did. And he is usually right there beside him doing it, too. He loves his big brother and still gives him plenty of hugs. His feelings can get hurt when Connor runs off with older kids, leaving Ryan behind.

Ryan doesn't have the gregarious personality that Connor has. Ryan is more hesitant, better in tune with the environment. Ryan will sit back and watch things first, taking it all in. He is such a smart little boy. Paul thinks he will be an engineer some day. He can take anything apart and quickly put it back to together again.

While Ryan loves to play with his brother, he also enjoys taunting him. I don't know if it's the second child syndrome or not, but Ryan knows what buttons to push to make Connor go mad. He just taunts him without reason, and Connor cannot ignore it.

Ryan can let things roll off his back, while Connor needs to talk everything out. Those two boys have had their fair share of hitting, punching, and kicking one another. Someone ends up crying and running to Mom and then they both get to spend some time in their rooms. Within ten minutes one of them has usually gone into the other's room and they're already talking about their next adventure together, having forgotten the past incident.

28

After

The weeks continue on, one blurring into the next. Not much changes each day. Paul goes to work all day, every day. We hardly see each other, barely speak to one another. I think I repulse him. I know my hygiene is disgusting, but I don't care. The phone rings, the doorbell rings, but I don't answer them. I don't want to talk to anyone or have anyone see me. I am content to be in my bed and dream.

I hear the back door open on a Friday afternoon at two o'clock and Paul is coming upstairs. I hear him talking to someone from work on his cell phone. Why is he home in the middle of the afternoon? He doesn't usually come home until seven o'clock or later. This makes me nervous.

He comes in our room and sits down on the chaise lounge, still talking on the phone. He glances at me once, and I believe he doesn't like what he sees. I'm in bed, as always. I showered a couple of days ago, I think, so I can't look *that* bad. When he hangs up, he just stares at me with a look of nothing on his face. I stare back.

"I'm taking you to see Dr. Hansen. Get dressed. You have an appointment in fifteen minutes."

"Well hello to you too, honey. And why do I have a doctor's appointment? Am I sick? Is there a problem?"

I'm feeling my heart beat too fast right now. How dare he boss me around.

"Anna, you are depressed. Dr. Hansen is a psychiatrist and she can give you medicine so you are not so sad all the time. Please, do this for me. I am trying to help you. I love you, Anna, and we cannot continue to go on like this. You know it's the truth. Please, I am begging you."

In my heart, I know what he says is true. I am depressed. I physically can't move, my body is limp, and my brain is on hold.

I have good reason to be depressed. Maybe medicine will help me. I'm just too bushed to get out of bed, put clothes on, get in the car, and walk into Dr. Hansen's office. That sounds like a lot of work.

Paul walks into our closet and comes out with my favorite jeans and gray t-shirt, socks, bra, and white Nike tennis shoes. He pulls the covers off of me, and lifts my old scrubby t-shirt over my head. He dresses me like I am a child. I don't really feel myself doing anything. I'm just watching it occur.

After I'm dressed I walk into the bathroom, brush my teeth, comb my hair, and go to the bathroom. My hair is greasy, I look awful without makeup, and I need deodorant. But it's too much work to put it on, so I skip it.

We get into Paul's car and I sink into his nice leather seat.

"You are going to feel better soon, I promise you, Anna. I will not let you waste away your life. We will get through this together."

Dr. Hansen prescribes an anti-depressant for me. She says I need to take it daily for three months. We will talk then about whether or not I feel as though the medicine is helping me. She also wants me to come in and talk to her once a week. I'm concerned that I may become a zombie. "How will these drugs affect me?" I ask.

"You shouldn't be as tired, and you should be in better spirits. Anti-depressants affect your brain's chemistry, adjusting it so that hormonally you should be able to deal with life better. The drugs can't *solve* your problems, and they won't take away the pain. But they should assist you in having a clearer mind, and in having more energy so you can get out of bed every day and function."

"Actually, I'd *like* drugs to take away the pain, Dr. Hansen. That's what I really need. Every minute of my life right now is painful. The pain is so deep I've just learned to accept it as part of my body's fiber now. I want the pain to go away so I don't constantly hurt. If you don't have that, I'm not sure anything else will help me. Drugs to help me 'deal with' the death of my babies isn't what I'm looking for. I want to have my life back *with* them, not without them. No one seems to understand that."

Paul raises his eyebrows at Dr. Hansen with that "I told you so" look. I grab the sheet with Dr. Hansen's prescription written on it and yank the door open and walk out. I go straight out to the car. I feel like an imbecile, I feel like everyone has been talking about me behind my back. I feel like a loser. Paul is dealing with our children's deaths, why can't I?

29
After

I begin taking the anti-depressants daily. Paul gives me a pill in the morning and one at night. I agree to it because I figure it can't hurt. I don't notice anything different though. I'm still sad, mad, pissed, furious, depressed, and angry.

I meet with Dr. Hansen every Tuesday morning now. After a couple of weeks of taking the pills, I notice that I am sleeping during the day a little less. I still spend most of my days in my bedroom, but now I am watching TV more, paging through magazines more often, and looking at photo albums of the kids more too.

I'm not happy by any means, but I do acknowledge that perhaps I'm not a zombie. It has been five months, two weeks, three days, and thirteen hours since the car accident.

***

Paul tells me he thinks the medicine is helping me. He says he has caught me with a semi-smile on my face a few times. I purposely do not smile when he says this, although it's hard for me to hold back a smile and he knows it. We have had dinner together in the kitchen a few times in the past few weeks. We are talking more, and he is coming home earlier some evenings. He will sit up in bed with me some nights and watch TV with me or he will read his work stuff.

I have a few goals for each day now. My first goal is to shower every morning before noon. I realize I feel better after the warm water hits me. My second goal is to spend a couple of hours outside of my bedroom every day. I generally sit in the kitchen and watch TV there, or I wander around the house looking at the kids' pictures. But that makes me sad, so I mainly try to keep myself in the kitchen.

I know I'm still grieving, but I'm not yet certain how to stop the grief. It clings to me, and I don't want it to go away totally either. I realize that someone is buying our groceries, doing our laundry, and basically doing my job. I know Tammie used to come over a couple of times a week, but I haven't heard her lately. I ask Paul about it, and he tells me that he has been doing everything. That is why he comes to bed so late. I feel like a child.

I've been forcing myself to talk to Paul, have a conversation with him every day. About nothing, or about what I've seen on TV or read in the newspaper. Or I ask him about work. He seems pleased with my progress. But I realize we haven't touched each other, literally, in months. Not a hug, not a kiss, not a hand laid across an arm…nothing. I feel removed from him completely. As though he were someone from a former life.

30

Before

Eighteen months after Ryan was born came our little sweetheart, Cassy. After our very first pregnancy ended in a miscarriage and our hearts were broken, Paul and I decided not to use any form of birth control anymore. So I went off the pill and we decided to let God's will give us our direction in life.

I must admit that neither Paul nor I thought that we would get pregnant as quickly as we did with our three kids. Apparently God knew that we were older parents and needed to get moving if we were going to have a family. And I thank God that I was able to have my children for the short time that I did get them.

I had always told Paul that I wanted to have both boys and girls in our family. Having been raised with two sisters, I wanted to experience both genders in our family, if possible. After having two boys, I told Paul we would go for as long as it took us to have a baby girl.

Of course I didn't really mean this, and it scared Paul. He was as overwhelmed as I was with two little ones, and I know he wondered if we could even handle a third. He prayed for the third baby to be a girl so we could conclude our family.

God must have heard his prayers.

We found out in an ultrasound that we were expecting a girl. We were so excited! To have pink in the house would be so very fun after lots of blue. And this could mean that our family was complete. Needless to say, about a month after Cassy was born, Paul very willingly had a vasectomy. Neither of us was certain if we could survive a fourth child.

Since Connor and Ryan arrived before their due dates, I was certain that the third child would be early as well. When my due date had come and gone, I was not a happy momma. I had gained forty pounds, I was fat, ugly and miserable.

I needed this baby out of me. Dr. Foster said we could induce labor if I wanted. *If* I wanted? Oh please, God, if you don't take this baby out soon I may burst.

So on May seven, I went in to have my baby girl. It took a lot longer than I thought. Paul and I went into the hospital at five in the morning, and nothing moved along real quickly. They gave me two doses of Pitocin to induce labor, broke my water, and finally, at seven p.m. I had horrible cramps.

I thought I needed to poop, so I sat on the toilet and pushed. Paul ran for the nurse at the station and the nurses insisted that I get off the toilet. Why I didn't realize that the baby was coming is beyond me. It all happened so quickly. I had an epidural, so I hadn't been feeling my contractions. So when the baby was coming, it was very sudden.

Thankfully I didn't have to push for hours as with the boys. Cassy was born quickly and I was so tickled to have my baby girl. She was good sized, weighing in at eight pounds and eleven ounces. My parents were able to stay at our home with Connor and Ryan while Paul was with me in the hospital.

The boys were so thrilled to hold their new sister and give her kisses. I was worn out, but couldn't have been happier. When Cassy was born I called her 'my little butterball.' She was round, rosy, and bald like Ryan. She was as sweet as could be; a very easy baby.

After high maintenance Connor, anyone would seem easy, but she was really a good baby. She watched her brothers, loved the dog, and was content as long as someone was nearby. She just went with the flow, and has always tagged along real well.

She is such a sweet thing. Cassy can be a princess one moment and a tomboy the next. Her feelings can get hurt by her brothers and she will be in tears, and then ten seconds later she is off chasing them to the sand box. She is shy in public, but once you get to know her she doesn't stop talking.

At home she never shuts up. She will tell me every detail about her day at kindergarten, while I can't get an ounce of information out of the boys except for, "It was fine."

Having a newborn, a one, and two year old at home was interesting. Our tiny little rental house was cramped with the three kids, all their baby and toddler stuff, and our brown Labrador retriever, Penny.

The house was always a disaster, and I felt like I did in-home daycare, which I guess I did. Even though I had exactly what I wanted now with my three wonderful children, it wasn't what I thought it would be. Paul was gone a lot, and I was stuck at home taking care of little ones all the time.

Our marriage took a hit during this time. I remember in sociology class at Iowa State in my Marriage and Family class, that the reported toughest time of a married couple's life was when they had young kids. I didn't understand it at the time, of course.

Until you have little ones of your own, you don't know the meaning of multi-tasking. Paul and I would fight about anything. We both perceived that the other had it easier. He couldn't understand why I was so tired all the time. I would get so mad when he would decide to work late or go out with the guys for a beer after work. I needed him at home, dammit. Some days I was barely surviving and he had the audacity to come and go as he pleased.

But somehow you work through it. Talking to my girlfriends helped a lot, because I discovered that Paul looked like an angel compared to many of their husbands. Paul loved his family, he did spend a lot of time with the kids and I, and I trusted him completely. He might have been a jerk at times, but overall he had a heart of gold.

31
After

I am scared that Paul is having an affair. If he is, I'm not sure I could handle it. I poked through the dirty clothes in the laundry room today, thinking about throwing in a load of clothes, and I found a scrap of paper in his pants pocket that said: Nicole, eight o'clock, Ridges. My heart stopped when I read the note. Who the hell is Nicole? Ridges is a fancy restaurant on the west end of town. Paul took me there a few years ago for our seventh anniversary. He didn't like it, claimed it was too fancy for him. So why is he meeting a Nicole there now?

This note puts me into a tailspin. Should I call Paul and ask him right now what is going on? Should I wait until he gets home tonight and confront him face to face? Should I barge into his office demanding an explanation? Or should I forget about it and trust him? Have some faith in the man, Anna. I'm sure it was a business meeting with a client. I've never heard him mention a Nicole, though. And he usually tells me about his co-workers and clients.

He would absolutely not betray me this way after what we've been through, would he? Our three kids died in a car accident along with my parents six months ago. During that time period he could not have had time to have an affair. He is a better man than that. Would he really go so far as to be unfaithful to me after our kids died?

But why *wouldn't* he seek outside attention? It's not like I've been the perfect wife to him the past six months. I've been depressed and in bed every day. I've soiled our bed sheets. I have stunk with my own body odor. I have offered him nothing by way of a marital relationship. Who wouldn't understand if he looked outside the marriage for some comfort?

But God help me, if that man abused my trust in him I will kill him. I am so mad right now that I am about ready to march into his office and confront him in front of everyone. I'd probably be the laughing stock, though. I'm sure everyone but me knows that Paul and this slut Nicole are having an affair. Aren't the wives always the last ones to know? I've been at home mourning the death of our children, and he's been out screwing around on me. If he thinks he can get away with this, he has another thing coming.

32

Before

When Ryan was a toddler, in his four year old days, he would tell me twenty times a day, "I love you, Mommy."

I always responded with, "I love you too, Ryan." Some days it got old. I mean, how many times can a person tell you they love you?

What I wouldn't give now to hear those words.

Ryan was the most challenging toddler of my three kids. He would scream when he was upset. It drove me nuts. He was also the most physical, and so he would physically just get in his brother's or sister's way too often. I had the most challenging time dealing with his outbursts. If I yelled at him, it didn't faze him. If I remained cool and calm, it didn't change his behavior.

I sometimes lost my temper and spanked his butt. That had an effect on Ryan, but I wasn't proud of it. Sending him to his room also made his behavior stop.

His outbursts lessened and he often was the best behaved child. But when he blew, he blew up. But Ryan was also a sweet, cuddly boy, too. He needed lots of hugs, and asked for them often. I called him my Jekyll and Hyde, for one minute he was a saint, and the next minute he was a little devil. As he got older, his temperament leveled off and he generally controlled his outbursts much better. He could still be a little stinker at home, though, teasing Connor and Cassy to no end.

What always amazed Paul and I, was that his teachers at school always complimented him on his great behavior. Apparently he behaved very well at school. At least they didn't see the worst of him. Many days he would run off the bus and immediately pick a fight with his brother. We waited for the inevitability of his outbursts to occur at school, but they never came, thank goodness.

Ryan was such a smart little boy. He loved his video games, the computer, and anything physical. We were amazed at his attention span for a five year old. He could sit and play his video game for an hour and not move a muscle. Try to get that boy to sit still at church for an hour, now that was another story. If he enjoyed doing something, then he went all out. Ryan also had such a soft side to him. He loved pets and stuffed animals. He adored Penny, our brown lab. He always wanted a new stuffed animal at a toy store. His bedroom was filled with every kind of animal possible. He was our tender hearted child.

33
After

I'm fretting about Paul's alleged affair daily now. I decide not to confront him about it. I'd rather catch him in a lie or in the act. I'm trying so hard to be normal around Paul now. I am clean and dressed when he comes home and I have dinner with him that I have prepared myself. I talk to him and try so hard to be positive and pleasant.

He compliments me on my progress. He reminds me that next week I have my three month appointment with Dr. Hansen to discuss my medicine. He thinks it is working great. After dinner tonight he tells me that he has to go back to the bank for a few hours. He has to prepare for a big meeting tomorrow.

"Not a problem," I tell him. "You do whatever you have to do. I'll just be here at home cleaning and picking up. There's a good movie on tonight I want to catch. I won't wait up for you."

He takes all of this in stride, and it doesn't seem to faze him. Boy, he could be an actor he's so nonchalant about it. He gathers up his briefcase and folders, grabs his car keys off the desk, and says, "See you in the morning, then."

"Bye, Hon. Don't work too late," I say with my best smile.

I listen to the garage door go up, his car leave the garage and then the garage door goes down again. I run out into the garage and get my Toyota mini-van going. I drive the two miles to his bank, making sure he has a good head start on me. I don't want him to see me at all.

I feel like a stalker. I never imagined myself doing this. I know where he always parks, and his car is not there. In fact, there are no cars in his bank parking lot. Maybe he stopped to get gas along the way, or ran a quick errand. I drive away and come back fifteen minutes later. Still no sign of Paul.

I sit and think. Now what in the world is he doing? I have just caught him in a lie. He distinctly told me that he was going to the bank to prepare for a meeting. He's not at the bank. Why would he lie to me? And where could he be?

Many nights I have no idea what time he comes home. It is all adding up to one big affair, if you ask me. Is he that big of a schmuck? I would never have believed it. I think I am handling this pretty well, considering my history with tragedy the past few months.

After waiting thirty minutes a block away from his bank and still no sign of his car, I decide to drive towards Ridges. I am fuming. I don't appreciate being lied to. You only lie if you're trying to hide something or you're guilty of something. Paul has no reason to lie to me if he's innocent. Maybe I should feel hurt or sad, but I don't. I'm pissed off and ready for a fight.

I drive through the parking lot of Ridges. I weave up and down the rows of vehicles, looking for Paul's silver Volvo. It's not in the lot. I drive around the block that Ridges is on.

There it is! There is his damn Volvo. I know his license plate number and there it is. Well, I'll be. That little puke. I pull into an empty spot and think. What should I do now? I'm in a sweatshirt and jeans. I could just bolt inside the restaurant and walk around the tables until I find Paul.

And then what? Do I make a scene? Everyone would just think I'm crazy.

"There's Anna, she's not been right ever since her parents and kids died in that awful car accident," they'd whisper. They'd probably feel sympathy for Paul.

I could go home and wake up when Paul does decide to come back, if he even decides to come home tonight. For all I know he and Nicole will go to the Highland Hotel after their dinner. He probably hops into our bed at five o'clock in the morning. And I've thought all along he spent the night with me. I have been so naïve. Here I have been trusting my husband all these years. He's probably been screwing around behind my back for years, for all I know.

I could just leave a note on the kitchen table that says, "Decided to leave you. Have a great life with Nicole." But then I'd miss seeing his reaction. I've always liked to watch people squirm. Catch them in their lies. The heat rising up their necks to their faces. They can't look you in the eyes anymore. I don't want Paul to get away with it too easily.

I decide that I need to see for myself who this Nicole babe is. I want to see how pretty she is. I want Paul to see me and I want him to feel guilty. I get out of my car and I go inside Ridges. It smells so good in here. Everyone is very dressed up and I instantly feel self-conscious. I know what I look like, and it's not pretty. The maitre de approaches me with, "May I help you, Maam?"

"Hello. Yes. I'm sorry that I'm under dressed. But we have a family emergency at home and I need to find my husband right away. Paul Dawson. He's having dinner here and I need to talk to him right away. Please," I plead.

The maitre de glances at the reservation book and says, "I'll be right back, Mrs. Dawson. I'll let Mr. Dawson know you're here."

My word, the schmuck is really here! My stomach is in knots and I feel dizzy. I watch while the maitre de goes across the room. I start to follow him from a distance behind. I have got to see Paul's face when he sees me.

I feel time slow down. Everything seems to be happening in slow motion. I hear forks and knives clank against china plates as steaks are being cut. I hear laughter and the clinking of wine glasses, toasts to happy times. I turn into the next room and see the maitre de bend over a man's shoulder from the side, whispering in his ear.

There is a woman sitting across the table from Paul. A very pretty woman. I don't know her. A woman I've never seen before, with shoulder length blonde hair, dressed fashionably, having dinner with *my* husband. Paul is starting to stand up, taking his napkin from his lap and setting it on the table. The woman nods in understanding to Paul.

I approach the table. The maitre de turns around quickly, almost bumping head first into me.

"Oh, Maam. I thought you were waiting at the door. I found Mr. Dawson. Would you like to come with me to the front?"

"No thank you. I can talk to my husband right here. Thank you for your help though."

The maitre de is unsure of whether to stay or go, and he reluctantly begins walking away back to his podium.

"Anna, what are you doing here? Is something wrong?" Paul has the gall to say.

"Oh, I just thought I'd stop by at your bank tonight to surprise you, and I guess the surprise was on me. You weren't at the bank working late like you told me. You lied to me, Paul. And then another surprise, you're here having dinner with Nicole. Care to explain this to me, oh husband of mine?"

I'm actually kind of enjoying this moment, if one can enjoy the moment when they find out their husband is a lying bastard. The woman is looking down at her plate, uncomfortable with the situation. She's dabbing her mouth with her napkin repeatedly, probably wondering if she should get up and head to the ladies room to avoid a nasty scene with her lover's distraught wife.

Paul is talking in whispers, attempting to keep this conversation quiet. I am purposefully speaking loudly, hoping everyone in the restaurant hears me. I can see out of the corner of my eyes that people at nearby tables are watching us. Paul has always hated a scene. I know he is embarrassed and I am loving every moment of this. He caused this scene.

"Anna, let's go talk in the lounge," Paul begs.

"Oh, no thanks, Paul. I'm quite fine with talking right here. I'd like to meet your friend here. Hi, I'm Paul's wife, Anna. It's so nice to meet you..."

The other woman looks at Paul for help as I hold my hand out to her. She reluctantly shakes my hand and says, "Hello Anna. I've heard so much about you. I'm Nicole Wakefield."

I knew it! I feel like I solved The Mystery of The Cheating Husband. A real Nancy Drew am I. Only I never imagined I would be the main character in this ugly drama.

"Well, well, well. It looks like you've just been busted, Paul. I think you have a lot of explaining to do. Maybe you've told Nicole the truth, and then again, maybe you haven't. Nicole, I hope Paul told you that he has a wife. A poor wife at that, these past few months. Maybe Paul forgot to mention to you that our children were killed six months ago. But he seems to be moving on just fine. Apparently it hasn't affected his sex life. It was real nice meeting you, Nicole. I hope you enjoy dinner with my husband. Although he already had chicken casserole at home with me tonight. He must be very hungry tonight."

Paul is mortified. He's just standing by the table, unsure of what to do. Nicole has remained seated this entire time. I twirl around and as quickly as I entered the scene, I leave.

Now everyone is craning their necks around and looking at Paul. I'm smiling. This was worth it. I wonder if Paul will just sit right back down with Nicole and finish their wine and dinner together, or is he walking after me? I'd put money on the former option.

I drive home, get in bed and dream.

34
After

Something interrupts me just as I'm beginning a good dream. I hear Paul come into our room. He turns on the light and changes out of his clothes.

"Anna, can we talk?"

Do I ignore him or should I deal with this? I decide I really do want to hear his lame excuse.

I roll over and say, "Paul, you're the one who has some talking to do, not me."

"You're right, I owe you an explanation. First of all, I am so sorry that I lied to you, Anna. You deserve that apology. I told you I was going to the bank to work, when in fact I knew all along that our business meeting was at a restaurant. I should have been honest with you up front. But I did it because I didn't want you to get the wrong idea."

"Well that sure backfired on you, Paul. Because now I do have the wrong idea, but I'm guessing it's the *right* idea. Any husband who lies to their wife about going to work late at the office, and really meets a beautiful lady at a fancy restaurant is hiding something. So...how long have you been cheating on me with Nicole? The day after the kids were killed? The day after their funerals? When, Paul? Or was it even *before* the kids' accident? I deserve to know the truth. You got busted tonight, so you might as well own up to it and tell me the truth. Give me something to really be depressed about. At least I can explain this one easily to Dr. Hansen. A cheating husband is a good excuse for anti-depressants, don't you think?"

"Anna, you've got it all wrong. I have not been having an affair with Nicole. She was sent here from corporate to work on an international account. I am her supervisor while she is at the bank. We have had to work closely together on this project, and I'm sorry to say we have had to work many nights together as well. We just cannot get everything done during the work day."

"Interesting, Paul. I didn't see any notebooks, papers, or files out on the restaurant table. In fact, it didn't resemble a working dinner at all to me. Don't lie to me. I know what I saw. I say my husband at the fanciest restaurant in town allegedly "meeting" another woman for work. You didn't tell me about it, and you got caught. It's really pathetic, your timing to have an affair."

"Anna, I swear to you that I haven't slept with Nicole. I admit that we have become friends, and that we talk about our personal lives. She is separated from her husband at the moment and going through a difficult time. I have obviously been through a terrible time, so we do commiserate together. But I have not cheated on you. I want you to believe that."

"I believe nothing you say as the truth right now, Paul. You have destroyed my faith in you, when I needed it most. I thought you were the one bright spot in my life. I thought you were the reason I was choosing to live. And now I come to find out that you have been lying and cheating on me. I don't even know what to say to you."

My heart is dead. I feel as though a stake has been driven through my chest. The love of my life has stepped out on me! Who would have thought? I am finished with this conversation and I go to sleep.

When you are sorrowful,
Look again in your heart,
And you shall see that in truth,
You are weeping for that which
Has been your delight.

—Kahlil Gibran

35

Before

In my dream it is Ryan's fourth birthday. He always loved the anticipation of his birthday more than the other kids. He loved gifts, cake, decorations, the parties, blowing out the candles, and just the attention that was bestowed on him for his special day. He would pile up his gifts on the kitchen floor for weeks before his birthday and try to guess what was inside of each one.

I can see his beautiful shining face so clearly. His white hair and devilish blue eyes. Ryan would unwrap his gifts with a fury. He needed to see the surprise so quickly. He never did have much patience for anything.

On his fourth birthday Paul and I had given him a battery powered four-wheeler that he could drive. It was a big, outside toy and he drove it around all winter long. When Paul showed him the four-wheeler in the garage, Ryan just stared at it without much emotion. Unusual for him. He's usually a squealer. He walked over to the four-wheeler and Paul showed him the forward and reverse pedals, and how to steer it. Ryan just hopped right in, put the Velcro seat belt around him and drove down the driveway.

You'd have thought the child had died and gone to heaven that day. He drove that four-wheeler until the battery died. We had to recharge it that night so he could ride it again the next morning. The four-wheeler had a seat for two people, and he would frequently let Cassy ride with him. I have so many pictures of Ryan in that four-wheeler. I always told Paul we were in trouble, that in a few years he would be wanting the real thing. Ryan definitely had a need for speed.

The night of Ryan's fourth birthday as we were getting the kids into bed, I lay down and snuggled Ryan in his bed. He was so sleepy he could hardly keep his eyes open.

He rolled over and gave me a "cheek hug" as we called them, and said, "Mommy, I love you so much. I never want to leave you." And he drifted off to sleep. I watched him for a few minutes, just mesmerized by his chest rising and falling with each breath, thinking about how I was the luckiest mom in the world.

Book Two

Trying To Move On

36

I'm sick of being sad. I'm tired of lying in bed all day. It's pathetic that I don't have a purpose in life anymore. The medicine that Dr. Hansen gave me must be working a little bit. I do seem to have a little more energy. I don't need to sleep as much. My head does seem a little clearer. My kids are still dead, my parents are still dead, and my husband is still a lying cheater.

Paul continues to stick to his story. He swears up and down that he did not sleep with Nicole. He admits that their friendship did get too personal. But Nicole is out of his bank now, and he promises me that he will never see her again. I want to believe Paul so badly. But being mad at Paul has given me a renewed source of energy.

I wonder what I should do now. Should I look for a job? I'm not sure who would hire the crazy woman. What was my college degree in again? Oh yeah, Business Administration. I need a purpose. My life calling as a mom is over, and now I need a new calling.

My sister Abby asked me if Paul and I would consider trying to have another baby or adopting. I balked when she said this out loud. I'm sure many people have wondered about this, though.

I must confess it has entered my mind. But then the thought leaves as quickly as it entered my mind. I'm forty years old, and I am done having babies. Been there, done that. And plus, I don't want different children, I want *my* children. I want the ones that I gave birth to. But I know that period of my life is over.

There are thousands of children all over the world that need parents. We could adopt three kids if we chose to. But the thought of filling up Connor, Ryan, and Cassy's rooms with other kids makes my skin crawl. It would never be the same. I don't want to try to replace my babies. I can't replace them. They were unique, one-of-a-kind kids. And if I can't have them, then I don't want anyone. That may seem like a childish way to go about it, but it's what I feel.

A woman from Catholic Charities called me last week. She wondered if I would be interested in coming to their seminars on grief counseling. Immediately I was insulted, because I assumed that she thought I needed grief counseling.

But then I realized she wanted me to speak to the people on grief. I told her I was still mourning myself, that I wasn't sure I had anything to offer to others. She said that I would mourn forever, but in different ways. I got depressed listening to her, and told her I wasn't a good public speaker and I wasn't ready to share my story with the public yet.

So I know I don't want to adopt, get pregnant again, or be the poster mom for parents who have lost their children. People apparently just don't realize how fragile I still am. They can't tell that I could break into pieces at any given moment? I've barely been out in public the past eight months. Going to the grocery store is still a challenge for me. I don't like people looking at me, and I really don't like people talking to me. Maybe I'm coming across as confident? That's a laugh!

I'm also not sure if my marriage is going to last. I used to never, ever doubt that one thing in my life. My sacred marriage. Other things may have been questionable, but never my marriage. Paul and I are strained at best now. We pass each other in the house, not touching or talking unless we have to. He is still attempting to be nice, to make an effort with the marriage. I will have nothing to do with him. He can just go have dinner with Nicole every night for all I care.

37

It's a November winter in Iowa and it sucks. It is freaking cold out, extremely windy, snow is on the ground, and it will continue to be this way for oh, four more months. My dad used to say, "When you're bored, why not travel? There's nothing better for the soul than a trip to another part of the world." How right you were, dad. I'm thinking I need to get away from here. The Caribbean is calling.

I call Abby, my dear sister. She and Courtney have been so kind to me these past nine months through my ordeal. I toss out my idea of her going on a cruise with me. She immediately says there is just no way that she can make it work. She begins to cry, she feels so bad telling me no.

I tell her not to worry about it, that it was just a whim I had. I thought it would be cathartic for both of us to get away from it all for a week. Abby says there is nothing better she would like to do, but she is so swamped with work, and her husband is out of town a lot lately, leaving her with no one to help with the kids. I completely understand her predicament, but still I am disappointed. She is mourning the death of our parents yet, too. I ask Courtney as well, but she can't get out of work either.

Next I call Tammie. I give her the same proposition I gave to Abby and Courtney. Tammie is quiet, and then I hear her classic war cry, her rolling of the tongue yelp she does when she's drinking.

"Anna, you are right, we need this trip. I would love to go with you. Let me talk to Jack tonight about it and I'll call you tomorrow."

Ooh, now I'm a little excited about the prospect of getting out of Gannon for a week. The Caribbean has always been a favorite destination of mine.

Paul and I have been to the Cayman Islands, Jamaica, the Bahamas, Cozumel, and Belize. I realize that I don't want Paul to go on this trip with me. I need a girl's trip. I need to sort things out with Tammie. I need to drink margaritas, lay in the sun by the pool, and get everything off my chest with my best friend. Maybe she can fix my life. I know I shouldn't get too excited about this trip. Tammie might not even be able to go. But just the thought of it is making me smile.

I get on-line and start researching cruises. I have never been on a cruise. Paul never wanted to go on one. He thought they would be too boring. There are so many cruising choices. Eastern Caribbean, western Caribbean, Alaska, the Mediterranean or the Mexican Riviera. I just want warm weather for one week. I don't care what islands we port at. I print up different travel itinerary possibilities. I have never been to the Virgin Islands, so St. Johns, St. Thomas, or St. Martin are sounding great to me. Aruba, Antigua, Turks and Cacaos…I'm feeling warm all over now.

Paul surprisingly comes home for dinner tonight. Drat, and of all the nights I was really hoping he would work late. I wanted to think about my vacation without him. I suppose I should tell him what I'm thinking about doing.

"Paul, I'd like to get out of the house and out of Gannon. I need a little get-away vacation," I begin.

"That is an awesome idea. I've been thinking the same thing. Let's just go away and have some time alone, Anna. I miss you and I know we need to talk and just be alone together."

He is looking so warm and loving at me, I almost feel guilty, but not quite. I just have to think about the name Nicole, and my distrust of him comes back at high speeds.

"I've asked Tammie to go with me, Paul."

His smile slowly drops from his face, and I see the recognition creep into his eyes.

"Oh, I see. I suppose that would be fun for the two of you to do together. A girl's trip. But if for some reason Tammie can't go, just let me know, and I'd be happy to go with you, Anna."

It's a little late to be a loving husband at this point, Paul.

"Thanks, but I feel like I just need to get away from it *all* right now. My life, my marriage, my town. Nothing is making sense to me right now, Paul. I just need to step out of my life for a week and put things back in perspective. I knew you'd understand."

I get up from the dinner table to get more milk for us both. I put my hand lightly on his shoulder. His hand grabs mine. I pull away. I just can't do it. I just can't pretend that he has not broken my heart. I want it to heal, but it's not time yet.

"I want you in my life, Anna. I will not give up on our marriage. I am with you forever. Please don't ever forget that. I understand that you need time to figure things out on your own level. But quit telling yourself that I had an affair. It is simply not true. I don't know what else I can say to make you believe that. I did not have an affair, and I feel like I am being punished for something I didn't even do."

I leave the kitchen and go upstairs. I want to take a nap, but I end up watching TV instead.

38

I'm waiting impatiently for Tammie to call me back. I couldn't sleep at all last night wondering what I'd do if she said she can't go. Would I go by myself? Would I break down and ask Paul to go with me? What if Tammie *can* go? Should we do it? I've never been on a girl's only vacation since I've been married. The last time I've been on a trip with only girlfriends was in college during spring break, and I'd rather not conjure up those drunken memories.

The phone rings, and I grab it before the second ring.

"Aruba, Jamaica, ooh I'm gonna take ya!" Some bad singing is coming from the other end of the phone, but I know instantly that Tammie is able to go with me.

"Can you handle a week with me, girlfriend? Because I am so in!"

"Jack doesn't care? Are you sure?"

I want to make certain that Tammie doesn't back out on me.

"He thought it was a wonderful idea. He just wanted to check our savings last night, make sure we had it padded a bit before I gallivant off to the Caribbean for a week without him. Oh, Anna, I'm so honored you asked me to go. I know this trip will be just what you need."

"As my best friend, I warn you now. I reserve the right to be intoxicated, to sleep in until noon if I feel like it, and to tell you things that may abhor you, but you are not allowed to repeat them. If you accept these terms, then you are in," I tell Tammie.

"I promise I won't disappoint, Anna. Your most heart felt secrets are safe with me. You've always known you can trust me."

Yes, but I always thought I could trust my husband, too, and look where that has gotten me.

39

For the next three weeks I am happy thinking about the upcoming vacation with Tammie. Paul seems put-off whenever I mention it. But he claims he's glad that I'm happy about *something*.

I realize that my husband and I have not had sex in nine months. I'm just really not attracted to a cheater anymore. The thought has crossed my mind that Paul could be spending a lot of time with Nicole while I'm gone. But weirdly enough, this thought doesn't upset me. It's pretty pathetic when you're not even jealous of your own husband cheating on you. That says a lot for the state of my marriage. I wonder if we'll still be married in a year.

The day finally comes when we fly out of Des Moines to Miami. I have bought magazines, books, and brought a journal to write in. I brought my iPod to listen to my music, too. Tammie and I just can't seem to stop talking, though. I'm not getting any reading done on the flight.

I'm trying hard to be happy. I made sure I had plenty of my anti-depressants along for the week. I'm nervous about going off of them. Dr. Hansen said I might need them for years. As long as they are helping me. Although I'm not supposed to drink much alcohol while on these anti-depressants. That could be a problem on this trip.

We stay overnight at an Embassy Suites near the Miami port. We can't get on the ship until the next morning. Tammie and I sit in the hotel bar and watch a college basketball game, drinking white Russians and sampling the appetizers. We both get a quick buzz, and realize that we're not quite the drinkers we were back in college.

Two men send us a round of drinks, and then come over to our table. They are not bad looking, but I'm really not in the mood for their talk. They ask if we mind if they sit down. I notice that they have on wedding rings, and it is obvious that Tammie and I do too. Tammie looks at me and I say, "I'm sorry guys. I just buried my three children and parents, so this trip is all about death and dying. I'm afraid I won't be very good company tonight."

The two men are gone in a heartbeat.

"I guess they figured their chances of getting lucky tonight with us were pretty slim," Tammie laughed. "You know, Anna, you do play the death card whenever it suits you."

I'm not sure how to take this comment. I don't know if I should be offended, or if she's right. I hadn't thought of it that way before. Tammie always tells me the truth, even when I don't want her to.

"Please don't be mad, honey. I didn't mean it as a criticism. I wasn't really in the mood to pretend to be interested in their lives anyway."

"Do I really pull out my trump card when necessary?" I ask.

I think she's right. No one can beat me at the game of life when I mention my big issue. I pull it out and slap it on the table when I'm frustrated, when I feel I'm backed into a corner, or when I'm just crabby. Everyone should feel sorry for me, because they have no idea the hell I've been through. I have every right to be a victim if and when I want to.

"Anna, you know I would only say this to help you. Only you can decide when you have had enough of being a victim.

Only you will know when you are ready to stop letting life happen to you, and when you decide to take control of the reins again. You can choose to wallow in your grief, and if you choose that I would understand. You have every right to never get over your ordeal. But there is another road. You can choose to take the path where you begin again, Anna. It will be a bumpy road, and sometimes there will be hills to cross. But you know I will always be in the car with you. Sometimes I will be driving the car for you, and other times I will be in the back seat quietly giving you directions."

Well, there goes my buzz. A little reality slapped in the face always gives me a headache. We tip our waiter and head up to our room, ready for tomorrow's cruise.

40

The cruise ship is one big ship! I had no idea it would be this large. My goodness, it's like a small town. We chose to go on the Royal Caribbean Fascination. It is eighty-five degrees and we are sweating. But we don't care. Back in Iowa it is ten degrees and Gannon is covered in ice. The cabins are smaller than I imagined. I hope I don't get too claustrophobic. We immediately change into our swim suits and grab lounge chairs on the lido deck by the pool. I could get used to this life, I think.

"Do you miss Paul?" I know Tammie is waiting for an honest answer, not a smart ass response from me.

"Honestly, I haven't thought much about him. Tammie, I'm afraid my marriage is in the trash can. I don't know how I feel about Paul anymore. I'm so hurt and mad at him. I feel betrayed and yet I know I still love him. I just cannot get over the fact that he had an affair with another woman. It just pains me to say it out loud. After all we have been through together. He knows the death of our kids about killed me, and yet he chose to be unfaithful to me. It just blows my mind."

"How do you know Paul slept with Nicole? Did you ever catch them in bed? Did Paul admit to you that he slept with her?"

"No, and actually he repeatedly tells me that he did not have sex with her. I guess I just don't believe him. I caught him in one big lie, so I'm not able to believe anything he tells me. He claims they worked together and that they were friends, and that's all. But it was an emotional affair, an affair of the heart, if nothing else. Maybe that's what hurts the most, that he chose to confide in another woman regarding our marital problems. I just imagine him talking about me and my problems, our sex life or the lack thereof, with another woman. How dare he! I have no respect for him anymore, Tammie. Why would I want to stay married to a man I can't respect?"

I am getting myself worked up and I wave my hand to the pool waiter. Man, I need a beer. Where is he when I need that cute little Pablo the waiter?

"For what it's worth, Anna, I believe Paul. I scolded him myself, telling him that he really screwed up. He knows it, and he feels horrible. He needs to regain your trust. And he understands that it may take awhile before he can get your trust back."

Pablo delivers our bucket of six Miller Lites. I just might continue this Caribbean cruise for the next month.

"My therapist told me that fifty percent of married couples who experience the death of a child end up divorcing, Tammie. Fifty percent! She said that everyone copes differently, and so many couples struggle to grieve together and work through the issues of the death together. I guess I'm just not feeling very confident about our marriage to begin with. I'm not sure we can withstand the struggles we've been through. Plus, every time I'm around Paul I'm reminded of what we lost. I think of our kids, I think of the death, I think of the funerals. It's like I can't get beyond the bad. I don't know how to create a life with Paul without our kids in it. There, I said it. The truth is out."

"We'll work it out together, Anna. I'm here for you. You and Paul may not make it. And then again you might. I think only time will tell what happens with your marriage. But just don't rush into any quick decisions in that area. It could take years for you to figure it out."

We both lay back in the lounge chairs, sip our beers and relax at that. She is right. I want answers now. I want my marital problems solved today, and that just isn't going to happen. I can worry about it all I want, but it won't do any good. I know I need to decide what I want from my marriage. The ball is in my court.

41

The food on this cruise ship is to die for! I have never in my life seen so much food. I'm going to gain ten pounds this week alone, and I don't really care. I just keep eating and eating. I've lost fifteen pounds since the kids died, so I do have a little room to grow, I guess.

I think I'd like to work on a cruise ship. Everyone is always so happy on vacation. Well, almost everyone. I see the parents yelling at their kids and it breaks my heart. Just let them have some fun. Relax, and don't worry about being ten minutes late for dinner. Just be glad you have your kids, I want to say.

Tammie and I spend every day on the deck, by the pool, drinking, reading, and snoozing. It really couldn't be a better trip. In the evening we shower, get dressed and go to dinner. We sit with different people at each meal, meeting interesting people and annoying people.

A Max Harms from Indiana quizzed Tammie and I repeatedly about our lives. He wouldn't quit. It's like he wouldn't stop until he knew our stories. I so badly wanted to play my trump card, but I held it in my hand all through dinner. I could tell Tammie was proud of me. I don't need to tell everyone my sad story. It's really none of their business.

We got off the ship at St. Thomas for a day excursion. We walked through the downtown shopping area, buying this and that trinket for people back home. Tammie has to go into every Harley Davidson shop around the world, as Jack loves his Harley. So Jack got a few St. Thomas Harley Davidson t-shirts. I found a cool emerald ring that I bought for myself. I would never before have spent that kind of money on something so unnecessary for myself. Am I vain or in therapy?

Tammie and I had pina coladas at lunch, and then when we got back on the ship that afternoon we continued with the Caribbean themed drinks one after the other. I enjoyed the Mai Tai's, while Tammie favored the Rum Runners. All I know is that the waiters here are heavy on the tequila.

We got drunk. And I mean, sloppy, hanging on each other drunk. We were so funny, too! We laughed, and reminisced, and talked to people from all over the world. I was having the time of my life. With only two days left of the trip, I was already starting to feel sad about going back to my real life.

This is what it's like to feel happy again, I thought. And then I instantly felt guilty. Here I am, in the Caribbean nine months after my three kids and parents were tragically killed, and I am able to vacation like nothing ever happened. What kind of a horrible person am I?

Then I immediately go back to knowing that this is the purpose of this trip. To feel happy again. That feeling was lost for so long on me. I know I shouldn't feel bad about laughing and being happy, but part of me does. Tammie took one look at me and knew what I was thinking. She put her arm around my shoulder and tried to whisper something in my ear. Her weight pulled me over her and we both fell backwards in our chairs to the floor.

We looked at one another and cracked up. Now this was funny! A young man was at my side asking if I was all right. He helped me up, but I just continued to laugh. My mascara was running down my face, and my stomach muscles hurt from laughing so hard. Tammie was still rolling around on the floor guffawing. Someone was trying to help her up too.

The young man picked up my chair and helped me back into it. Man, he was handsome.

"Are you sure you're ok?" he asked.

I still had the giggles, but I assured him that nothing was broken and that I would be fine. Tammie sat up in her chair then too. The music started roaring a loud dance tune, and before I knew it the handsome young man and I were walking out on the dance floor together. I had trouble dancing to the fast music, so I took his hands and pulled him closer. He smiled a beautiful smile at me, and we danced to the rock n' roll tunes.

Tammie was next to me dancing too, with another man, this one about her age. We had smiles pasted on our faces, having the time of our lives. Boy, was I going to have a headache in the morning.

Young handsome man pulls me close and we move to a slow song. I don't remember the last time I felt this good. And wow, did Handsome feel good against me. The new touch of someone different was jolting my senses alive. I'm sure the alcohol helped my nerve endings as well.

Handsome's hands were caressing my neck, and I begin to melt. The butterflies in your stomach kind of melting that occurs with puppy love. I am partly embarrassed by this and partly electrified by this knowledge. This young man is driving me crazy! Why haven't I felt this way in years? It is good, it is healthy to feel like this. I don't hurt. I'm not sad, and I'm not in pain. This is a good thing. I look around for Tammie but I don't see her.

Handsome says, "Want to get out of here?"

His smile melts me again, and I feel like jello. I think I might follow him around like a puppy dog wherever he goes if I continue to feel like this. I really don't answer him, but we start walking away anyway. I'm looking for Tammie but there are so many people I can't begin to make out where she might be. My vision is blurry at best.

We walk along the outer deck for as long as we can. We go inside onto one of the decks, and I can no longer stand up very well by myself. We are walking down a hall with cabins on either side. We stop and Handsome opens a cabin door and pulls me in behind him. This is a suite! Tammie and I have a cabin, but this appears to be a First Class Suite.

I walk around looking at the differences in Handsome's cabin from mine. It is much bigger, and he has a huge bed. He has a private balcony. I go to the sliding glass doors and look out at the blue ocean. Am I really here?

I feel arms wrap around me from behind. He is warm and feels so soft. He came out of the bathroom and now I smell minty toothpaste and cologne. Mmmm, he smells good. Handsome presses his soft cheek against the back of my neck and I feel my legs begin to give out. I am light headed from his touch. I am queasy in the stomach from his delicious scent. He walks me closer to the giant bed and he kisses me. He grabs my chin with both his hands, something Paul has never, ever, done, and he kisses me softly and gingerly. He handles me with care, like I am special to him.

I am so very sleepy, but his touch is like magic to me. I kiss him back, knowing I am kissing someone other than my husband. Knowing that I am being unfaithful to my ass of a husband. Knowing full well where this is going and wanting it so very badly.

Handsome turns the lights off and some soft music on. We fall on the bed. He is so gentle, as if he is in no hurry whatsoever. He pulls up my shirt to my neck, respectfully. He places soft kisses all over my stomach, my sides, and moves up to my chest. I am going to burst, I think. Is this foreplay? Paul was never much into foreplay.

I want this man tonight. I don't even know his name. I doubt he knows my name. It is wrong, and yet it is a beautiful thing. No one will ever know, and I am pretty sure I can live with the guilt. Will I tell Tammie tomorrow?

He slides my pants down to the ground. My shoes are already off. His touch is so soft, I just can't get over it. Are they teaching these moves in college now? I wonder if he is thirty yet? Will he regret this tomorrow?

My lips are swelling in anticipation. I have been acting as though I'm not sure if I want this, but now I stop pretending. I pull Handsome down on me. He yanks his shirt off and unzips his pants. I can't see much in the darkened room, but I can feel everything. Thank God he has protection. I'm glad he can't see my face so well. He would see the crow's feet around my eyes, and the lines around my mouth. He might stop his magic if he saw me for what I truly was.

But he doesn't stop, and I don't want him to. He is respectful, and moves with grace. He makes me feel ten years younger, and I feel gorgeous. He stares into my face, and brushes the hair away from my eyes.

Handsome could be a movie star, I think. With these moves, he could make anyone believe in him. He lies down beside me, and now that we are both exhausted, he puts his muscular arm around my neck and we immediately fall asleep. The room is spinning a bit for me, but I am drunk on happiness and so, so tired.

42

I open my eyes and from the light behind the curtain I can tell that it is morning. I am alone in this bed, and it is not mine. The men's clothes scattered around the cabin remind me of last night.

Last night's events come tumbling out from my fried brain. Oh my word, I just had sex with a complete stranger! My head is throbbing, and I am smiling. Last night felt good. My body is sore. Every muscle feels like it's been through an aerobic work out.

But I realize that I am not feeling regret. For the first time in a long time, I am happy and I am smiling. When was the last time that I could say that? I am a married woman, and I should feel some shame and guilt for what I did last night. Waiting… waiting for the shame and guilt to surface. Nope. Not yet anyway.

I go back to sleep and wake up two hours later. It is now ten in the morning. I put on my outfit from last night, put some toothpaste on my finger and run it through my mouth. I attempt to comb my hair and straighten the wrinkles in my clothes. My attempts fail.

I open the cabin door and proceed in my walk of shame to the elevators. Luckily not many people are around. I take the elevator up to the eighth deck and find my cabin. I knock on the door, praying that Tammie is inside, as I don't have my purse or room key. I hear movement inside, and I breathe a sigh of relief.

I'm uncertain as to how much I am going to tell Tammie. Should I keep last night as my little secret, or should I include Tammie in my naughty indulgence? Tammie looks horrible. I obviously woke her from a deep sleep. As she opens the cabin door, she doesn't really even glance at me. She dives right back into her bed. I do the same, and we sleep for another few hours.

"Ok, what in the world happened to you last night? I lost you on the lido deck. And I have your purse, by the way. Since you left it on the table and disappeared into thin air. I was going to report you missing pretty soon here if you didn't come home." Tammie has her eyes closed, thankfully, and looks very sleepy.

I peek out from the covers and nonchalantly say, "I ended up passing out in that college boy's cabin. He was so sweet to let an old lady throw up in his bathroom and then let me sleep off my drunkenness in his cabin. I don't know where he spent the night. He must have found some young thing and took off to have a wild night with her." I'm wondering if that story sounded lame or true.

"Well, I have not been that drunk since college, Anna. My head is still pounding. But it was worth every minute. Did you see me dancing? Was I good or what? I bet I danced with ten different men last night. I just had the best time. One guy kept trying to talk me into checking out his cabin with him, but my will power prevailed. I kept flashing him my wedding ring and telling him he didn't want the wrath of my husband on him."

I manage, "It sounds like you had fun, then. I feel awful. Should we sleep off our hangovers in here today, or go back out on the lido deck?"

Tammie is already getting up and picking out a swimsuit for the day. I guess we'll be back at the pool today. I hope I don't run into Handsome again. I *think* I would recognize him. But I just don't want to have to deal with talking to him or the awkwardness of "what now."

But I never do run into Handsome again. For the final two days on the cruise ship, I never see that beautiful man again. In a way it is a relief. I decide to keep the secret all to myself. I was unfaithful to my husband. That's not really something you want to brag about to your best friend. Although I would trust Tammie completely with that information. I know she would never tell Paul. But she would have reason to judge me differently now.

I'm not sure how I would feel if she told me that she cheated on Jack. I would be disappointed in her, I know that. So I just don't mention this one little detail. I won't ever. To anyone. It will remain my secret that I take to my grave.

Tammie and I have some good heart to heart talks the final days of the vacation. She tries not to press, but she does guide our conversations to my future. What do I see myself doing when we get back home? How do I want to live my life now? What do I want out of my marriage?

She asks some really good, tough questions. Most of them I do not have answers for. But I know I need to think about these things. This trip was so good for me. I do feel like a huge weight has been lifted off of my shoulders. I can breathe better now.

I travelled outside of Gannon and was reminded that there is life outside of my nightmare.

Now just what in the world am I going to do with my life?

43

After the cruise, I feel better equipped to handle things. My coping skills are better now. I'm still not sure what I want from my marriage. I'm not sure if I want to be in it or not. And I think that is painfully obvious to both Paul and I.

We have drifted apart. Dangerously apart. If he came to me today and said, "Anna, I want a divorce," I think I would say, "Ok, Paul." I'm not sure I would fight for our marriage. I need more time to sort it all out.

I still don't know if I can trust Paul. I don't know what his relationship with Nicole was. I was so hurt by his lie. I wonder what else he has lied to me about over the years.

Who is my husband? Do I really even know him? He spent so much time traveling when the kids were alive, that he could have done about anything and I wouldn't have even noticed. I was too busy with the kids. Now the kids are gone. Now I am forced to take a hard look at us and redefine our marriage.

I realize now that the affair I had while on the cruise was my pay back to Paul. At any other point in our marriage I would have been hit with a profound sense of guilt. But if I'm honest with myself, I actually feel as though now we're even. He cheated on me with Nicole, and to get even with him, I cheated on him with Handsome. I'm not proud of this recognition. I'm honestly not even sure who I've become anymore. I don't recognize my actions, my thoughts, or myself at all.

After the cruise it is as if I have forgiven Paul concerning the Nicole affair. My own affair showed me how inconsequential it really was. The sex was amazing, and I can't say that I definitely regret it. It's not something I plan to do again. It's not me. But it helped me to get over my heartache with Paul, so I'm ok with it. How sick am I?

The anti-depressants must be helping me. That or with time I am able to enter into society again. I go to the grocery store and I run all of the household errands. Now I go to church on the weekends and sometimes even by myself during the week. I go to the fitness center and work out with Tammie three mornings a week. I feel as though I am slowly entering back into society.

Paul and I are in a routine now. We see each other at the dinner table most evenings at six o'clock. We have dinner together and talk about our days. He usually goes back to the bank in the evening, has a meeting with a client, or maybe once a week he stays home and we just watch TV together.

I hired a housekeeper to come in and clean once a week. The house seems so big now without the kids here. I tell Paul that I wonder if we should down size, look at smaller homes now. He doesn't want to talk about it, and so we don't.

If you are going through hell,
Keep going.

—Winston Churchill

44

It is excruciatingly painful for me to see my friends with their children out in public. It just tears at my heart, knowing full well what I have lost. I watch Tammie with her three children. She opens the car door for them, she laughs with them, and takes their backpacks from them as they get into the car.

Such simple, unexciting activities that we take for granted. My heart just aches when I see those every day moments that I never appreciated. What a blessing it is for parents to get to pick up their kids from school. What a blessing it is for parents to get to read to their children at night time, to help with baths, get their babies into their pj's.

I about lost it on a mother the other day at the grocery store. I could hear her yelling at her kids an aisle over. She was rude and mean, and treating them very poorly. I couldn't see what was happening, but just from the tone of her voice, I knew that those kids did not have a happy life with her. I hurried to turn into the next aisle to watch the mother and kids. The mom looked tired and frustrated, with three little ones. The kids were tired and crabby and didn't want to follow their mom. There wasn't enough room in the cart for groceries and kids.

Just as I was about ready to ask if I could help her with one of the children, she yelled at the little boy, yanked him hard by his shoulder, and began paddling his bottom. I didn't know what to do. I was behind her, so I don't think she saw me there at all. By now the little toddler was crying and screaming. The mom turns and finally sees me but doesn't appear to be embarrassed at all. I am dumb founded. I want to tell this mother that she might not have tomorrow with her children, but I am unsure of what she might say to that. I am just so very sad that this mother gets to have her three children, and I don't.

It is also difficult to watch TV without crying. So many commercials have families in them. So many TV shows have parents and children in them. I never realized before how the fabric of our society revolves around families. Everywhere I turn I am reminded of my loss. I cannot go one day without someone or something being thrown in my face regarding the death of my kids. Paul used to change the TV channels quickly when something came on that he thought might bother me. Now he doesn't even try. It's just not worth it. I have to learn how to cope with it.

By the way, Paul appears to be doing just fine with our loss. He chooses to not talk about our kids. When I bring them up, he quickly changes the subject. I am appalled at his avoidance. I have asked him numerous times if he would go to couples counseling with me, but he says that he doesn't need it. He thinks it's great that I am going to see Dr. Hansen, but he doesn't need it.

At some point he is going to have to deal with it.

***

I still think about Handsome sometimes. At times I wonder if I dreamt him. I never saw him again on the ship after our evening together. Did I make him up? Was he just a fantasy of mine? I know he wasn't, but it's as though he just appeared in my life when I needed him, and then he disappeared as quickly.

It has never occurred to me to tell Paul about that incident. What would be the reason? To hurt Paul? To get it off my conscience? I can live with it. In fact, I think I feel that the score has been evened now. I had a one-night stand, and Paul had a something. I still don't know what it was. But I know it was cheating.

Dr. Hansen told me that people need to let go of the things that are eating them alive inside. If we can forgive and forget and move on, we are much more likely to be healthier emotionally. Carrying emotional baggage for years is about the worst thing you can do to yourself, she says. At some point it becomes a part of us and we don't even realize that we need to get rid of it to be happy and healthy. She encourages me to cleanse myself by telling her anything and everything that is in my mind. She won't judge me, and she says I can trust her. I do trust her. I just don't see the point in telling her about Handsome. He's my little secret.

45

The anniversary of the accident is approaching. It has been almost one year. When I think about it I start to have trouble breathing. Dr. Hansen says it is an anxiety attack. She has scaled back on my anti-depressants and I tell her I think I need more. She thinks I can handle it on my own, that I shouldn't be reliant on the medicine to get me through the anniversary.

So where am I one year later in my life? Let's see...I'm a wife with a poor marriage. I am a former mother who lost her three children. My parents have died. My biggest achievement in the past year is that I can now go out in public without having a full blown panic attack. I aim to leave the house once a day, whether it is just to go to the grocery store, post office, bank, or even to just drive around town.

Dr. Hansen wants me to shower daily, exercise, and get out every day. I know having these routines has helped me, but I still crave a bigger purpose in my life. I need a reason besides buying food and mailing bills to get up each morning.

I'm not sure how I want to spend March eighth. Should I hole up in my house or should I leave town? Either way, I know it will be a sad day for me. Paul will go to work as usual and pretend that all is fine with the world. Does he *have* a heart? If I could do what I really wanted, I would spend the day watching home videos and looking at all of the scrapbooks I made for the kids throughout their short lives. I just need to *remember* them. It feels like so many people want me to forget my kids, while I want nothing more than to remember them. They touched my heart so deeply, and there is no way anyone can take them away from me.

At dinner I ask Paul if he will go away with me on March eighth.

"We could go anywhere for a two to three day trip," I suggest. "You love Vegas. Why don't we spend a few days there gambling, shopping, eating, going to shows? I think it would be a great little get away for us both."

Paul doesn't look thrilled about the idea. "I'll check my work schedule and see if it's a possibility, Anna."

Yeah, sure you will. You sound absolutely thrilled about spending three days with me. It won't happen. I know right now that I will end up spending the entire day by myself watching our home videos and crying my eyes out while Paul is at work all day.

I feel brave. "Paul, can I ask you something?"

He hesitates with the fork midway to his mouth, the meat loaf slipping off the fork onto his plate.

"Sure honey, what's up?" He won't look me in the eye now.

"Do you still want to be in this marriage? Or would you prefer that we get divorced?"

He finishes chewing his food slowly and stares at me.

"Now why would you ask a silly question like that?"

He throws the ball back into my court, taking the coward's way out of talking about it.

"Oh, I don't know. I just want us to be honest about what our marriage is right now. We've been through a lot of changes this past year, and I don't feel that our marriage has necessarily held up. We never see each other. When we are together we have a difficult time making conversation. I have no idea what to do with our marriage right now. And I look into the future and I guess I can't see where we'll be in even five years together. I just want to know what you're thinking."

He appears to be contemplating how to respond to me. I think I caught him off guard.

"I guess I see our future together pretty much like it's always been, Anna. I have a great thing going at the Bank, and I don't see me making a change in my career. I thought we always planned to be in Gannon forever. I think we need to adjust to our misfortune, make our lives what we want them to be. I'm just waiting for you to decide how you want to live your life, I guess. I know what I want."

"So you're ok with our marriage, then?"

"I think our marriage isn't much different than it was before when the kids were alive. I worked a lot, I came home for dinner, and we spent our weekends together. I think you are the one who has all this empty space now, Anna. Your days used to be filled with the kids. Now your days are lonely. I think you need to look for a job or find something to fill your days with. You can't expect me to fill the void in your life."

I know he's right, but he says it so cold, without warmth or emotion. Was Paul always this clinical, this heartless? I swear he is not the man I married.

"It seemed to me that the vacation you took with Tammie was good for you. You came home with an improved attitude."

Oh goodness, if he only knew the reason for that.

"I think it was good for you to get out of Gannon and see that there are so many other ways to live. Many people have full lives without children, Anna. Unless you've changed your mind on that issue. But you've told me quite a few times that you don't want to adopt or try to get pregnant again. And I'm ok with that. Now *you* need to be ok with that. So what do you want to do with your life now that you are childless?"

"How can you be so heartless, Paul? Our kids were my life and they were ripped away from me. I will never get over that. They will constantly be a part of me. If you're waiting for me to 'just get over them,' then please know that is *never* going to happen."

I am yelling and I throw down my napkin and leave the room.

Man, I am mad at that cold hearted puke. I hear him coming after me. I plop down into a chair in the living room.

"Anna, I didn't mean to imply that you should forget about our kids. Of course you shouldn't. I may not talk about them every day, but Connor, Ryan, and Cassy are on my mind every day. I just can't function if I allow myself to think about them all of the time. I *do* have my work to make me think about other things. And I know that's part of your problem. You are searching for that something else to give purpose to your days. I don't know how to help you. I've tried to just let you figure it out on your own time. Please don't take that for not caring."

He's right, as usual. I just don't want to admit it. It's easier to blame him for my unhappiness. Sighing, I lean forward and take his hands in mind.

"Paul, I'm going to counseling. I'm dealing with the loss of our children. I get up every day and force myself to live. I'm not happy about it, but I am doing it. And I think I've come a long way in the past year. But understand that I will have bad days and bad months. I'm trying hard to put on a smile and move forward, but part of me doesn't really want to. Part of me wants to be with them so badly. Part of me wants to not wake up in the morning. And the biggest part of me just wants our old life back with the kids in it."

I look around at our living room. The walls are filled with photographs of our kids. The hall's bulletin board still holds their school artwork from last year. I haven't been able to part with one thing of the kids. I honestly don't know who I am without my kids in my life.

Who is Anna Dawson?

46

And so my journey continues. My search for myself. My soul is wounded, and it needs to be repaired. Paul and I go back into our daily routines of simple existence. Paul tells me that he could go to Vegas with me over the one year anniversary of the accident if I want to.

I think about it for a day and decide I would probably ruin the trip with my mood. I can't imagine celebrating that day. So I end up holed-up in the house. I watch old home videos and look through all of the scrapbooks I made for the kids over the years. I wander through each of their rooms, refolding clothes and putting them back in drawers. I haven't taken anything out of their rooms. Tammie raised her eyebrows at me when I told her this. I know it may seem spooky to others, but I can't get rid of anything of the kids. It seems wrong to me to want to do so.

And so I continue to live in the past. My dreaming of the past has turned into daydreaming. When I go to the fitness center and get on the treadmill, I plug in my iPod and daydream of days gone by. I constantly associate everything I see or do with "when the kids were alive…"

My head knows I need to move on, but my heart hasn't bought into the idea yet. People tell me that I look great. I have lost weight, and I exercise a few times a week. I grew my hair out past my shoulders and I started coloring it a shade lighter. The circles have slowly gone away from under my eyes. I still don't feel good, but it is nice to hear people say that I look good.

Looks can be so deceiving.

47

Every mom I know fantasizes about what they would do with a free day. A day with no kids. With no responsibilities to the household. My friends and I used to discuss this.

Of course, now no one discusses much with me anymore. But we all used to say we would spend a free day doing any of the following: reading, sleeping, watching a movie, scrap booking, or just lounging around the house doing nothing. Well my fantasy has apparently come true.

Now I get to do all of this any day of the week. I have read too many books the past few months. I have rented every movie possible, and I know all of the TV shows by heart. I don't scrapbook anymore. I have no reason for that.

But the irony doesn't escape me. Now that I have every day as a free day, I have no idea what to do with all of the free time. I would trade places with anyone. I would never, ever again fantasize about not having my kids around. Be careful what you wish for, Anna.

48

On the dreaded one year anniversary of my kids' deaths, I decided to begin a journal. I talk to myself all the time, and I am feeling a need to write. Just get it all out.

Dr. Hansen suggested this months ago, but I didn't have the energy then. So I started writing letters to the kids. It made me cry, but it felt good to get it all out. I still can't get over the fact that my kids will never graduate from high school, never go to college, never get married, and never know the joy of having kids themselves.

But as a woman of faith, I also know they are in the best place possible. They are with God in heaven, and it is this one piece of knowledge that keeps me from going insane.

What happened to my perfect life? Either I was too arrogant or too naïve in my thinking a year ago. I sincerely thought I had it all at that time. I felt humbled and blessed by what the Lord had given me. A year later I am still in shock over the detour my life has taken.

I used to feel guilty for all of the richness my life had. Now I feel empty and am left wondering what in the world happened. I am fearful of each day now, wondering what changes will come my way. Instead of looking forward to the future, I fear it. My glass is definitely half empty now.

49

Three months ago Tammie decided that she and I needed a girl's night out once a month. So we go out to dinner and a movie and catch up. The past three months we have seen The Curious Case of Benjamin Button, Bride Wars, and Pink Panther 2 at the theater. She is careful in her selection of movie choices on my behalf.

Tonight we are going out on our fourth movie night and I am looking forward to it. I like to listen to Tammie ramble on about the community gossip, what she and Jack have been up to, and her job. She doesn't mention her kids, I notice, unless I ask about them. Some nights I ask about them and sometimes I don't.

I am over being angry when I see people staring at me and whispering behind their hands. I just don't care anymore. Tammie and I are eating at our favorite Mexican restaurant, El Jimos, and I am loving the Chile con Queso and chips. We refrain from ordering a second jumbo margarita. We want to see a movie after dinner, too. On a whim, I almost decide to tell Tammie about Handsome. But I can't get a word in, as she is going off about her jerk of a boss again. The moment is lost and so I don't bring him up. Later I am glad I kept the secret to myself.

I am so thankful for Tammie's friendship. I try to tell her, but she waves me off, knowing that we will both be crying if we have this conversation. We know the truth. We both need each other, and we value the friendship more than we can describe. I have learned that having good women in your life makes you more solid. Tammie and my sisters have always grounded me. I have always been able to tell them my insecurities over the years, and they always know how to pick me up.

50

Paul comes home from work with a big smile on his face. "I've got some interesting news for you, honey."

Crap. Oh no, I think. What can this possibly be? I'm nervous already.

"The Bank has an opening for a Vice Presidency, with the outlook of Presidency in two to four years, at the Des Moines office. They called me and want me to come and talk to them about it next week. What do you think?"

I can tell Paul is excited about this. His eyes are shining and there is excitement in his voice.

"Are you really wanting to leave Gannon, Paul? You've always told me that you wanted to be in Gannon forever."

His big smile starts to fade. He takes off his sport coat and hangs it over a kitchen bar stool and sits down.

"Well, a lot of things have changed since we moved to Gannon, obviously. Even a year ago I did think I could spend my whole life here. But with the accident, now I'm not so sure that's a good idea for us. Maybe it's an opportunity for us to start fresh, Anna. Maybe this is just what you and I need. We could get rid of some of the memories that are holding us down here. A new chance at life."

I'm not even sure how to respond to this. Am I supposed to be happy?

"I...I don't know what to say, Paul. I'm honestly surprised and caught off guard. I wasn't expecting this, ever. Is it what you want?" Is all I can muster.

"I don't know. I'm as shocked as you are on the offer. But the more I thought about it this afternoon, I figured it wouldn't hurt to look at it. Let's go talk with the Bank next week in Des Moines. We'll drive down for the day and just talk to their management team and see what they have to say. I know what the offer will be. Essentially they need a new President in a few years. It would be the same job for me there, just at a much bigger bank, with many more financial incentives. I think the bigger question is, do we want to leave Gannon?"

He's right, and I know it. It's just that I've been holding on for dear life here. Holding on to what, I have no idea. The thought of leaving Gannon means I would be leaving my kids behind. They are buried here. When would I get to leave flowers at my kids' grave sites? I feel a panic attack just thinking about never being close to them again.

51

I agree to go with Paul to Des Moines to talk with First National Bank. Actually I tell him that I will talk with the bank people for an hour. Then I want to spend some time on my own driving around Des Moines by myself.

I know Des Moines, as we lived there for eight years, but I know it has changed. I need to really look at the homes, the churches, and the shopping districts. But if I'm going to move there, I need to figure out if it's a good fit for me.

Paul asks me if I want him to set up an appointment with a realtor.

"She could drive you around, Anna, and you could tour a few homes if you'd like," Paul offers.

But I don't want to. I need time by myself to get a feel for it.

***

The First National Bank of Des Moines people are marvelous. They are all first class professionals. We are treated well at a small reception at the Bank. Paul already knows many of the officers and Vice Presidents from previous work.

I feel a little left out, and I sense that they are all gentle with me. No one talks about their children. They keep it all very stream lined to the bank, housing, and shopping advantages in Des Moines. I know they are all aware of our children's deaths. Some of them came to the memorial services.

After my obligatory hour at the bank, I take Paul's Volvo keys and I just drive aimlessly around the city. Des Moines is the biggest town in the state, with over 300,000 people. I realize that I do miss living here in many ways. The suburbs around it have grown immensely in the past decade as well. The small, rural farming communities in Iowa have seen serious decline, while the state capital has been thriving.

There are aspects of the city life that I miss. The restaurant selection makes my mouth water. Olive Garden, T.G.I. Friday's, Macaroni Grill, The Fourth Street Micro Brewery, The Cheesecake Factory. I need to drive at least an hour from Gannon to hit any of these restaurants.

The malls also make my head turn. The super Wal-Mart and Target get me thinking. The beautiful newer churches are appealing. I park and walk into a brand new St. Thomas Catholic church. It is breath taking. It is a combination of old cathedral and modern. I wonder how many years the pledge cards are for.

After a lunch at Applebee's and stops at Target and North Pointe Mall, I am ready to pick up Paul. He just texted me that he will be ready to leave in half an hour. I am anxious to hear what he thought about his day.

The drive home consists of mostly Paul talking about what a great opportunity this new position would be for him. In fact, if it worked out, he could see another move up even after the Des Moines position, possibly. He was treated well, and he knows he has a lot to offer their bank, too. He told them he and I needed a week to discuss it. I haven't heard him ask me yet what I thought about the whole deal.

"We have a week to think about it, Anna. Did you have a good day driving around? What are you thinking?" Paul finally asks.

"There are pros and cons to wherever you live, Paul. There are things about Des Moines that I would appreciate. But they are mostly material things. Like better shopping, more variety in restaurants, the concert venues, movie theaters, Broadway shows. I'm not sure bigger is better. I don't know anyone in Des Moines anymore. It would be like starting over."

"Well, isn't that the whole point, Anna? It's a chance for us to begin a new life together. We can put our past pains behind us and build a new life together. I, for one, think it is exactly what we need right now."

I am appalled by his lack of a human heart beating inside his chest. Has he so quickly forgotten about our three children? Did it take just over a year and, wammo! They're gone, let's move on.

"Paul, I'm not looking to forget about our kids. I'm not looking for a new life. I'm quite happy with our current one, thank you. I'm not certain I can even imagine what it would be like to leave my friends in Gannon. Every memory I have of our kids is in Gannon. I'm scared that if we leave, we'll leave the kids there too."

"I'm not suggesting that we forget about the kids, Anna. I would never suggest such a thing. I'm only offering that a move will physically take you away from some of the pain. We will always have our memories, our pictures, and our videos. No one can take the memories of our kids from us. But don't you agree that you might be healthier in an environment where you aren't constantly reminded of Connor, Ryan, and Cassy?"

I really hate him. I do. I've just figured out the truth of the matter. I hate this man. Why did I ever think he was the man of my dreams? He is evil. I do not understand how he can dismiss our kids from our lives as though they didn't exist.

I choose to not talk to Paul the rest of the drive home. He is pissed at me for tuning him out as well. It's our dysfunctional way of going through life now. We just basically ignore one another. Three days later he leaves me a note stating that he needs to let the Des Moines Bank know what he is thinking. Can I have an answer for him this weekend?

The truth is that I'm scared to leave Gannon. Because, yes, that would mean that I'm leaving the kids. Without them and their memories, will they fade from my mind? What kind of a mother forgets about her kids, ever?

What if I find a great new life in Des Moines and move onward? What if in five years I can't conjure up a picture in my mind of my kids? Who would do that to their kids? I can't bear to think that I might be able to let them go. I think it is my cross to carry, that I need to remember them forever. I need to keep them close to my heart. Paul will never understand that.

52

The dreaded talk. I've already made my decision and I know that Paul has made his. I can see it in the way he walks, in the way he has been getting out of bed earlier every morning this week. He's excited. He has a new project to work on. A new goal.

He tells me that he thinks we should take this opportunity. It is an opportunity for him professionally, as well as for he and I personally. Des Moines is only two hours away. I can always drive back to Gannon whenever I want to visit Tammie and the kids' grave sites.

It's not like we won't ever be back, he says. He'll probably have bank work to come back to once in awhile, anyway. I could find a decent job in Des Moines. Hasn't that always been one of my biggest complaints about Gannon? That there were no career opportunities for me here. Well, now here's my chance to start a career for myself.

He's obviously thought all of this through. I tell him I have thought about it long and hard this week. And I'm not moving. Not now and not ever. He is shaking his head at me. Looking at me like I'm not as smart as him. I explain to him that my heart is connected to Gannon. It would be like ripping my heart out if I had to leave Gannon, I explain to Paul. Part of me knows that it seems like a good idea to leave, to forge on ahead with a new lease on life.

The deal is, I don't want to. I know it's wrong, but I still want my old life. I want my three kids alive again.

"Anna, I'm going to only say this once. And I'm sorry if I hurt your feelings by saying this. But you are crazy. The death of the kids has left you not right in the head. You are living in the past. It's like you think the kids will magically reappear some day in the near future. It's not going to happen, Anna! They are *dead*! The quicker you come to terms with this, the quicker you will be able to move along in life. I thought all of the counseling you have had would have helped you more. But you are still stuck in the unrealistic mind set that somehow the past will come to life again. I just cannot live like this anymore. I am going to take this job offer in Des Moines. I need to get out of Gannon and live. If you want some time to think about it, then that's fine. Come in a few months if you want. But I cannot stay in this house, living with death all around me, like you choose to do. You need to move on, Anna. Everybody thinks so."

His words sting. Paul gets up and goes upstairs. I sit on the living room couch for awhile all alone. I feel bad because I know he's right and I don't want to admit it. I also don't want to do anything about it. Paul's right. I am crazy.

53

Paul is moving to Des Moines in three weeks. He has begun to pack some things in boxes, tape them up and label them. Boxes are lining the upstairs hallway and the kids' bedrooms. I'm not even sure what he is taking. I should be concerned, but I don't care. He can take whatever he wants.

I ask him one night if he wants a divorce. He says no, but I don't believe him. I think that he is too proud to divorce me. It would make him look like a bad husband if he filed the papers. He will wait for me to do it. I know he doesn't want to hurt me. We both know that this marriage has been over for more than a year now. I truly thought we would beat the odds. How wrong I was.

A small moving van comes the morning of his big move. He isn't taking much furniture, as he has rented a furnished apartment downtown close to his bank. For his new life without kids or a wife, he is taking his Volvo, his clothes, everything that was in his study, his books, cd's, computer, and only a few photographs of me and the kids.

As I look around the house, it is surprisingly still full. You wouldn't even know he had moved out unless you looked in his closet or study.

I'm sure the pain will come in time, but right now I don't feel much. My husband is leaving me. I talked to Tammie and Dr. Hansen about it. They are both concerned that I don't seem to care. They don't understand that I truly *don't* care. I loved Paul eons ago. That love has died. Our marriage is over and I wish him well. I truly do.

I think of him as a good friend who I have shared many good memories with. In some ways it is a relief to see him drive down the street. I heave a big sigh, and feel a sense of freedom. Now I can do whatever I feel like without wondering what Paul will think. Now I can make my own life, the life I want. Not the one Paul wants.

Paul told me he will wait for me. He will make sure I am taken care of financially. He thinks in a few months, I will discover that he was right. I will then move to Des Moines to be with him and everything will be ok. We'll see. I smile as I see his silver Volvo turn the corner, out of my sight.

The best way to mend a broken heart
Is time and girlfriends.

—Gwyneth Paltrow

54

I am a free woman. I have no one to take care of. I have no shirts to iron for my husband. I have no lunches to pack for my kids. I have no one to worry about except for myself. I don't know what to do with myself. I don't think I have ever been truly alone.

I moved from my parent's house at eighteen to college, and then from college in with Paul. I've always had someone telling me what I should do. What I should think. Who I should be. I am not a Banker's Wife anymore. I don't need to be a Good Girl anymore. Who should I be now?

My daily rituals don't change much after Paul leaves me. I exercise at the fitness center daily. I cook and bake and go to the grocery store and run my errands. I pick up my house. I read many books and watch a lot of TV and go see many good movies with Tammie. I go to church daily now, because I can. Because my schedule allows for it.

I read the newspaper every morning, the same one I've been reading since junior high, The Des Moines Register. I know I am secretly looking for any news of Paul. But I don't ever read anything about him.

Paul calls every Sunday to check in on me. He asks the same questions. How am I feeling? What am I up to every day? Do I want to come visit him for a weekend in Des Moines, just to try it out?

I enjoy talking to Paul. He knows me better than anyone, well, except for Tammie. But he knows me well, and he knows that I am not ok. I wonder how long he will keep calling me on Sundays, how long he will continue to financially support me. Will I receive divorce papers in the mail unexpectedly, or will he warn me?

He says he really likes his new job. That he is very glad he made the move professionally. It was his time, he said. He says that he wishes things would have turned out differently for our family. He knows that I am lost in my sadness for our kids. He admires my devotion to them. He can't imagine marrying a better mom for his kids. I wonder if he has met a woman. Someone that doesn't have serious issues like me.

55

I continue talking with Dr. Hansen. She assures me that I am making progress. She wonders if I made the right choice regarding Paul. She asks what am I going to do with my life now. I tell her that is the million dollar question.

I write in my journal every day. I just write, and write, and write. I have never gone back and read anything. It just helps me to let my thoughts out. I know most of it is dark and gloomy. I'm actually kind of scared to read it. I'm not sure I want to see myself for who I really am.

I'm sitting at the backyard pool drinking lemonade and Tammie walks in through the gate. I expect to see three kids behind her, but thankfully she is all alone.

"Hi Stranger. Mind if I join you?" she asks.

"That would be awesome. I need a friend right now."

I put down my journal and stretch. I bet I've been out here for three hours. My butt is sore. I go get us some more lemonade.

Tammie surprises me. "Would you care if I read some of this?"

I look back and she is holding up my journal. I hold my breath for a moment. That is me in there. Those are my private words, and most of them are ugly.

"If you think you can handle it, go ahead. But I must warn you, it's not pretty."

When I come out with the lemonade Tammie is curled up crying on the lounge chair. She doesn't even look my way when I sit down beside her and pour her a glass of lemonade. I lay back and close my eyes. Periodically I peer over at her, but she is still engrossed in her reading of my most private thoughts. I turn the outdoor music up just a little louder so I can close my eyes and let my mind wander.

Tammie is poking me in the leg. Her lower lip and chin are trembling.

"Wake up, you. We need to talk."

"I warned you about reading it, Tammie. I have used that journal as a tool to take away some of my hatred and bad thoughts. I'm embarrassed, actually, that now you can see me for who I really am. Please don't leave me as your friend."

"I cannot believe that you have been living like this, Anna. I knew you were in pain, but I didn't know the depths of your pain. I am so sorry. I feel like I have been a bad friend. I want to be here for you more. Please tell me what I can do."

"My life has been horrible for the past year. You have done exactly what I needed you to do. You have always been there for me, not judging me and not giving me free advice. You are my confidant and my best friend. You've seen me in my darkest moments, and you're still my friend. What more could I ask from you?"

56

I find out that after a year and a half, Courtney still hasn't gone through mom and dad's home. She says she really wants Abby and I to do it with her. She has gone to their home a few times, and it is just too overwhelming and too emotional for her to do it by herself. I completely understand. I tell her that I can drive to Mason whenever they want to get the job done. We agree to all meet at mom and dad's house in two weeks. Courtney wants to get the house on the market by spring.

I look forward to this time that I get to spend with my two sisters, although it is under sad circumstances. I didn't envision us doing this task for many years yet. We agreed to a three day get-together. We plan to go through everything in their home, with each of us taking things as memories and whatever else we think we might use. I'm really only thinking about a few items that I'd love to have.

Mom and dad's wedding portrait has hung over their bed for as long as I can remember. I'd love to have that. Any photos of them would mean a lot to me. Dad had saved everything we ever gave him over the years—father's day cards, pictures that the kids drew for him, letters we wrote to him while in college. He was pretty sentimental.

Anything with his handwriting on I would cherish. If I could just have one more day with them! To hug them, tell them how much they meant to me, to thank them for everything they did for me throughout my life. I know they knew these things, but it would have been closure for me to know that I was telling them these important things before their death.

As it stands, I am left with nightmares of the terrible head-on car crash with my three kids in the back seat. Who saw it coming first? Who screamed the loudest? Did my kids even have a moment of anticipation of the crash? Or did it take everyone by surprise? I will never have peace with these questions. They will haunt me forever.

Courtney, Abby, and I hug and cry before we even unlock mom and dad's front door. It is difficult to be back at our childhood home knowing that the familiar sights, sounds, and smells are forever gone. As we walk through the foyer, it amazes me that everything looks the same as I remember. Mom was never a great housekeeper, and so the house is littered with everyday items. A few newspapers by Mom's favorite brown leather recliner, dad's pillow on the couch, their shoes on the front door rug.

We hang our coats in the closet and just wander around the house, laughing, reminding each other of silly statements and funny times we had in this home. I thought perhaps Courtney would want to move here and live in Mason. But she doesn't have any desire to do that. I think I just wanted to preserve the home. I'm not quite ready to give it up. The thought of it being empty and for sale makes my heart ache.

We walk upstairs to our old bedrooms. I literally stop in my tracks when I see Cassy's suitcase in my old room. The orange and yellow polka dot weekend case is thrown open with most of its contents strewn around it, in typical Cassy fashion. Her favorite teddy bear, Harry, is on my old twin bed. Her blanket and a blue sweater are on my bed, too. Tears run down my cheeks and I slump onto my bed. I hear Abby and Courtney in their rooms, and I wonder if Ryan and Connor's suitcases are in their rooms as well.

So on the day of the accident they did come here first. I've always wondered what they did on that dreadful day. They picked my kids up at four o'clock in Gannon that day, and left right after that. They had to be in Mason shortly after six o'clock, unless they stopped somewhere along the way, which is unlikely. Maybe they would have stopped at a convenience store for a quick snack.

So what were they doing out on the highway at nine o'clock that night? Just a few miles outside of Mason, coming back into town? I've never figured that one out.

My sisters come inside my old room and look at me. I tell them what has bugged me about the night of the accident.

"Obviously, they came home first, and the kids brought their suitcases up to their rooms. Mom probably made them dinner. I don't understand what they were doing out on the highway that night."

"Maybe we can drive out on the road tomorrow, Anna. Visit the accident site if you want. We can drive along the high way, see if we can come up with any ideas of where they may have been."

Abby offers this suggestion and it makes me catch my breath. I want to do it. It would be good for me to do it. But I will need both of my sisters with me.

57

We turn on some Steve Miller tunes and get busy. Courtney brought dozens of boxes and we decide to begin this project upstairs. We each start in our own former bedrooms. Mom had kept our rooms pretty much the same since the day we moved out of them.

We each had taken things over the years, but she never did redecorate our bedrooms or turn them into project rooms like so many people do. The grandkids loved coming to look at our old dance trophies, track ribbons, and pictures from prom. My Sean Cassidy poster still was tacked into the wall, right beside my corkboard still filled with class pictures from high school. It was like stepping back into time.

We boxed up all of our personal possessions, reminiscing over past boyfriends and simpler times. I wasn't sure where I would even put these boxes of memorabilia, but I knew I would take them home. It was actually kind of fun, just spending this time with Courtney and Abby.

Over the years our lives each went different ways and we just didn't get to spend the time we wanted with each other. Maybe that would change since mom and dad were gone now. We finally crashed after midnight. My brain was mush and I was emotionally drained.

The next day we decided to start in dad's study. That would be a hard room, so we wanted to get it over with first. So many memories of dad in his cherry wood paneled study.

He would retreat to his study many evenings when we girls were watching a TV show in the family room that didn't interest him. He would turn on his own little TV, lie back in his big leather desk chair with his feet up on the desk, and read a book or page through a magazine. Mom would bring him in a cup of coffee and a snack before bed each night.

If I wanted to talk to dad about something serious, I always knew to do it when he was in his study. He was always at ease and happy in his study. He had pictures of us hanging on his walls. Photos mom took from family vacations at Disney Land, fishing, swimming, and Christmas photos. It was *his* room.

I remember asking dad if I could have my own car in this room. I asked dad if I could go to the prom as a freshman in this room. I would talk to him about what I wanted to be when I grew up, where he thought I should go to college. This room gave me comfort over the years and it did now too.

I knew Courtney and Abby felt the same way about dad's study. We could all feel dad's presence within these walls. I started with dad's desk, Courtney took the filing cabinet, and Abby started taking books and knick knacks off the shelves and boxing them up.

"You guys, there are files in this cabinet with our names on them. I wonder what dad has in these," Courtney turned around holding three file folders with each of our names on them.

We each took a seat and opened up our files. Inside mine there were pictures he had cut out of the newspaper over the years when I was in high school. Pictures of me on the basketball team, pictures of me in the band, choir, and musicals. Pictures of me on the golf team, Homecoming. I had no idea that he cut these out of the paper, let alone saved them. I could tell Courtney and Abby were looking at similar mementos as well.

My file contained cards I had given him over the years and letters I had written to him when I was in college. There were pictures of me from my senior year in high school and my sorority formal at Iowa State. My love for him multiplied as I leafed through my folder.

At the very back was a sealed envelope with my name handwritten in dad's penmanship. My heart fluttered. I turned the envelope over and the date was written on it. Dad had written this four years ago! Next to the date were his words, "Please open and read after I have died. I love you with all my heart, Dad."

We all had these same envelopes, and we tore them open together.

I was excited and nervous at the same time. It is an odd feeling to know that dad wanted us to read these letters after he died. What in the world would he tell us now? Abby was laughing and crying at the same time. I could tell we were all nervous. My letter stated:

My Dearest Anna,

If you are reading this letter, then I have obviously passed on to another life. I am so sorry to have left you. My greatest accomplishment in my lifetime was my three daughters. God blessed me with you and I loved you more than you can ever imagine. Now that you have three kids of your own, I know that you can understand the depth of a parent's love. How you love your three sweethearts, Connor, Ryan, and Cassy, is what I feel for you. That parental love never lessens, as my love for you continued even as you grew to be a beautiful adult.

I look up to see how Abby and Courtney are doing. They are both engrossed in their letters, and it appears that we all have many pages of dad's handwriting, so I go back to my letter.

The smartest move I made was to marry your mother. I fell in love with her when I was young, and I never fell out of love with her. She is an amazing woman, and I hope she outlives me. We both felt that our family time together was our most cherished memory throughout our marriage.

Our home was never quite the same after you girls left for college. I loved the drama and excitement that three daughters brought to our household. It was so quiet when you all grew up and left. But I was so proud of each of you. The bond between you, Courtney, and Abby will hopefully continue throughout your adult lives. For after your mother and I pass on, you will only have each other. Please take care of your sisters.

I am so proud of all of your accomplishments, Anna. You were such a joy as a daughter, and life just came so easily to you. Whatever you did, you did it well. People always loved you, and you just fit in so seamlessly into any environment that you entered. I know you will adapt through your life no matter what comes your way.

I will always remember walking you down the aisle of St. Paul's Church the day you married Paul. You looked so very beautiful and I was so proud to be your daddy. Paul loves you very much, Anna. When he asked me for your hand in marriage, I told him that he better always take care of my Anna. He knows you are a special one, and I know he will always be a loyal, faithful husband to you.

More proud moments of mine with you are the three days you called to tell your mother and I that you blessed us with grand babies. Connor, Ryan, and Cassy are so lucky to have you as their mommy. I know you will make a wonderful mother and make your kids your number one priority in your life. There is nothing more important in this world than your family, Anna.

If there is one thing that your mother and I taught you, I hope it is that family always comes first. I know in my heart that you will do everything in your power to watch over your children so nothing bad comes their way.

I honestly look up to see if dad is standing in his study. Can this letter be real? My heart is about ready to break in two. Can he make me feel *more* guilty?

Although I worked hard to take care of my family over the years, I must admit to you now that I was not perfect. My love for you, your sisters, and your mother should never be doubted. But I did fail in some areas that I think as an adult you should know about. I am a coward to be telling you this after my death, I know. I should have owned up to my failures years ago, but I could never find the right time. I feel you deserve to know the truth of who your father really was. I just pray that you don't hate me after you are finished reading this letter.

I look up again to see how Courtney and Abby are doing.

"Can you believe this?" Courtney asks. "I'm almost afraid to read the whole letter. Do you think all our letters say the same thing?"

"Hush. Let's just all finish reading our letters and then we can compare," says Abby hurriedly.

The secret that I could never get enough courage to tell you girls is this. When I was a little boy, my grandfather abused me. I've never told anyone but your mother this secret. It is so horrible for me to even tell to you. I've been ashamed my whole life worrying that someone would find out the truth.

Being abused by a man you adored and trusted changes everything about your life. As a seven year old boy, I certainly didn't understand it at that time. When the abuse continued until I was ten, I knew then that it was horribly wrong and that I was horribly dirty.

Finally, at age ten I broke down and told my father. That night my father kicked his father out of our house, and we never saw grandpa again. I truly don't know what ever came of the man, for we never spoke of him again. I have harbored guilt for this, even now feeling that somehow it was all my fault. I was thankful that my father believed me and got rid of the problem, but I never felt at ease with my own father after that. I think he looked at me differently, as though he was ashamed.

All of this I have carried with me, never getting professional help. I know today, at age sixty-two, as I write this, that there is still time for me to seek out counseling. But I just don't want to anymore. I have carried the burden for so long, that I am used to it. I just want you girls to know who your father really was, both the good and bad parts. I think the abuse may explain a little bit about me for you. I know I was distant at times. I wasn't comfortable seeing you girls unless you were fully dressed. I know I was over protective of you when you began to date. I couldn't imagine what I would do if someone hurt my girls.

I told your mother about this secret after we were married. She expressed nothing but love and understanding and told me that she would love me forever. I'll never forget her unconditional love for me and my failures.

In many regards I'm surprised that your mother stayed with me all of these years. She would have had good reason to leave me. I suffered from depression for years. The fear of my abuse being found out was carried on my shoulders every day. I thought for sure someone from work would find out who I truly was. An old man with a dirty past.

My depression became unbearable for your mother. She grew frustrated with my lack of desire to do anything. I put up a good front for you girls. I'm guessing you never would have thought I was depressed. I didn't want you to know. I didn't want you to worry about me.

I'm not proud to be telling you this. I do it because I want you to know the truth about me. I know you girls always thought I was 'Dad of the Year.' And when you were young and growing up, I was a better person.

So if you ever struggle with depression or abuse, please make me proud and get professional help. I never did, and I believe that was the biggest mistake I made. My pride got in the way. Hopefully I raised better daughters than that. I know genetically many flaws can be passed down, and so I pray that I have not passed on my shortcomings to my beautiful girls. If so, I apologize and beg for your forgiveness.

I never knew who my parents really were at heart. Their generation and the ones before them didn't discuss openly the skeletons in the closet of their ancestors. We were all left to wonder, or we were told lies. I want you to know who your father was, the whole truth, albeit not always so pretty.

Know that I loved you Anna, and that you were always a blessing from God. I pray that you, Paul, Connor, Ryan, and Cassy have a wonderful, happy life together. You are so lucky to have such a loving family.

I will always love you with all my heart,

Dad

I am emotionally spent. The gravity of dad's message sinks in. I didn't really know who he was. I'm too shocked to cry, and too heartbroken to know that he lived years with a weight on his shoulders that he didn't think he could get off until his death. Now I know the whole picture of dad...but did I need to? Why did he feel the need to write us these letters? To clear *his* conscience? Or did he really have *our* best interests in mind?

We all finish reading our letters at about the same time. Abby looks like she is in shock, and Courtney looks tired. We discuss the letters, and none of us would have guessed dad's secrets. We feel really bad that Dad carried the abuse and depression with him his whole life, never letting any of us help him. But we are glad to know the truth in the end.

We wonder if mom left us notes as well. Are there more secrets from the crypt that we don't know about? We go look in mom's dressers and in her desk in the kitchen. But we don't see anything that resembles a sealed letter like dad's. We continue in the study, boxing everything up, labeling it to go with Courtney, Abby, or myself. Things none of us want we are donating to the church.

What I thought would be a few fun days with my sisters has turned into a stressful time because of dad's letters. We are still shocked by his admittances. We never would have guessed that he had been abused as a child or that he suffered from depression. We feel horrible that he didn't trust us enough to tell us about it in person. It does change things for me. I look at dad differently now. I wonder if that will change over time. After all, he is still the same father that I knew.

After the letters, we are speeding up the process of going through the house. Courtney wants the grandfather clock, the living room furniture, the washer and dryer, and mom and dad's bedroom set. Abby says she will take the kitchen appliances, the dining room table, chairs, buffet, the family room furniture, dad's treadmill, and mom's Lexus.

I have told them that I really don't plan to take anything big with me. I don't need furniture or cars. We split up the decorations, the photos, the personal items of mom and dad's. We each take boxes, trying to just split things evenly. We are civil and there is no fighting over material things. We are nostalgic, remembering past good times with our parents. We cry, retell a favorite old story, pack a few more boxes, and then repeat the cycle.

This experience has been good for us. It has brought some closure for Abby, Courtney, and I. I'm hoping it will bring the three of us even closer together. I worry that we will all go back to our own lives, and not see each other very often. We don't have the central location of mom and dad's home anymore, or the excuse to see our parents. But I have faith that we will continue on as a family unit, my sisters and I.

Courtney asks if we should take a break and go for a drive. I know where this is headed. Abby and she exchange a look.

"Are you up for it, Anna? We don't have to do it if you don't want to."

"I know. I think I need to. But only if you both come with me. I can't do this alone. I would also like to stop at the Mason Police Station. The officers told me that I could stop in anytime and look at the accident reports if I wanted to. I think I'm ready to do it now."

We drive out of Mason. Courtney drives slowly in Mom's, now her, blue Lexus. I am sitting in the front passenger seat, holding on tightly to the door handle. My stomach feels sick, nauseous. Abby is in the back seat, and she puts her hands on my shoulders, giving me a little shoulder rub.

We were told the accident happened three miles outside of Mason on the north side, on County Road M59. We know this route. You would take M59 out of Mason to catch the interstate to head north to Minneapolis. Why in the world would dad and mom have my kids out on the road at nine o'clock in the evening? It just does not make sense to me.

The state troopers had told Paul and I at the hospital that dad hit a semi truck head on coming up over a hill. We watch the odometer in the car. At just past three miles, we start heading up a steep hill. Tears come to my eyes. They are burning. This is the last path that my kids took before the awful crash.

Courtney slows down and looks over to me. She takes hold of my left hand. As we drive up and over the hill I can imagine how dad swerved into the center lane and never knew what hit him. Vehicles drive fast out here. They are approaching the interstate and going over the speed limit. I let out a big breath as we go up and over the hill.

Courtney slows down and pulls over to the shoulder. I think my sister can read my mind. I want to get out of the car and just walk around here. Luckily during the middle of the afternoon there isn't much traffic out here. The three of us get out of the Lexus and walk back towards the top of the hill.

There is no sign of any type of accident on the road. I expected to see black tread marks on the highway, red stains on the road, broken glass and uprooted trees in the ditch. There is really nothing remarkable about the site. It has been over a year, I guess, and things have been cleaned up and washed away.

I never did see dad's Tahoe after the accident. The police said that it was towed away and we could go look at it at the salvage yard later if we wanted to. The police needed to keep it for a couple of weeks for their reports. I never had a desire to look at the Tahoe. It would scar my memory for life, I think.

As we stand on the shoulder of the road, at the site where our parents and my three children were killed, I can envision the accident. I can hear the screeching of metal on metal. I know it happened quickly. I want to believe that none of them suffered. I don't want any of them to have been in pain. Quick, swift deaths, and hopefully they never even knew what hit them.

"What happened to the driver of the semi truck? I remember the police saying that he was taken to the Mason Hospital for injuries as well. Did either of you ever hear if he was alright? And I don't remember his name. I wonder if he is ok," I think aloud.

"From what I remember, Anna, he broke a couple of ribs in the accident and needed stitches on his forehead. Maybe some other minor injuries. I don't remember his name though. He was a truck driver working for a trucking company out of Oklahoma. He drove this route for about four years. And the police investigation found that the truck driver was not at fault. They said he was in his lane, and that dad swerved into him head on," Abby tells me.

This makes me swallow hard, with a lump in my throat. What in the hell was dad doing? It was nine o'clock at night, so they would have both had their headlights on. Didn't dad see the truck's lights coming up over the hill? Was he turned around towards the back seat talking to the kids? I am mad all over again. I want to know what happened, and realize that I will never know the truth. It is infuriating. I want someone to blame, I want someone to tell me it was their fault. I want answers.

Courtney and Abby walk back to the car. I stand on the shoulder for a few more minutes. This is where my babies were found dead. This is where the jaws of life had to cut open dad's SUV to free them from the wreckage. An ambulance came and took my babies to the hospital. And where was I? I was back in

Gannon, partying. I was at Nick's Pub having my third margarita and boozing it up with my friends. I was tickled that I was free for the weekend. My wish had been granted. No kids for the weekend. No kids for life.

58

Courtney drives the car back into Mason and we head down-town to the police station. None of us have been here before. I ask them to please both come inside with me. I may not be strong enough to do this alone. I need my sisters with me.

Abby talks to the officer at the window. She gives him the basic information of why we are here. She points back at me and the officer shakes his head as if in understanding.

"Anna, they need you to fill out a form requesting to look at the files from the accident." I take the clipboard from the man in uniform and sit down to fill out the form. Date of accident. Names of people involved in accident. Reason why I want to re-view the police report. Names of officers involved at the accident scene. I don't remember their names. I hand the clipboard back to the officer.

Within five minutes a different officer walks toward us and calls my name. The three of us follow him back to his office.

"Mrs. Dawson, I am Sergeant Tanner. I was one of the of-ficers at the scene of the accident. I filled out these reports and I would be happy to let you review them. I will also answer any questions that you may have. Why don't you sit here in my of-fice and read over the reports. I'll come back in a little while and then we can talk."

Sergeant Tanner leaves and hands me a manila file folder. I look at Abby and Courtney and they both give me the head nod. Go to it, they are saying. I take a deep breath and open the folder. I start reading the officer's report, but it is detailed and I begin to skim it. Actually there are two officer's reports in here, both saying about the same thing. I page through to the end, and see some pictures from the accident scene. I can't help myself, I have to look.

It is awful. Dad's blue Tahoe is crumpled like a tin can. It looks like it is about one third the size that it should be. My kids are still in the truck! The next picture shows the firemen using the jaws of life to cut open the side of the Tahoe. I can see mom and dad's heads in the front seat. They don't appear to be moving. Should I continue to look at these pictures?

I slowly flip to the next page. More pictures. I cry out at the next picture. It is Cassy and Ryan in the middle seat. They are crammed up to the front seat, and the third row seat is on top of them. It is difficult to see, but Connor's little body is partially hanging down from the top of the hood.

I can't bear it. Tears are dripping down my cheeks.

"Anna, you don't have to do this," says Abby. They are peering over my shoulder at the pictures too, and they quickly sit back down. They don't want to see it either.

I take a deep breath and continue to look at the rest of the pictures quickly. It is what I thought it would be. I quickly flip past the pages of my babies lying on the ground dead. Their bodies don't appear to be mangled or destroyed, but you can just tell that they are not alive. My beautiful angels! It breaks my heart that they had to die this way, at so young of an age. Without me there to take care of them.

The report states very matter of factly that a head-on collision occurred on County Road M59, three miles outside of Mason at approximately nine o'clock that evening. The truck driver reported that when coming to the crest of the hill, a vehicle just ran right into him. Both vehicles were estimated to be traveling at about sixty miles per hour. That is like a car driving one hundred and twenty miles per hour directly into a brick wall. Dad had no chance. The semi truck driver endured because of his big truck.

A car behind dad witnessed the accident and said that dad's truck just did a quick swerve right into the trucker's lane. The witness, Calvin Hartford, thought maybe the driver fell asleep. Maybe he was reaching for something? He said he could see the lights coming up over the hill and held his breath as he saw the crash occur. He slammed on his brakes and immediately called 911. He rushed out of his car to the scene. He helped the truck driver out of his semi.

Mr. Hartford said there was no way to get into the Tahoe. It was smashed up so badly that he was afraid to touch anything. Within minutes the police and fire trucks arrived and they began to get the passengers out of the Tahoe. It all sounded familiar to me. No ground breaking news here. No answers to my questions of "Why?" Why did this have to happen? Why did dad swerve into the lane of an oncoming semi truck? No one can give me the reason for the deaths.

I hand over the folder to Abby so she and Courtney can look through it. They hold their hands over their mouths and cry as they read it too. The pictures are horrible to look at. It puts you right at the scene. It doesn't leave any guesses as to what happened regarding the accident. It's quite obvious really. Five innocent people died for no good reason.

Sergeant Tanner comes back into his office and sits behind his desk. He asks if we have any questions for him. I can't bring myself to speak. I am in such despair. I was really hoping to feel better after seeing the report, but I feel worse.

Courtney asks if they have any indications as to why our dad would have swerved into the oncoming semi. Sergeant Tanner says no, that it is really difficult to ascertain why it happened. Since it was dusk out, the witness couldn't tell what he was doing in the car. The semi truck driver saw head lights coming up over the hill, but didn't realize until too late that the lights had moved into his path.

"We'll probably never know why," Sergeant Tanner says sadly.

I want to leave now. This was a mistake to come here. We drive back to mom and dad's home in silence. I feel guilty for putting Abby and Courtney through this too.

"I'm sorry. I didn't mean for all of us to go through this heart ache."

"Anna, we are all mourning. You lost your kids and your parents, but remember that Courtney and I lost our parents too. We know your loss is greater than ours, but we still grieve. We need to get through this together. The three of us need to stick together and keep in better contact with each other. Even though we live hours apart, it's easy to pick up the phone or shoot a quick e-mail. I love you two and I want us all to stay together. We are what is left of our family unit now. I don't want to see that ruined too," Abby sobs.

We are all crying and hugging now. We go into the house and it surprises me that it is relatively empty. The boxes are all over the floor and there isn't much left to do. We go to bed and finish up in the morning. It is time to go home now. We all pack some boxes in our cars and the rest will be shipped to us.

I drive home thinking about how grateful I am to have my sisters. We have always been close as siblings, and now it's all we have left of our family. I vow to keep in touch more often with them. To call them more and to visit more. I love them.

Giving up doesn't always mean you are weak.
Sometimes it means that you are strong enough
To let go.

—Author Unknown

59

Paul still calls every Sunday to touch base with me. After being gone for two months he stops asking if I'm going to move to Des Moines with him. I think he now knows that answer. After four months he sometimes forgets to call every Sunday. It grows to every other Sunday, and then maybe once a month. I know I can call him anytime too, but I don't. I look forward to our conversations, actually, knowing in my heart that we will never live under the same roof again.

Paul has been doing great in Des Moines, of course. He has been traveling a fair amount for the First National Bank and enjoys that. He is seeing a lot of the world, he says. I notice that he hasn't invited me to travel with him on any of these trips. Not that I would have gone. He has been to Europe several times, he has been to Florida, California, Arizona, and Massachusetts. He has been asked to speak at many conventions. I am proud of him and of course I am not surprised that he has achieved success. Now he doesn't have a wife or three kids to hold him back. He can work late without feeling guilty.

I want to ask him if he has met someone else. He seems so happy that it is hard for me to believe that he hasn't. He has not come back to Gannon once since he moved out. I haven't been to Des Moines either to visit him.

In my heart I know that I want a divorce. I find it easier to cope now without Paul in my life. I never, ever imagined I would be saying that, but it's true.

With Paul gone, now it's as though I can start over. Paul goes hand in hand with the memory of our kids. I cannot separate the two. I wonder if he feels the same way.

60

After six months of being separated from Paul, the doorbell rings one Friday afternoon. I am surprised to hear it. People have stopped bugging me. No one calls me or comes to my house anymore. I'm guessing it is the UPS man. The bell rings again and I peek out the dining room window. It is Paul! How strange. He could have driven his car into the garage or used his key to open up the door.

I open the door and we stare at one another. I know instantly why he is here. His eyes look sad and I know he is miserable doing this. I know we are over. It is what I want too, but still it sucks.

He sits on a bar stool at the kitchen island while I open a bottle of our favorite white wine. Paul used to drive miles out of his way in Missouri to stop at my favorite winery to buy Golden Chablis. We have gone through many bottles of this over the years. We small talk for awhile, knowing we are putting off the inevitable.

He tells me about his apartment. How it is strange to him that he likes the quick five minute walk to work every day. He parks his car in the underground garage and doesn't even take it out every day. He is a workaholic and he knows it. He is committed to his bank and that gives him reason to exist.

Paul asks me how I've been. He looks at me with sincerity when he asks this. I know he wants the truth, not just some shallow answer. I'm not sure what to tell him, really. I want him to know the truth. I'm not ashamed of the truth. I'm just not really sure how I am anymore.

I tell him that I'm lonely. I tell him about my routine each day. I talk about the fact that after two years now, I still miss the kids just as much. I tell my husband that I don't think I will ever fully recover from this loss. I'll never be the same again, I say.

He looks at me with wet eyes. He knows I have been brutally honest with him. He knows that I will never again be truly happy without our kids in my life. That he isn't enough to bring me out of my hole has to weigh on him.

I think that's why he eventually left me. He can't rescue me, for I won't allow it. I know he still loves me like the day he married me. My heart beams knowing that truth. Paul has always loved me dearly. But unfortunately, even his love won't bring our kids' lives back.

I ask Paul if he wants to spend the night here. He says no, that he has a room at the Highland Hotel downtown. That hits my heart hard. He says he wants to get a few more things out of the house that are his.

He says that we need to talk. He spoke with a lawyer in Des Moines about a divorce. He's wondering if that is what I want. I hate it when Paul throws the ball back into my court when we both know he's in charge of it.

I tell him that I do think it is time we divorced. I am sorry to say it out loud, and I start to cry. I tell him I am so sorry that I couldn't be a better wife to him after the kids died.

"This is not how I saw our life, Paul. Please believe me when I say that I have tried everything in my power to love you again. I don't think I'll ever allow myself to love anyone again. My heart is broken and I fear that it will never be fixed. You need to be rid of me."

He gets up and gives me a big bear hug. A brotherly hug. I am soaking his shirt sleeve with my tears.

"I am so sorry, Anna. I didn't see us ending this way, either. But I agree that we both need to go our own way now. I will always be just a phone call away, though. I want you to visit me in Des Moines anytime. I want you to call me and keep in touch. I want us to never lose sight of each other. Part of you will always be in my heart."

Paul was always good at melting my heart. He could always say the right thing at the right time. He is a very eloquent man. We both know that after today we probably won't ever see one another again. But I do want to part on good terms. We shared such a wonderful life together in the past. I'll never forget him.

We sit down at the kitchen table and sign the divorce forms together. I don't imagine that many couples do this as amicably as Paul and I. He says his lawyer will call mine here in Gannon and that we can work out the financial settlement. I trust him enough to know that he will be good to me. He will take care of me. This isn't about hating one another. This is about forgetting the pain associated with one another.

As if that's possible.

61

I call Tammie and we meet at our favorite Chinese restaurant in town, Wontons. I tell her I'm getting divorced. She chokes on her egg roll.

"What? When did this come about? Did Paul send you papers in the mail?"

I tell her the story and she just stares at me with bug eyes. "Only the two of you could make divorce look so easy. I'm sad for you both, though. You know you and Paul have been Jack and my best friends for years. We are so sorry to see it come to an end."

I guess I have really been expecting it for some time now. I'm not emotional about the loss of my marriage, nor am I shocked. I will always love Paul, but it became obvious that our future together was doomed after the kids died. We both reminded one another of the horrible tragedy that we shared. Independently, we don't have to be constantly reminded of it in each other's presence.

Tammie confides in me that she and Jack have not been getting along great the past year. Tammie has put on weight and she says they haven't touched one another in eight months.

"He doesn't find me attractive anymore, Anna. I can see it in his eyes. The way he looks at me now is like I'm repulsive to him. It hurts my feelings. He's put on weight too, so it's not like he's Mr. America. I feel as though my marriage is headed south. Maybe I'll be joining you in the divorcee club."

"Oh, Tammie, quit it. All couples go through this. Talk to anyone and they'll tell you the same thing. Relationships go through their ups and downs. As we age, so do our bodies, and it's not like it was when we were in our twenties and could have a quickie on a Saturday afternoon. Now you have kids and carpools and ball games. It never ends. The relationship has to change with the times."

We finish our sweet and sour chicken, crab rangoons, and egg drop soup. I hand Tammie a fortune cookie and open mine. I've never believed in the fortunes, but what the heck. I read mine and laugh out loud.

It says, "Romance is in your near future." Like that is going to happen.

Tammie reads hers, "You will face challenging times in the coming month."

"Great," Tammie shrugs. "More crappy times with my marriage. Just what I needed to hear."

As we leave Wontons, I can barely remember the years when the four of us used to spend hours here together over beers and drinks. Those days with our husbands seem like decades ago. We used to sit here and talk about our kids endlessly. We compared notes on our babies and gave each other suggestions on how to get through the difficult times.

I wish I would have known then that those times weren't even remotely close to being difficult times.

62

I am now officially a divorcee. I just received the papers in the mail today. After twelve years of marriage, it is over. I feel like I should be more saddened by this fact, but the truth is that the marriage has been over for two years.

So I have already gone through the grieving process of losing the relationship. I don't harbor ill feelings to Paul. Quite the contrary, actually. He was very kind to me in the divorce settlement. He promised that he would make sure I was taken care of, and he kept that promise.

Paul wanted me to keep our home, and that is really all I cared about. I can't let go of the memories here yet. I told Paul that he could take whatever he wanted from the house. Furniture or anything he needed. But he didn't take much. I think he wanted a clean slate. He was ready to start over with all new things.

I can't bear to let go of anything old. Paul will pay me alimony until I turn sixty-five, or until I remarry, whichever comes first. I can't even imagine me ever getting remarried. That is not in my stars.

So here I am at age forty-two, divorced, having buried my three children and parents, and no career. Money won't be an issue for me, but a reason to get up each morning is still a problem.

Although I function fine, I know that I am still depressed. My heart is still so very heavy, and I rarely find anything to be happy about. I go through the motions of daily life, but most of the time the motions are so routinized into my being, that I feel as though my body is just leading me.

My soul is very empty. I go to Mass almost every day, but it has yet to fill my heart with the longing that it is apparently searching for. I just ask God to please grant me peace and contentment. All I ask for is joy to be alive.

I thank God for giving me Connor, Ryan, and Cassy for the short time that I had them here on earth. I praise His name in glory. But I leave feeling empty and alone. I won't give up on God, but there are days when I definitely feel as though He has given up on me.

Father Daniel is so good to me. He tells me that I can call him any time, day or night to talk. I know he is worried about me taking my own life. He hasn't said it out loud, but I can see it on his face. We talk about heaven and how Connor, Ryan, and Cassy are living a pure, sin-free life with God our Father. We talk about how they are so very happy and not in pain. These conversations do make me long to be with them. I am jealous that they are in a better place and I am left here to rot.

I still go talk to Dr. Hansen once a month. I don't know that I have anything new to say anymore. Although some of the pain has subsided, I am what I am. I am a mother who lost her children and that will never change. I can only work on how I will deal with that fact.

As Dr. Hansen tells me, only I am in charge of making me happy now. *I* decide if I want to be happy or sad each morning when I wake up. I cannot rely on others to make my life full of life. She is so right about that.

I haven't talked to Paul in months. I so badly want to ask him if he is seeing someone. Part of me is ok with that thought, and another part of me would be so envious of him. I envy the fact that he is able to move on. I envy him for being stronger than I. I envy him for having the courage to face the truth and accept it. I don't know that I will ever accept the truth. I still long for the past. I still dream of yesterday and I want it back so very badly.

I've been journaling a lot lately. It has become the one thing I do look forward to each day. Since I don't really talk to many people anymore, my journal has become my main source of conversation. Dr. Hansen wants to read it, but I have yet to give it to her. It is so personal. All of my worst thoughts are in there, some about her. I would be ashamed to allow her into my most private thoughts. She might not like me afterwards. Only Tammie has read some of the journal entries.

Every Sunday I visit the kids at the cemetery. I bring something different for them each week. I like to bring fresh flowers in good weather, and I bring artificial ones in the winter. I like to say the rosary by their grave sites, as it makes me feel good thinking that my prayers are going to them.

It calms my nerves to be near them. I would truthfully go every day, but I know that would not be healthy for me. I talk to each of them, telling them what is going on in Gannon that I'm aware of. But honestly, my conversations are becoming shorter. I have lost touch with Gannon, their friends, the school, their activities. I don't really know what to tell them about anymore. Their dad has left me, the house is empty, and their grandparents are dead.

Their mother's soul is floundering.

63

Almost a year to the date of our divorce, I get a call from Paul. He has to come to Gannon for a bank meeting and wants to know if he can take me out to dinner. I hesitate…wondering why he wants to take me out to dinner. I know he has been back to Gannon for previous bank meetings and he doesn't always call me. I hear it from Tammie or someone else who saw him here. I ask him if he would rather just come to the house. He says no, he would actually prefer not to come to the house.

So I meet him at Ridges, of all places. My heart beats a little too fast remembering the Nicole incident here years ago, how I am sure I embarrassed myself, but didn't care. That seems like so long ago. Now I'm waiting for Paul, as my ex-husband, to have dinner here with me. I can count on one hand the number of times he took me out to eat here when we were married. Interesting how things change.

I see Paul walk in alone. He looks great. He is graying a little more above the ears, but of course it looks distinguished on him. He looks like he's been working out. He's very fit and trim as he was when he was my husband. He's all dressed up in his business suit and tan trench coat. He so looks like a banker.

Paul and I hug, and he gives me a quick kiss on the cheek. He smells like Paul. Thank God I dressed up in my black A-line skirt with my favorite white blouse. Paul always liked this skirt. He said my calves looked sexy when I walked. We hang up our coats and go sit down.

I am surprised at how easy it is to talk to Paul. I know we really did love each other in our former married life together. We had such a great thing for a long time. I still get butterflies when he looks right into my eyes. And yet, I can't bare the thought of what he reminds me of. My heart is still so fragile. My soul is left open to the world when he is around me. I see Connor in Paul's face, his smile, and his mannerisms. I have to look away or I will begin to cry.

After Paul orders us appetizers and drinks, he says that he needs to talk to me about something important. Oh no, I think. I knew there had to be a reason for this dinner. He didn't just want a social outing with his ex-wife. And silly me to accept his offer to meet in public.

I can't throw a big fit or walk out on him at Ridges. Actually, I could, but he knows me better. I probably won't. I'd be less likely to do it here anyway, than at our, now my, house.

My mind is racing. He's accepted a job with First National Bank in Europe. He got fired. He made a huge mistake thinking he wanted to divorce me and now he wants me back.

Paul takes my hand across the table and clears his throat. He looks nervous.

"Anna, I've been wanting to tell you about this for a long time now, but it just never seemed to be the right time. Anyway, I wanted you to hear it from me. I want you to know that I'm getting married this weekend."

My heart stops. I did not see this one coming. I feel betrayed and hurt. Why is it so easy for him to move on, while I am stuck here? I truly love this man, and yet I don't want to be married to him. And then again, how dare he be happy without me?

Paul sees that he has surprised me. I know he wants to spare my feelings, so he starts rambling on so I don't have to say anything yet. He knows I need to get my composure back.

"Victoria and I met through friends in Des Moines. She is an Interior Decorator in Des Moines and has been divorced for five years. She has two kids in high school and they are great kids. She shares custody with her ex-husband, and it works really well for them. I know I should have told you about her before, but it was always so awkward, Anna. I didn't know how to tell you."

"Were you seeing her while we were still married?"

That's all I really want to know. Was he living in Des Moines, free of his depressed wife, while I was here trying to recover from our children's deaths? His hesitation tells me what I need to know.

"Anna, I swear to you that we were not in an official relationship until after you and I divorced. I did meet Victoria when I moved to Des Moines, but we didn't start spending time together until I knew you and I were getting divorced. I wouldn't do that to you. Please trust me on this one."

Yeah, like I trusted you before and then I found you here, at this restaurant with Nicole. Did I ever really know this man?

"Honestly, Paul, I'm happy for you. Please don't feel pity for me. I'm not upset. I knew you would get married again, and I wanted you to. I am happy for you. Some day I'd like to meet this Victoria."

I try so very hard to be as gracious as possible.

"Actually, she came to Gannon with me today. I can give her a quick call and she can come and meet you right now, if you would like."

Boy, did he have everything planned out or what? His whole little scheme is falling into place for him. The distressed ex-wife did not make a scene when the distinguished banker tells her that he is getting remarried. How perfectly perfect for him.

I'm not sure what to say to this. On one hand, I'd like to meet Paul's new wife. I want to put a face to her and make sure she is good enough for Paul. On the other hand, then it will be very real and I will have to face the facts. Sooner or later I guess I need to anyway.

"Give her a call, Paul. I'd like to meet your Victoria," I surprise myself and say.

Within minutes a short, dark haired woman joins us. She has a great smile, and is not at all what I had pictured. I envisioned a tall, blonde, big boobed, leggy thing for Paul. I like this Victoria at first glance. She looks to be about my age, which relieves me.

Paul introduces us, and we order more drinks and dinner and have a surprisingly nice conversation. Victoria tells me how she grew up in Missouri, got a job at a Design firm downtown Des Moines and has been there ever since. She married a man who turned out to not be faithful to her, and so she divorced him.

She has two high school aged kids, Matthew, 17, who is into basketball and golf. Her daughter, Bethany, 14, has autism and is a special needs student. Victoria tells me about her work in interior decorating and I think that she and I could be friends if we met under different circumstances. I can see why Paul fell in love with this woman.

If Paul is looking for my approval, then he has it. Victoria is down to earth, considerate, and seems very genuine. She and Paul aren't all touchy feely, lovey dovey. But they definitely seem to have a good connection and are in love. I am truly happy for Paul, I think.

I ask about their wedding this weekend. Victoria tells me that they are having a very small ceremony in Des Moines. Nothing big or fancy. I notice that neither one of them invites me. Not that I would attend, but it would have been nice to have been included.

We all decline dessert, as I believe we have discussed everything that we needed to. It is time to move on. I appreciate it that Paul did tell me in person that he was getting remarried. I would have been devastated to hear it from someone else in town. And I hope he will be happy with Victoria. I think he made a fine choice. A real woman, not some younger trophy wife.

I drive home by myself and the tears come, nonetheless. I am sad for me.

I am still alone.

They say that time heals all wounds
But all it's done so far is
Give me more time to think
About how much I miss you.

—Ezbeth Wilder

64

I can't seem to help myself. My need to sift through the kids' things is still there. I know I am living in the past, and I can't seem to get out of it yet. Periodically I just wander into one of their bedrooms. I will start in one drawer, and then just go through everything.

I mean *everything* in their room. The other day I was in Cassy's room and before I knew it, three hours had gone by. I looked at every piece of clothing in her closet, and I took out every doll, toy, and book on her shelves and just held them. I have memories from every item in her room. I can picture her smiling face asking me to read another book to her before bed.

"Just one more, please, Mommy?" What I wouldn't give to do just that.

I was always a snoopy mom. The kids each had their private drawers where they hid their most precious things. They wouldn't let their siblings look in there. But I always did. I wanted to know what girls were giving their school pictures to Connor. I wanted to know what their most precious things were to them. It was usually something they found outside at recess. A flat, smooth rock. Or a toy given to them by a friend. Nothing of great monetary value, but special to them, nonetheless.

So I felt that I knew exactly what was in my kids' rooms. Even before they died, I could tell them where any toy was when they couldn't find it. The play room upstairs was another story. I didn't spend a lot of time in there. It was always pretty messy and we kept too many toys in there, so it never had a prayer to stay clean. It didn't bother me, though. I never saw it and the kids loved it.

I had thoughts of going through the kids' things the past few months and giving away some of their toys. Not all, mind you, just some toys and things that I could part with at this point. But I had never gotten around to it.

Today I thought I might attempt to pick through the play room and see if I could at least begin sorting all the junk in there. Maybe there were a few toys I could give to the preschool or daycare in town.

I organized the Lite Brites, the Sorry board game, the kitchen set, the pirate ship, the Thomas the Train tracks. I sorted through American Girl doll clothes, fairy dolls, Barbie clothes, and Fancy Nancy books. I was on a roll.

I came across the kids' sketch pads and coloring books. They all three really enjoyed drawing pictures and coloring. Connor was old enough to write beginning stories, and I was amused at his 'books.' I found numerous notepads and sketch pads with their beautiful drawings. My heart couldn't take looking at them at the moment, so I put them aside to look at later.

That evening as I lay on the family room couch watching my favorite Sunday night TV show, I paged through their drawings. Ryan had drawn many SpongeBob and Patrick episodes. He was actually not a bad artist for a seven year old. Cassy always drew pictures of she and I. She wrote 'I heart Mommy.' I was saving all of these beautiful pieces of artwork. I was thinking about framing some of them to hang in my bedroom, actually.

65

I finally decide to call the Mason police station and ask if I could get copies of all the reports from the accident mailed to me. I will be glad to pay for it, I say. I know I have gone to the station and read through everything, but it was done quickly and I'm sure I missed a lot of details. I just want to read through the entire accident on my own terms and see if there are any clues that I may have missed.

A few things remain a mystery concerning the accident. First of all, why they were out driving at that time of night? Where had they been? They were coming back into town. Mom and dad told me their plans for that weekend with the kids, and they didn't mention anything about leaving town that night. What caused dad to swerve into an oncoming semi? The coroner ruled out a heart attack or any sudden illness that would have caused dad's driving to be impaired. He was not under the influence of drugs or alcohol.

I have swerved many times while driving, and they all have been when I was turning around to talk to the kids in the back seat, to hand them something, or when reaching down to grab something. My best guess is that dad turned around to talk to the kids.

But why didn't mom warn dad that he had swerved over to the wrong lane? Wouldn't she have noticed? They both should have seen the oncoming headlights of the semi truck approaching over the hill. It was nine o'clock at night, but it wasn't pitch black out yet. It was that hazy color, where you need your headlights, but you can still see without them. I am so mad at mom and dad. Couldn't they have prevented this accident if they had just been more careful?

The Mason police officer wants to know if I want the pictures included. I think about this for a moment. Do I? The pictures were really difficult to look at. But then again, they might help me fill in the blanks. I tell him to send everything. I want every last shred of information, no matter how miniscule. He says the package should arrive in a few days.

I pace around the house for three days. I need to read through the reports. I am driving myself mad thinking about it. I don't know what I think I am going to find, but I have become obsessed thinking about it. I know I am searching for answers that everyone has told me don't exist. I know that nothing will make me feel better. Yet I continue to yearn for the secrets.

67

On day three the package arrives. The folder is bigger than I remembered. I spread everything out on the kitchen table and get down to work. I read every page, highlighting anything that I think I might want to come back to. I cry when I read the pages. They are not easy to read, nor do I really want to live it all over again.

Hearing the story of my children's deaths will haunt me for the rest of my life. I know I will have bad dreams tonight and that I will be grumpy for awhile. But I need to do this.

The reports don't tell me anything I didn't already know. Everything is very clinical, stated very matter of factly. No opinions, no subjective comments. It is all very professionally written. I stop and catch my breath when I see the name of the semi truck driver. I had missed his name somehow the first time I read through the report with Courtney and Abby.

His name is Boyd Cornell. His address is listed as 7438 Cormick Road, Stillwater, Oklahoma. His phone number is listed as well. I highlight his information. I don't know why this seems important to me right now. His first hand account is listed in the report, but it doesn't say much. He reported to the police that it all happened so fast. That as he came up over the hill, he saw headlights but didn't notice they were coming right at him until it was too late.

The impact left him with a couple of broken ribs and a cut on his forehead. He was taken to the hospital via ambulance after my family was taken there. I notice that Mr. Cornell was not cited for any traffic violations. He was found not to be under the influence of any drugs or alcohol, he had an impeccable driving record, and the police report states that the collision was ruled an accident.

I wonder what good it would do if I were to call Mr. Boyd Cornell? Would he even want to talk with me? I wonder if he feels any guilt associated with the accident. After all, it did leave five people dead. Five of my family members. I wonder if he worried about a lawsuit. Paul and I never even considered a lawsuit. We had a couple of lawyers contact Paul in the months following the accident to see if we might be interested in pursuing legal action. We were not in the least bit interested. What was done was done. No amount of money could make us feel better, and we didn't want to have to relive the accident again. We didn't blame the truck driver. The police said it was an accident, so we believed them.

But what if Mr. Cornell could tell me something that I don't know? Would it make any difference? There are so many things left unknown about the accident. Any shred of information that could be shed onto the picture could help. Or am I grasping at thin air here?

I should call Paul and ask him what he thinks. Should I call Boyd Cornell? I know that Paul would tell me "no." I decide to sleep on it. I read through everything again, this time not looking at the horrible pictures of my dead babies and parents. In fact, I remove the pictures and put them in an envelope and stuff it in the kitchen drawer.

68

For the next week I stew about whether or not to call Boyd Cornell. He might not still be at the same address or have the same phone number. He may not live in Stillwater, Oklahoma anymore. Even if he does, he may not speak to me. But then again, he might. I decide to take my chances and just try the number.

I leave a message on his answering machine, explaining who I am and I leave my phone number. I'm betting anything that he won't return my call. I'm not sure that I would. I try to stay at home for the next three days, hoping to hear the phone ring. My phone rarely rings anymore. Most of my friends have given up on me. I must admit that I'm not much fun to be around anymore.

On a Thursday evening after I finish my spaghetti dinner, the phone rings. I know it is Mr. Cornell before I even see the caller id.

My stomach does a double flip. He talks with a hint of a southern twang. He apologizes for not getting back to me sooner. He had been driving a route to California. We small talk for a minute, and then he is silent. I realize that I must get to the point of why I called.

"Mr. Cornell, I'm guessing you might be surprised that I called you. I have put much thought into this phone conversation, and I am very nervous."

We both give a little nervous laugh. "I want you to know that in no way do I blame you for the accident. I have read through the police reports numerous times, and every account ruled the accident as just that, a terrible accident. It has been very hard for me to live with, wondering *why*. As a last resort, I just thought possibly you might be able to shed some information about the accident that I haven't heard already. Anything that you might remember, anything at all," I plead with him.

Mr. Cornell hesitates. The second hand on my kitchen clock is moving very, very slowly. Time almost stands still for me. It's as though I'm waiting for the hammer to strike, waiting for some awful crash.

"I truly wish I could tell you something that would help, Mrs. Dawson. My life was changed the day of that accident as well. I'll never forget what happened, and even though it wasn't my fault, I'll go to my grave feeling guilty. After that accident, I asked to transfer trucking routes. I can't even bear to drive back into Iowa again. Now each week I drive to California and back."

I want to hear firsthand his version of the accident. "Could you tell me what happened from your perspective that night, Mr. Cornell?"

"Well, I had been to Minneapolis and was heading back to Oklahoma, my usual weekly route. I knew those roads. I had driven them almost weekly for years. I knew that county road I was on, and I remembered that hill. I could see headlights coming up over the hill, but they didn't appear to me to be in my lane. All of a sudden, when I saw the truck coming right at me, it was too late. I keep thinking that if I had noticed it sooner, I would have had time to swerve into the ditch. Maybe he would have missed me. I feel like maybe there was something that I could have done to prevent it."

"We all know it wasn't your fault. My father, for whatever reason, swerved right into your semi truck. The witness behind him saw the whole thing. So we know it was my father's fault, but we just don't know what caused him to do it. Medically the autopsy reported that he was fine. The kids were all buckled in their car seats. I don't know if he was looking behind him, talking to the kids, and accidentally swerved, or what happened."

For the thousandth time, I am recreating the accident in my mind.

Mr. Cornell clears his throat and then adds, "The strange thing was how I swear I saw your father gripping the wheel tightly and staring right at me at impact. It's like he was frozen."

I freeze at this comment. "You saw my father's face right before impact? I didn't read that in the police reports."

"I told an officer that when I gave him my testimony at the scene. He was writing things down. I just assumed he included that too, Mrs. Dawson."

This new piece of information has my heart racing and my mind reeling. Get a grip, Anna.

"What else can you tell me about that? Do you remember *anything* else?" I beg.

"I told the officer that what I saw only lasted a fraction of a second. But when I came up over the hill and saw his truck coming right at me, I saw his hands on the wheel, at the ten and two spots. He had a purposeful look on his face, and he was staring right at me, too. I told the officer that if I didn't know better, it almost looked like he meant to drive right into me."

I'm shaking and I feel weak. I did not expect this. Anything but this. I can't understand why it wasn't in the reports.

"That's all I saw, Mrs. Dawson. It all happened so quickly. And I could be wrong. Maybe he was frozen because he saw it coming too late as well, and didn't know how to react. I had never been in an accident before, and it happened so quickly that

I didn't have time to react. The sudden impact was awful. But because I was sitting up high in the semi, I had an upper view a little bit. I remember a woman in the front passenger seat, and she was looking out her window. I don't think she saw it coming at all. But you have to remember it was just getting to be dusk, and so I could have seen it all wrong, too. I'm just telling you what I remember."

"Thank you so much, Mr. Cornell. I appreciate your time and your honesty. If you ever think of anything else, will you please call me back? I'm trying to put together the pieces of this puzzle, and it's not making much sense."

"If I were you, Mrs. Dawson, I would just let it be. I'm so sorry you lost your family, but some things we never get answers to. It will drive you crazy thinking about it. If I could go back in time and change the outcome, I would do it for you in a heart beat."

What a nice man, I think. I feel horrible that he has to live with this over his head for the rest of his life. I am stunned by what he told me. It doesn't make any sense to me, though. Dad wouldn't intentionally drive his Tahoe into an oncoming vehicle, would he? That would mean...that would mean the worst possible thing. That he meant to kill himself, his wife, and my kids. What would cause him to want to do that? I cannot and will not believe that he purposefully drove head on into an oncoming truck.

I'm not sure I could live with that.

69

I'm at Mass one Wednesday morning, saying the rosary, minding my own business. The emotions suddenly hit me hard, like a jolt to my system.

I feel myself reel back to the pew, and go soft in the knees. I am so sad that my parents have died. For years now I have grieved more over my children. But all of a sudden, out of nowhere, I realize that I am so very, horribly sad that my parents are gone. I miss them. I miss not talking to them every week. I miss not strategizing with them on where they should travel during their retirement. I miss not golfing with dad. I miss not shopping with mom. I miss my childhood with them, and I miss the security they gave to me.

Mom and dad were always there for me. Only a phone call away, they would come to Gannon and help with the kids anytime I asked. They celebrated every birthday, holiday, and school activity with us. I know now that I took them for granted.

At times they really bugged me, too. I grew impatient with the repeated stories dad would tell me again and again. I didn't always have time for them their last few years of life. I allowed them into my life when it was convenient for me. And now I wish I could have them back. I would be a better daughter to them. I would tell them that they were wonderful parents and grandparents. I would tell them how I was always proud of them as my parents. That I had so much respect for them.

Father Daniel comes over and puts his hand on my shoulder. I didn't even realize that I was sobbing out loud. My head is resting on the pew in front of me. And I am bawling like a baby. He takes me by the elbow and we go inside the face to face confessional at the back of the church. The rosary continues to be recited without me.

I attempt to gather myself as much as I can.

"Anna, I'm here if you want to tell me about it," says Father Daniel.

That's all I needed. I open up to him. I expose my broken soul to him. He only glances at the clock once. I know he has to go start Mass in just a few minutes. But everything is pouring out of me at the moment. I tell him about dad's abuse and depression, about the possibility of the accident being intentional. I am mortified that my life has come to this. I am so distraught that I think I truly would rather be dead.

Father tells me to stay in the confessional during Mass and he will come back here when Mass is over to talk with me. He leaves and I lay down on the floor in fetal position. I close my eyes and go to sleep.

I hear Father Daniel come in the confessional. The door closes and he sits down on the padded chair. I don't get up. I just look at him. I know I am pathetic. I begin to cry again. Father says some prayers for me. He helps me back up into the other gray padded chair.

I can't stop crying. We sit next to each other for what seems like hours, me crying and him praying. My shoulders finally quit heaving and my sobs slowly subside. Now I am spent. I am emotionally drained of all thoughts.

"If you trust in God, He will help you, Anna. You have got to put your faith in Him, and He will show you the way. You will be so much stronger with Him than without Him. You need Him right now."

I know Father Daniel is right, but I don't know that anyone can help me anymore. Grief for my parents has just hit me, and hard. I truly feel as though even God has given up on me.

When we are no longer able to change a situation
We are challenged to change ourselves.

—*Victor Frankl*

70

I never truly understood my mom. She was a great mother, always there for us, providing a wonderful home, and childhood experiences for us. But she kept us away at a safe distance emotionally. We just couldn't break through the glass shield that surrounded her most private thoughts.

Mom was raised in a very Catholic household in Freeman, Iowa. She went to Catholic schools and was the youngest of five kids, with four older brothers. Her father was a physician, so she grew up fairly well to do in small town Iowa. I think she was spoiled growing up, and my dad just continued to spoil her. I don't know why she kept people at arms length, but I know that she was not close with her mother, either.

I used to be envious of my friends' relationships with their moms. They seemed like friends more than moms sometimes. Tammie tells her mother everything, both the good and the bad. They can go on girl's weekend trips together and be friends. For some reason, that kind of relationship was never an option with Mom.

Courtney, Abby, and I have discussed this at length. We all agree that it wasn't us, that Mom was either frightened to let us get too close, or else she didn't know how to let people in. Knowing what I now know about Dad's abuse and depression, I'm guessing she kept up a façade for people. She wanted the public to see a perfect marriage, a perfect family. She didn't want people to get too close, for fear of knowing the truth.

I'm guessing that Mom was really a lonely person. She kept her secrets hidden, and never let herself be vulnerable. It makes me sad knowing that I could have been there for her, had she allowed me to be. We had a good superficial relationship, but I tried numerous times over the years to have her tell me about her family. She just wouldn't talk about them. It's like she put her childhood behind her. There must have been something bad that happened that she didn't want to talk about.

I know that Mom loved my Dad very much. It must have been all she could do to watch her husband deal with his issues on his own. She hid her pain well, I will give her that. I never would have guessed that Dad had been abused.

I feel as though I should have tried harder to get closer to Mom. I wish I could have had more time to get closer to her, to figure her out better. I am just now realizing how heartbreaking it is that they were ripped away from me too soon. I've been grieving over the loss of my kids for so long, that the loss of Mom and Dad is just hitting home.

71

I heard that Paul and Victoria bought a big, new house in West Des Moines. I'm sure it's gorgeous, as Victoria probably decorated it herself. Paul is thriving in his new life. His career is booming and he is remarried, with two step children. He has a new life with a new wife. His old wife is stuck in the middle of hell.

I don't long for Paul in a sexual way, but I do long for the companionship that marriage provided. Just knowing that you had a partner, someone to go to events with, brought security and contentment. It's that best friend forever concept. You just know they will always have your back, no matter what. I miss that.

When Paul and I were at Iowa State, I think it was our junior year, he was spending a lot of time with a wild fraternity brother of his, Cody Morrison, whom I did not care for. When Paul was with Cody, it was like he was a different person. He treated me differently, and not so kindly.

They drank too much together, and Cody was a ladies man. I was worried that Paul would ruin our relationship when he was out with Cody. Plus, I missed not being the one that Paul preferred to spend time with. It was as though Cody was Paul's new best friend forever. I was jealous, and I became really insecure about it.

When I talked to Paul about it, he got mad and said I was being ridiculous. He was just spending time with his fraternity brother, for God's sake. He told me to stop acting like his mother. I was hurt and pissed that he chose Cody over me.

I missed the friendship *we* shared together. The studying together at the library, the jogging in the morning together. After a few months Paul figured out that Cody was a jerk and stopped spending so much time with him. All of a sudden I was now ok to hang out with again. I'm embarrassed to admit that I welcomed him back with open arms.

But it's that feeling of being connected to someone so closely that I miss. When you're married, if you have a good relationship, you feel secure. You can tell each other everything, and you don't worry about your spouse cheating on you or leaving you. You just know that you are partners in life together. It is a great feeling. And that is what I miss about Paul.

72

It shouldn't matter, but it matters greatly to me. *How* my family died is important. If they were killed in a car accident, then they were victims. If they died at my father's hands, then it was intentional. And those two different scenarios are eating me up inside.

I don't want to believe that my dad could drive his truck head on into an oncoming semi. I don't know how anyone could do that to your spouse and your grandkids. What would be so bad that you had to take them with you? If you need to take your own life, well then all right. But did you need to take innocent people with you?

My heart tells me that there is no way in hell my father would have done that to me. He would not hurt me that way. He could never intentionally take my kids from me. He knows they are the world to me.

But my head has doubts. Things just aren't adding up like they should be if it was a true accident. Maybe Dad was afraid his secret would come out.

What kills me is the not knowing. Instead of moving forward with my life, I am stuck in the past. A day doesn't go by that I don't think about all of the possibilities. Was Mom going to share Dad's secret?

73

Tammie has an English degree from The University of Iowa. She has always been a good writer. She writes a column in the Gannon Gazette once a month. It's an editorial, usually about a hot topic in the local news. She has guts to write what she thinks. People in town can get so upset with her views. I respect her for having the courage to say what most of us only dare to think.

She has worked at a small publishing firm in Gannon for eighteen years. The owner, old Malcolm Robinson, announced that he wanted to sell the firm. He is eighty and is finally going to retire. His kids aren't interested in the publishing business and he wants Tammie and Jack to buy his business.

Tammie has practically run the firm for years now anyway. Malcolm has been a stinker to work for the past decade, as his mental health has depreciated and his temper has grown icy at best.

I tell her I think they should go for it. It will mean taking on some serious debt, but the business is doing great and I believe in Tammie. The company has focused on publishing smaller works for upcoming authors, schools, and the government. I know Tammie will take the business to a higher level. It will mean longer days and more stress, but I know she can handle it.

They decide to take the leap and buy the publishing firm. Tammie immediately offers me a job. I think she is doing it out of pity's sake, so I don't take her seriously at first.

"Anna, I mean it. I really do want you to work with me. I need a good office manager, and you are a great business woman. I don't know the financial side of publishing as well as I should. You would be an asset to the company. You don't have to work full time. Just come in whenever you want, and I'm sure it will work out."

I tell her I appreciate her kindness, and that I will think about it. I could use something to do with my life right now. I'm not sure this is exactly what I had in mind, but I guess you never know what will come your way tomorrow.

I've definitely learned *that* life lesson. I don't know if I could be at the office forty hours a week. I'm thinking twenty to thirty would be good. I don't want to let Tammie down. What if I say yes, and then do a bad job? What if we lose our friendship over this? Don't they say to never to mix business with pleasure? I tell her I need a week to think about it, and maybe by then she'll come to her senses and rescind her offer.

I mull the job offer over in my head for a week. Tammie and I always had each other to bitch to about our co-workers, bosses, and a bad day at work. What if Tammie complains to Jack about me? I couldn't stand to lose my only friend.

I tell Tammie what I'm feeling and she assures me that in no way will our friendship be affected by this. I don't know that I believe her. I don't want her to hire me just because I'm her best friend, and because I'm beautiful. She's laughs, and guarantees me that my beauty is definitely the reason she wants me at her office.

74

I can't believe how smug I was three years ago. Boy, God sure humbled me quickly. Three years ago I thought I had it all. I was living the life of my dreams. Up to that date, I really believed that my life was charmed. I had a great childhood, I went to college, married my college sweetheart, moved to Gannon, and had three beautiful children. I appreciated my good fortune, I really did. I know now that I was so naïve back then.

My life hadn't known misfortune or cruelty up to that point. And the reality is that I didn't think bad things would come my way. I didn't even consider it. So when my picture perfect life began to unfold, I didn't know how to deal with it. I had never dealt with adversity before. Not of this magnitude anyway. If I ever had a problem, I always had my parents to fall back on for advice. They always gave me unconditional love and support. Now that's gone, too.

And then there was Paul. I know now I was attracted to him in college because he gave me the security that I wanted. I needed him to make the big decisions in my life, I needed him to lead the way for us. And now he's gone, too. Now I'm stuck with me, and it's not so much fun being me at the moment.

Without my parents, without my kids, without my husband, who am I? I was always a daughter, a mom, a wife. Now I'm plain old Anna and I'm quite boring, scared, and uninteresting. I still have thoughts periodically of ending my life. I really don't want to, but at times I feel it would be easier.

The constant dull ache of pain that I live with would be gone. Or would it? What if I killed myself and then I still had to live with the pain in my afterlife? I'm banking on God's will that if I hang on, I will only have to suffer here on earth. That when I die according to God's terms, then He will not make me suffer anymore.

75

It's Sunday night and I'm just settling down to watch my TV shows. I am sipping my favorite tea, munching on popcorn, and I have my favorite fleece blanket on top of me. The doorbell rings. It's Tammie and I know what she wants to talk about. I've been avoiding her all week. We sit down together and small talk. But then she digs right into the heart of the matter.

"So…are you coming to work for me, or not? I need to know, Anna. I only have two more weeks until Jack and I sign the papers and take ownership. I'm interviewing for other positions, and I need to know if I should be looking elsewhere for an office manager. You are my first choice, and I'd be honored if you would join Robinson Publishing with me. What do you say?"

I can tell she really, truly wants me to do it. I just so badly don't want to lose her friendship. If I lose her, I will be so lonely.

"I have been thinking about it, Tammie. And actually, I want to take the position. I'm dragging my feet because I'm worried that if it doesn't work out, then our friendship will suffer the consequences. I can't bear to lose you."

"How about if we just try it for awhile, kind of like a temporary position. Why don't you come in this week, you can meet with Glenda, the current office manager. She only has two weeks left, and then she is retiring too. She can show you around the office and you can see what she does. Come in all week, if you want. Just take a peek and see if you think you can stand me for eight hours a day. And I promise you, I guarantee, that if it doesn't work out, we will still be friends for always. I'm not leaving you, Anna, ever. I don't even want you worrying about that. If the job doesn't work out, then fine. I trust that our friendship can endure this."

I know Tammie is right. Deep down I believe in my heart that no matter what happens, we will always be there for each other.

"You know what, I'm going to do it."

Tammie gets up out of the recliner and comes over to my couch and gives me a big hug.

"I'm so glad. It will be great getting to see you every day. And if you decide it isn't the job for you, then tell me, Anna. My feelings won't be hurt, I promise."

And just like that, I appear to be employed for the first time in ten years. I barely remember what it feels like to go into an office every day. I may need to update my professional clothes. I'm sure mine are out of fashion by now.

76

On Monday morning I am at Robinson Publishing at eight o'clock. I notice that Robinson Publishing is directly across the street from First National Bank. Just my luck. I had forgotten about that. I'm actually nervous. I have butterflies in my stomach and I wonder if everyone knows that the only reason I have this job is because Tammie is my friend.

Glenda is a frumpy, older woman who looks like she could have a heart attack at any moment. She seems thrilled to have me here and can't wait to show me around. I think she'd leave today if she could. Glenda tells me she has worked for Malcolm Robinson for twenty-five years. No wonder she looks grumpy. Anyone who could put up with that old grouch for that long needs their head examined.

I get a tour of the office. I see Tammie in the conference room meeting with a dozen or so people. She gives me a wink as I walk by the windowed room. Glenda shows me the ancient kitchen where I can go for my morning and afternoon breaks. She introduces me to the publishing crew, and I realize I don't know anything about publishing. I do know human resources, accounting and managing an office, though, so hopefully I can learn the publishing details later.

Glenda talks to me about payroll, insurance, the phone system, and the general nuances of the business. She tells me that everyone is so excited that Tammie is the new owner of the business. Tammie has worked at Robinson Publishing since college, and she has worked her way up and has been the Senior Publisher for over ten years. Old Malcolm knew he had a special something in Tammie when he hired her years ago.

I sit down and take a look around the office. I see all the people in their offices, at their cubicles, I hear the machines running, the computers clicking, and the phones ringing. It feels good, really, to be back in my old element. I hope I can hold up my own here. I spend the rest of the day basically following Glenda around, watching her and meeting people. I know I can do the job. Things are coming back to me, and it doesn't appear to be rocket science. I know mentally and emotionally I will need to be tough, though. I can't let my bad days bring me down.

I go into the office the rest of the week and continue to be a sponge. I want to show Tammie that she made the right decision in hiring me. I enjoy the adult conversations and realize that work is where people hear the town gossip. Everyone seems to know some little tidbit about someone or something. I cringe when I think about how I must have been a hot topic of conversation for a long time.

No one talks to me about the past, though. They all keep it light and surfacey. I wonder if Tammie instructed them on what *not* to say around me. If she did, I appreciate it. I don't need a breakdown on my first week at work.

77

Tammie and I go out to Wontons and to a movie on Saturday night. She wants to hear all about my first week at the publishing firm, what I think. I tell her I'm envious of her. She has a bright future. She has goals, a reason to get up every day. I never knew that her career was such an inspiration to her. She has always worked since I've known her. I had stopped in her office a couple of times over the years, but it was always brief. I listened to Tammie vent about the frustrations at her job, yet I knew she loved it. Now I understand why.

I thank her for giving me this opportunity. She knew all along that I just needed to get out of my house and focus my energy on something else besides my family. Just the thought of my new career gives me hope for a brighter future.

I still think about the worst every day—my kids, my parents, my failed marriage, and why did the car accident happen? But when I'm at work I can't obsess over these thoughts as much. I don't have time.

I'm beginning to see why Paul got over the tragedy before I did. He went to the bank every day and could channel his energy and attention on work. If he had been at home all day every day like I was, I'll bet anything he would have gone crazy too. It's interesting that every day at work now, I find myself looking across the street at First National Bank, just wondering if I'll happen to see Paul walk out of the bank.

I haven't told Paul yet that I have a job. We don't talk regularly anymore, as he is married and has a new life. I wonder if he's heard that I am working now. I hope he's proud of me. I hope he knows that I am trying so very hard to move on. Not to forget, but to move forward with my life.

78

It's been five years since the accident. I have been working at Robinson Publishing for one and a half years now. I love it. I can't thank Tammie enough for giving me a new life. She brushes me off every time I tell her that she saved me, but she really did save my life.

I am good at what I do, and I feel important. Tammie has given me a raise twice now, and I feel guilty. I don't want her to play favorites with me. She swears she isn't showing any nepotism, that I deserve everything I've gotten. We generally go out to lunch together most days. If she doesn't have a meeting with someone, anyway.

I look forward to our lunches. We try not to talk about work, but it's hard since we have that common denominator now. I have started asking about her kids more. At first it was like taking a knife and stabbing myself in the gut. But each time we talk about Gretchen, Carli, and Anthony, it gets easier.

I have missed her kids. They are now thirteen, ten, and seven. I want to be a part of their lives, too, but I haven't been able to bring myself to go to their games, yet, or watch them partake in activities that my kids should be in with them.

Tammie has invited me over to their house for dinner numerous times lately. She knows that will be a big step for me. I will have to allow her kids back in my life, and I'm not quite there yet. I like to hear Tammie talk about Gretchen's basketball team, and Carli's dance classes. She briefly touches on them and then we let it go. It's best not to dwell on it too much yet.

But I'm making progress. The more we talk about her kids, each time it hurts just a little bit less. I tell myself that my goal is to go to their house for Christmas this year. That's in four months, so I have some work to do. Tammie has invited me over for Christmas every year since the accident, and I have never gone. I have preferred to stay home and envelope myself in my memories.

79

Robinson Publishing is now Harmon Publishing. I'm so proud of Tammie. She has made some serious changes since she and Jack bought the business. The staff here respects her and in turn, she treats us with respect. The employees have grown to thirty-five people now. We publish manuscripts from all over the world. Tammie is a great business woman, and knows how to look into the future to capitalize on upcoming ventures. She amazes me. I am so proud to work for her.

A few months ago Tammie asked me if she could read more of my personal journal. I remembered that she had read some of it a few years back. I thought I mortified her by my private thoughts of death and destruction. I couldn't believe she was interested in reading more negativity from me. But I let her. She seemed nonchalant about it, so I handed over my four notebooks that I had been writing in since the year after my kids died.

A week later she called me into her office. I thought maybe I had screwed up the new payroll accounts.

"Anna, I'd like to publish your journals." She just stared at me and smiled. I felt sick to my stomach, thinking of all the horrible things I had written in my journals. Things about people that were just mean. Things that I wouldn't even say out loud to Tammie. Those journals were my inner most private feelings, and the purpose was for me to vent, to grow, and to forgive and forget. To move on.

I can feel myself getting angrier by the minute as Tammie continues talking, explaining to me why she thinks I should publish "my story." I'm pissed that she would even consider asking this of me. It's not her story, and it's sure as hell not her place to assume that I want to share my story with anyone. I already regret sharing it with her.

"Tammie, I'm going to leave your office now. But before I go, I'm only going to tell you this one time. Please don't ever ask me this again. I will never allow you or anyone to read my journals again. I can't believe you would even consider publication an option for me. You know how long it has taken me to get to this point. I'm not even close to being able to share my sorrow. I'm upset and hurt that you would ask."

I storm out of her office, trying to hold back my tears.

I grab my sweater at my desk and bolt outside. I exhale deeply in the cool air. I've always loved the fall in Iowa. The leaves turn gorgeous colors of gold, orange, green, and red. I take a walk around the block. My heart is still beating too fast. I feel betrayed by Tammie. I never imagined she had an ulterior motive when she wanted to read my journals. I feel as though she wants to expose my flaws to the world. Not that anyone would even want to read my journals. But how dare she assume that my material was for sharing. I didn't expect this from Tammie, my best friend. She has always had my back. Now she's trying to take me down.

I walk around another block, past Gannon Pharmacy, Hank's Hardware, First National Bank, and the Red Owl Grocery Store. When I look into each of the store's windows, I see only my kids inside. I can conjure up memories of my kids in every place down town. They loved to run errands with me. They were my little buddies, always one step behind me, experiencing life through my eyes, and me through theirs. God, I miss them.

When I go back inside the office, Tammie is in a meeting with some vendors. It's almost time to leave for the day, so hopefully I won't have to talk to her again. I believe she meant well, but she really messed me up. I'm sure she'll call tonight and apologize.

80

Four days later and Tammie still hasn't apologized for her inexcusable request. In fact, she continues her plead for me to reconsider. I tell her that it's a done deal. I will not even consider it, and I would appreciate it if she would drop it. Surprisingly, she doesn't seem hurt nor does she get mad at me. She lets it go. But I can tell she she's going to bring it up again.

To be honest, I do think about Tammie's suggestion. From her point of view, I know she thinks it is an honor to be asked to publish someone's writing. Many writers only dream about being asked if their manuscripts could be published. Would-be writers may search unsuccessfully for years for an editor, an agent, or a publisher. That I have a publisher begging to publish my writing would be a dream come true for any aspiring author.

But my story is not something that I want to share. I am horrified at the thought of anyone knowing how sick I was, how sad I continue to be, and how low my spirit has fallen. I am too proud to expose my vulnerabilities.

Tammie says it would cost me nothing, that Harmon Publishing would publish it at no cost to me, and that after they covered expenses, we would share the profits. I ask Tammie why she thinks my story would sell. She hesitates, then is gentle with me.

She tells me that although everyone has someone close to them die over their lifetime, I had a very unusual experience. To have all of my children and my parents die suddenly, tragically, is unique. She says the detailed account of my experience is what people will identify with. All of us have tragedy in our lives, but

I have documented my tragedy in a way that people can understand. Tammie thinks my story would sell. She thinks I could actually make a lot of money off of it.

On one hand, I feel complimented, I think, and on the other hand I am appalled. To even consider making money, of all things, off of my family's tragedy is incomprehensible to me.

I trust Tammie's professional judgment. If she thinks something will sell, she is likely correct. I'm just not sure that I am strong enough to share my personal catastrophe with the public. That's even assuming that anyone would want to read my story. I have serious doubts about that. But her pestering continues, and I finally tell Tammie that I will think about it, if she leaves me alone.

81

My daily life is busy now. I get up at six thirty on work days, and work from eight to five, Monday through Friday. After work I run errands if need be, buy groceries and supplies, go to the post office, pay bills, go the bank, whatever mundane living tasks need to be taken care of.

I go home and make dinner, nothing too fancy for just myself. I prefer pastas—fettuccine, linguine, or spaghetti. I may swing by a fast food place if I'm feeling lazy. But my evenings consist of watching TV, reading my books, or renting a movie. I still have a housekeeper come and clean every Friday morning, and that has been wonderful.

I go to the fitness center three or four times a week to exercise. Sometimes I take an aerobics class, yoga, Pilates, or a weight training course for a month. But usually I just hop on the treadmill with my iPod and walk for forty minutes. The exercise has helped me feel better physically.

I have trimmed down my therapy sessions, going only now on an as-needed basis. Which generally amounts to once every other month. When I'm feeling especially low, I call Dr. Hansen and just go talk with her. She is happy that my dreaming fantasies have dwindled down. I was living in the past for so long, and I'm trying very hard to still keep my family in my heart, but not fantasize daily about what my life was.

Dr. Hansen was surprised when I told her about Tammie's offer to publish my personal journals. At first she was protective of me, and told me that I needed to think long and hard about that offer. She thinks that if I would do it before I'm ready emotionally, that it could set me back years. On the other hand, if I'm ready to share my story, then she thinks it would be a huge step for me. It would be very healthy and help me to move on. I tell her I'm just not sure where I am yet.

I try to go to Mass before work some mornings during the week, and I never miss a weekend Mass. I feel as though my faith is holding me together right now. I have turned over my control to God and I think it's working. I try not to worry so much about my future now, knowing that He will take care of me. I know everything happens for a reason, but I still struggle with the reason for that accident.

Being at church brings a sense of peace to me. I feel closer to my kids when I am there. In fact, I don't visit them so often at the cemetery now. Probably three times a year I will spruce up their grave sites with flowers or decorations, but now I'm more comfortable talking to them in church.

I feel God's presence with me more there. I cling to the notion that my babies are safe with God and in a better place than earth could offer to them. I so desperately want to believe that.

Most weekends I spend by myself. I will go shopping, drive out of town and go to a movie. I will drive to Des Moines by myself and see a Broadway show. I just need to drive out of Gannon about once a month for a breath of fresh air. No one knows me in Des Moines, and I can walk around the mall without fear of people whispering about me.

Actually, if I'm totally honest with myself, the community of Gannon has been remarkably good to me. A memorial fund was set up at First National Bank after the kids died, and so many people contributed money to my children's memory. I didn't know what to do with the seventeen thousand dollars that was donated over the first few years.

Finally, last year I had the city purchase new playground equipment for the city park. My kids used to absolutely love going to the park and play. I felt good about giving the money back to the community who has supported me so well over these tough years. It's still difficult for me to drive past the park though, and see all the little ones running and laughing. My heart aches with a pain that I doubt will ever disappear totally.

Tammie and I still do our monthly girls' nights out, and I so look forward to those evenings. She is busy with her family, and yet she takes time to spend with me outside of work. She has offered many times that we could invite some other friends to join us, but I'm really not interested. I feel like I would have to open up to others then, and it's too exhausting to think about that.

Courtney, Abby, and I have a goal of getting together for sure every summer and at Christmas. We usually meet at a hotel with a water park in Des Moines, so Abby's kids can swim. I miss my sisters. I don't ever want us to lose touch of one another. Now that mom and dad are gone, they are truly my only close family left. We have a great time when we're together, and I cry every time we part.

82

I owe Tammie my life for giving me this job. I so enjoy getting up each morning now and serving a purpose. She even pays me well. I'd probably do it for free, but the money sure is nice.

Ok, I probably wouldn't do it for nothing. But I realize now that I am not so consumed by my personal loss when I have a task in front of me. I am now a part of something. I have an identity outside of being a mom and a wife. People expect me to be at work every day, they count on me. I am part of the Harmon Publishing family and I am proud to be employed by the Harmon family. Tammie knows how to make the business grow, and the employees know what they need to do to keep things rolling.

I had been searching for a new and different meaning in my life these past five years. I never, ever, would have guessed that a career would have given that to me. I had been so out of touch with the career world. Funny how we can adapt when we need to.

Tammie needs someone from the firm to take on more traveling in the U.S. She's telling me this at lunch and I suggest the senior editor, the advertising director, the assistant publisher. She says no, they are all busy with other responsibilities right now.

She wonders if I would be interested in helping the firm out by traveling maybe once a month for her. I am startled. I am an office manager, I'm in Human Resources, for God's sake. I really don't know the details of the publishing world. She says that she can train me for what I would need to know.

Mainly the travel would include representing Harmon Publishing at trade shows and conventions around the country. She wants to expand the market for Harmon. She says that sometimes she could go with me, but other times I would need to travel alone. I think it sounds like a great opportunity to get out of Gannon once in awhile, actually. I tell her I think I could do it, if she really wants me to. She says that next month I will need to go to Chicago for a four day trip. I'm excited already!

83

Christmas is in two weeks. I tend to fall apart this time of the year. Christmas was so special with my kids. They loved everything about the holiday. The warm feeling that the spirit of the holiday used to bring has all but vanished from me now. I can still be resentful when I see all the gushy Christmas commercials on TV. Christmas reminds me exactly how much I have lost. I struggle to remember that it is a Christian holiday. All I focus on this time of the year is family, and that I don't have one.

Courtney and Abby have begged me for years to join them at Christmas. I just don't want to. I would feel like an outsider looking in, a third wheel that really wasn't meant to be there. I don't want anyone's pity. I prefer to be by myself and exist in my vacuum of solitude.

Tammie has been asking if I'll join her family this year at Christmas, and she isn't taking no for an answer. I make an urgent meeting with Dr. Hansen, and she agrees with Tammie. She thinks it's time for me to join her family and learn to have fun again. I'm sweating just thinking about it. What if I freak out and have a panic attack in front of the Harmon family on Christmas Eve? What if I ruin their holiday? I'd never forgive myself.

Tammie tells me that they would like me to come over to their home on Christmas Eve, have turkey dinner with the trimmings and then sing carols with them. Gretchen plays beautifully on the piano, and the kids really want me to be there, or so she claims. It is stressing me out, but I accept her offer. Now I need to do some shopping for her family.

I find that I'm actually kind of excited anticipating celebrating Christmas again. It's been a long five year reprieve. I want to find something for each of the kids. I am out of touch with what kids are into right now. But I go shopping and just ask the sales clerks what a thirteen year old girl, ten year old girl, and seven year old boy would want. I spend too much money, but I am having fun. I haven't bought gifts for over five years, for anyone. I need something really special for Tammie. I don't even know how to begin to thank her for pushing me along my path towards peace.

A good friend is a connection to life,
A tie to the past,
A road to the future,
The key to sanity in a totally insane world.

—*Lois Wyse*

84

I make Tammie's favorite salad, the old standby strawberry pretzel salad/dessert. I bring a bottle of our favorite Chardonnay, and a book for Jack, which seems inadequate, but I didn't know what to get him. I can't wait to see the look on Tammie's face when she opens the gift I got for her. I really went out on a limb for her, and I hope she likes it.

I'm so excited as I'm driving to the Harmon's home for Christmas. They bought a beautiful, old home years ago and have spent countless hours redoing it. It feels as though you step back in time when you walk through the foyer.

The curved staircase, the oak floors with Persian rugs, the twelve foot high ceilings, and it's decorated for Christmas so beautifully. Tammie has Christmas music playing on a CD somewhere, and the aroma of dinner is wafting throughout the house.

My eyes begin to sting when the kids run to hug me. They have gotten so big! Oh, how I've missed Tammie's kids. I used to spend days on end with them, and now they seem like strangers to me. Anthony takes my hand and pulls me upstairs to his room. Tammie just let him redecorate it in a snowboarding theme, so he wants to show it to me.

Everything in this room reminds me of my boys at Anthony's age. I have a lump in my throat and it is hard for me to talk. I walk around his room and admire everything. Luckily, Anthony doesn't stop talking for even a moment. I doubt he even remembers my kids. He was two when they died.

We go back downstairs to the kitchen where Tammie offers me a glass of eggnog. We used to drink this by the cartons when the kids were babies! Carli takes me to see their ten foot tall tree in the family room. It is gorgeous. The presents under the tree seem to take up half the room. These kids are so lucky. I hope they know how fortunate they are to have Tammie and Jack for parents.

Tammie calls us all to dinner. We hold hands while Jack says the blessing and I am reminded of my own bottomless pit of grief. Why can't I just be happy? I continue to cling to the past and focus on the negative. I force myself to smile and praise God for His blessings. As we pass the turkey, stuffing, potatoes, gravy, salads, and rolls around, I can't help but just watch Tammie with her beautiful family. She has it all, I think. Just like I did. And in one awful, terrifying moment, it can be snatched away from you, never to see happiness again. Does Tammie know that this is a possibility?

I never did until it was too late.

I eat so much I unbutton my pants. The meal was wonderful. We head into the family room and the kids begin passing out presents. I am embarrassed at how many presents Tammie has for me. She shouldn't have. I only bought one thing per family member for her family. I am feeling guiltier by the moment here.

I watch the exchange of presents with her family, the hugs, and the squeals of delight when much hoped for presents are unwrapped. Her kids have turned out to be good people.

I'm so proud of Tammie. She has a rewarding career, a loving husband, and great kids. Tammie gives me a scarf, leather gloves, a watch, and some books. Her kids made me all sorts of Christmas pictures and cards. Their hand made gifts make my heart stop momentarily at memories that I am trying so hard to push back right now.

I see Tammie take the gift I brought for her. I'm nervous watching her open up my gift. I hope it's not too disappointing for her. I hope I made the right decision. She opens the lid and takes the tissue paper off. Her hand goes over her mouth and I see her shoulders buckle. Tears are coming down her cheeks as she pulls the scrapbook out of the box. I don't know yet if she's happy or sad.

For months I have been trying to come up with something meaningful to give to Tammie to show to her how much her friendship has meant to me over the years, but especially these past five horrible years. I truly don't know what I would have done without her support.

I started taking pictures out of my photo albums of us from the first year we met. Pretty soon I had hundreds of photos of Tammie and me, her kids, and my kids. I wrote a story for Tammie, one that started when we met fifteen years ago.

I told of times at my backyard pool, walks around town with strollers, playing at the parks, excursions to Des Moines to the zoo, water parks, amusement parks, ball games, soccer matches, and many days just spent at each other's homes. Our lives blended with one another's for so many years. I wanted Tammie to see what she means to me.

She has me crying now too. We get up at the same time for a big hug.

"Thank you, Anna. I can't believe you were able to do this. I am so touched, and I will always treasure these memories of our kids together."

We go into the kitchen to dry our eyes. Tammie pops open the bottle of Chardonnay that I brought for her. I'm feeling exhausted emotionally. I'm so thankful to be here, but I also want to run out the front door and go home to cry. My heart is so weary for my kids. Tammie and I share memories from the past that are in the scrapbook. I suddenly realize this is the first time I have done this. Talked about my kids with someone, shared stories about their lives.

We laugh and we cry. I want to get mad, but Tammie somehow always redirects my oncoming emotional outbursts. I am truly emotionally spent, and I tell Tammie I am just going to sneak out the back door. I can't bear good bye hugs from her kids. I thank her for a truly meaningful Christmas. I can't even put into words yet what this evening has done for me. I think I may have turned a corner.

85

As I'm approaching my house, I notice a car in my driveway. How odd. Now who would be at my house on Christmas Eve? As I pull in the driveway my heart sinks. Ringing the front doorbell is my cousin, Jessica. The one that I have never cared for. What in the hell is she doing here? She lives an hour away with her family in Sherman, Iowa. I drive into the garage and walk out towards the front door.

Jessica is smiling and has a plate of cookies in her hands. It is freezing outside, but I make her talk to me out here anyway, as I'm not sure I want to invite her in. The last time I saw Jessica was right before the funerals, and I told her to get the hell out of my house. Why would she think I had changed my mind since then?

"Hi Anna. Merry Christmas! Tom and I are driving through Gannon to Des Moines, and I wanted to stop by to wish you a Merry Christmas and give you some goodies. It's so good to see you. It's been too long, you know."

I immediately remember why I've never liked Jessica. She's so phony. She has that fake, plastered smile on her face, with her eyebrows pulled up too high on her forehead. She always has a hidden agenda. I don't know what her real reason for stopping here is, but trust me, she is *not* just trying to be nice to me.

"Well, Merry Christmas. You didn't have to stop here, though, on Christmas Eve. I'm sure you're family is anxious to hit the road. Where are Tom and the kids?" I don't see anyone else in the car.

"Oh, I dropped them off at the Diner downtown. I ordered two banana cream pies for dinner tomorrow. So they're getting those boxed up and having a quick snack. We're headed to my Mom and Dad's house tonight. I told them I just wanted to stop by and see you real quick before we left town."

We're both freezing and I'm still hesitating on whether or not to invite her inside. Against my better judgment, I do.

"Well, come inside if you have a minute then. It's freezing out here." We walk in through the garage and she puts the plate of Christmas cookies on my kitchen table. She sits down and appears to be making herself right at home. I know I'm going to regret this.

"Anna, I want you to know that I forgave you for how you treated me the day I visited you a few years ago. I know you didn't mean what you said. I didn't take it personally. You were very fragile at that moment and going through a horrendous time. So I don't hold it against you."

I can feel my blood starting to boil already. Same old shit with Jessica. She's such a pompous bitch. I choose not to reply to her opening statement. Instead, I sit down across from her at my table and just look coolly at her, hoping to make her sweat a little.

She makes a little nervous laugh, looks around the house. I know she was fishing for an apology from me, but she sure as hell isn't going to get it.

"Jessica, is there something I can help you with? Is there a purpose to this visit or did you just come here to insult me?"

I'm not going to pretend that we ever liked each other. I grew up with this girl who has never, ever been nice to me. She is two years older than me, and we were forced to play together as we grew up.

"Oh Anna, now please don't get that chip on your shoulder going with me. I only came to see how you're doing. I really do care, you know. All of the cousins, aunts, and uncles have been worried about you for years. It's like you've joined a convent or something since your kids died. I hear that you never go out in public, and that you just hole up in this house. I just wanted to see if you were ok."

I'm remembering back to when we were in high school. At the annual summer Newman Family Reunion, when Jessica and I were forced to pretend we liked each other. She was all nice to my face, pretended to be my friend. But the second I turned my back, wow. She could throw the knives at me.

She would ask our other cousins to join in some game, intentionally leaving me out. She would criticize what I wore, compete with me at everything. All the other cousins talked about how jealous she was of me. I knew that was the problem, but it was hard to feel sympathy for someone who is passive aggressive with you all the time.

And when we both got married and had kids, it got worse. I tried my best to avoid her at all costs. I was cordial to her face, didn't say anything negative about her to others. I didn't need to, everyone else did.

Jessica constantly compared her kids to my kids over the years. She had to tell me all about the volunteering she does for her kid's classes at their school. She talked about her kids' test scores, for God's sake. She was so concerned about every tiny little developmental stage her kid was in. She worried if they were behind. She worried that they wouldn't be smart enough. She was making her kids do flash cards regularly when they were in pre-school. She was so afraid that her kids wouldn't be exceptional.

Everyone talked about her serious control freak personality. Her husband, Tom, laughed about it a lot, making jokes when she wasn't around. We all felt so bad for Tom. He really was a good guy, and we all knew he was miserable with her. There's no pleasing someone like Jessica. She will never be happy. Nothing is ever good enough.

I am worn out physically and mentally, and I am not in the mood to trade insults with Jessica at this moment. I have just had a wonderful Christmas celebration with Tammie and her family, and I will not let Jessica spoil it for me.

Jessica is just staring at me, with that fake smile glued to her mouth, baiting me to insult her back. My hands are sweaty and my heart is beating fast. There is nothing I would like to do more than to tell this insecure bitch what I think of her. But then that will give her something to tell all the relatives. How she was being the good Christian woman checking in on her pathetic cousin, only to be bombarded with insults.

Her attempt to humor me has failed.

"Jessica, I'm only going to tell you this one final time. I meant what I said the last time you were here. You have never been a friend to me, and I feel so sorry for you. I don't want you to ever come to my home again. I find your patronizing attitude repulsive. You need some serious therapy, cousin. Now get the hell out of my house, and don't ever come back here again."

This is not the response she expected. I know she anticipated trading insults with me, and hopefully getting me to break down. Then she'd have a real story to tell the relatives. I stand up, open the back door, and wait for her to walk through. She is gathering her coat and she takes her tray of cookies with her. How thoughtful.

"I hope you can live with yourself, Anna. Everyone feels sorry for you. Not only because you've lost your family, but also because of who you've become."

I give her a gentle push out the door and slam the door loudly. I see her surprised face through the glass and I give a little smile and wave. I dead bolt the door and leave the kitchen. God, but she never ceases to amaze me. Merry Christmas.

86

I'm forty-five years old and I'm embarrassed to admit this, but I miss sex so much. I mean, I really crave it. I have been celibate for over five years now (ok, not counting that one night on the cruise), and I really crave it. I miss the intimacy, I miss the physical release that your body gets, and I mostly miss having that private dance that makes you feel so special.

Not that Paul and I ever had mind-altering sex. In our young days, yes. But as we got older, the sex occurred less frequently year after year. I'm not sure why. It's not as though I didn't want it anymore. And I'm sure Paul wanted it too.

Other couples would discuss their sex lives around us, and it always made Paul and I uncomfortable. That was just one topic that was off-limits for me. I didn't want to know what other couples did in their beds. And I didn't want to share that part of our life with anyone but Paul. I don't know, maybe both Paul and I were embarrassed to talk about it around our friends. Maybe we thought that our sex life was somehow inadequate compared to our friends.

I think the truth of the matter is that most couples have less sex as they grow older together. Some of it is due to age, I suppose. I am just more tired now than I was twenty years ago. I don't have the energy I used to have. My body is not in the physical shape it was years ago. If Paul wanted to initiate sex, then great. But I was never sure if he was in the mood or not. And the times that I did initiate sex with him and was rejected, hurt. I felt like he wasn't attracted to me. And it hurt my feelings. So I thought that he could just let me know when he was in the mood.

But now that I am a divorcee, I don't ever have sex. I am not intimate with another man, and I don't have a personal life to speak of. And I'm not interested in having sex with someone just to have sex. I need the relationship. I would feel like a whore if I just did the physical act without the love (except for that one time, and that did feel good—but I don't plan to make a habit out of it).

I've been alone for so long now that honestly I'd basically forgotten about sex. But for some reason, lately the need has been cropping up when I least expect it. My libido seems to have a mid-life drive of its own. I am anticipating menopause in the next few years, so to be day dreaming about sex seems odd for me.

Book Three
Moving On

87

I'm in the Des Moines airport by myself, flying to Chicago to represent Harmon Publishing at a national tradeshow. I'm nervous and excited about this trip. Tammie has been preparing me for the past month on my new duties for Harmon, and I feel confident. I understand what the firm does, who we are, and what we represent.

I'm still surprised she wanted me to do this for Harmon Publishing, but I told her I'd give it my best effort. If it doesn't work out, she has other employees who would jump at the opportunity to travel periodically.

On the plane I squeeze in between two men, who don't seem thrilled that the middle seat is now occupied. I know they were hoping for a little extra elbow room. The man by the window already has his ear phones in and is attempting to sleep. The baby two rows behind us screaming bloody murder may try his patience.

The man on my right has his lap top out and is busily typing away. I am squished in like a sardine. I kick my bag under the seat in front of me and thank God this flight is a short one.

When we're in the air, the man on my right pulls out some business files to read through. I notice that he has the same pamphlet about the publishing tradeshow that I do. What a small world. I ask him if he will be attending the Chicago publishing trade show and he says yes. We introduce ourselves and I find myself intrigued by this stranger.

His name is Pierce Seaton, from Des Moines. Pierce works for the state's largest publisher in Des Moines, Gibson Publishers. I have heard of Gibson, of course, and am curious to know more about this man.

We hit it off immediately and I find myself talking more to this stranger than I have talked to anyone in years. He has a sincere smile and his eyes are comforting to me. Plus, he's quite handsome. My stomach is in knots just sitting next to him. He is looking fine in a dark brown sport coat, brown turtle neck, and brown pants. He smells good, too. It usually bugs me that I can smell other people on airplanes. They usually stink, though. His smell is clean and fresh.

Pierce tells me that he is the Senior Editor at Gibson, having just moved to Des Moines three years ago. He actually grew up in Chicago and lived all his life there, until his move to Des Moines. I tell him that I live two hours north of Des Moines, in Gannon. He's heard of Harmon Publishing and says it is a very reputable company.

We end up talking the entire flight from Des Moines to Chicago. We talk about inconsequential things. I tell him that I used to live in Des Moines, and so we compare notes on our favorite restaurants and highlights of the city. We find out that we know a couple of the same people. I am actually disappointed when the plane descends. I have not had a normal conversation with a normal man in years.

When the plane lands we prepare to go our separate ways. I tell him I will probably seem him around at the convention center. We go our separate ways and I am proud of myself for having my first mature conversation with a man in a long time.

I take a taxi to the downtown Marriott and check in. I grab my briefcase and walk to the connecting convention center to register at the show. I realize I won't know anyone at this trade show. Tammie said it is my first step in establishing connections with others in our industry. She literally gave me pointers on how to schmooze, as she apparently didn't think I knew how. She was right in her assumption. It had been a very long time since I had any professional development.

I spend the rest of the day talking with vendors, with advertising execs, with editors, publishers, you name it. My head is spinning from all of the people I meet. There are too many names to remember, and I begin to collect business cards from people to assist my memory. All in all, it is a positive experience. By the evening, I decide to skip the entertainment offered for the trade show registrants. I just want to sit down and take my shoes off.

The line for the elevators is too long, so I head into the little sports bar just off the front desk. Aahhh, I find a comfortable leather pub chair and fall into it. The LA Lakers are in town playing the Bulls, so I watch the game while I have a Corona Light and order a chicken sandwich and fries.

I enjoy getting lost in the anonymity of the big city. All these people around me, and no one is paying any attention to me. It's such a relief. In Gannon, I feel like I always need to hide in public.

My sandwich and fries have arrived and I'm trying to decide if I should order another Corona Light or just have a glass of water. I see Pierce walk into the bar and head towards my table. He is smiling right at me! God, I am excited to see him. I feel like a teenager again, all giggly and nervous. There are three empty chairs at my table, so I have no excuse not to invite him to join me. But maybe he is meeting someone else here.

"Well, what a coincidence meeting you here, Anna. You must be a big Bulls fan too, I see." He really is good looking. I wonder if Tammie has ever met him in her professional outings.

"Hi Pierce. Have a seat if you'd like, unless you're meeting someone else here...?"

"No, I just wanted to catch the end of the game and get a quick bite to eat too. I'm tired of the convention center. After growing up here, I can't seem to stop myself from watching the Bulls play any chance I get. Even after Michael Jordan is gone and the team quite frankly stinks, they are still my favorite team."

So he sits down next to me and we have an enjoyable conversation with our meal. Pierce seems like an old friend, not some stranger I just met on a plane today. He orders chicken wings and a Coors Light. We laugh about the trade show today, and watch the game and just chat about nothing. When the game is over and his Bulls have lost, I assume he will leave. But it's only nine o'clock and I'm not quite ready to head up to the room yet, either. So we continue to talk.

He tells me that three and a half years ago he came home from work one day to surprise his wife and found her in bed with a young neighbor, a college boy. The young man was a son of friends of theirs. He was devastated and couldn't get over the betrayal. He tried for months to repair the marriage, but he knew in his heart it was over for him. They had tried for years to have children, and it just never worked out. He divorced his wife and took a job at Gibson Publishers in Des Moines.

I feel as though it's my turn to share my story, and I get suddenly sick to my stomach. I don't want Pierce to know my story. He won't want to be around me if he knows the truth.

That my life has been filled with pain and suffering, and that underneath my smile, I am a woman in need of help.

I keep asking Pierce questions, hoping to prolong the inevitable. But he is kind and I think he knows that I am not going to reciprocate in the disclosure of personal details.

Pierce hasn't asked me anything about my personal life. I find that very respectful. I saw him glance at my left hand, and obviously there is not a wedding ring on my finger. I like this man and maybe we'll have a friendship. I think he deserves to know the truth. He has told me about his situation.

I take a deep breath and say, "Pierce, there are few things about me that I think you need to know." He sets his beer bottle down on the table, and says, "Ok, Anna."

I tell him everything. Well, not everything, but all the important things. I tell him that I am divorced. I tell him that I used to have three wonderful children but they, along with my parents, were killed in a car accident almost six years ago. I tell him that I have had a very difficult time since this tragedy, and that I am still in the process of making my life whole again.

I tell him that I am sometimes a mess, and that I don't let others easily into my life now. I sigh and settle into my chair, taking a big chug from my beer bottle. I hope I haven't scared the shit out of this nice man.

Pierce just looks at me, almost in a surprised way. I'm so glad he's not giving me a look of pity. That's what I hate most. I'm expecting that he will be turned off by my bad luck in life, and now it will be uncomfortable between us. But this man surprises me.

Pierce tells me that he is so sorry to hear of my losses. He says he can't even imagine what I have gone through. He tells me that he understands divorce, and how that, in a way, is a death. It's a death of a relationship, he says. And I know just what he means.

Pierce tells me that when he was seventeen, he was driving his brother to school one morning. It was a cold January morning, and the roads were icy. They had the music turned up, and they were joking around. Pierce punched his brother, Colton, in the shoulder and the car swerved. He lost control and the car spun around and flipped over and over down an embankment.

Pierce had on his seat belt, but Colton did not. Colton died in that accident, because of Pierce's driving. He says he has never forgiven himself. He knows what losing someone you love feels like. He knows that it really never gets better, no matter how many years go by. He knows that until you have experienced the unseemliness of death, you don't know what it's like.

I am in awe of this man. Although we have experienced different circumstances, he knows exactly what I feel. I can see the pain on his face. I can hear the grief in his voice, even after thirty years. He can relate to my pain, and not dismiss it. He has had to live with the guilt for all these years. Asking himself over and over again, "Why did it have to happen?" And not getting a good answer, ever.

We talk for a little while longer, but now I am getting tired. Pierce senses my sleepiness and asks where I am staying. I tell him just across the street, at the Marriott, and he's staying there as well. We walk to the hotel together, and I tell him I'll probably run into him again tomorrow. I thank him for the company.

88

The next few days of the trade show are exhilarating. I love being in Chicago with all of these publishing people. The people are fascinating, the food is scrumptious, and I am learning so many new things about the world of publishing. I pray that I am representing Harmon Publishing in a positive manner.

I think I am getting some good leads on future business, while also taking home some ideas on how to improve our business in Gannon. I so want Tammie to be proud of me. I call her at least once a day back at the office just to report that things are going great. I don't tell her about meeting Pierce, as I'm embarrassed to say anything about him yet.

Every night Pierce and I both just end up back at the sports bar. We never made arrangements, but I think we both were looking for each other. Each evening I share a little more of myself with Pierce. I don't want him to see my soul, but I find myself feeling secure telling him my thoughts and exposing my open wounds to him. I keep expecting him to run away, to tell me that I am a crazy lady. But he also opens up to me and gives me a little picture of his life, too.

On the last night of the convention, Pierce and I realize we are flying back on different flights. He gets a little nervous, and asks me if he could have my business card. He actually blushes, I think, and wonders if he could call me sometime.

I am thrilled and amused. He looks like a school boy nervously asking his girlfriend to the dance. I attempt to be nonchalant about it, but I, too, am nervous. I haven't done this for a very long time. We exchange business cards and I jot down my home phone number on the back. I tell him I truly enjoyed meeting him, and I appreciated his company at the sports bar every night.

It's kind of awkward parting, but we end up shaking hands outside of the sports bar, and I'm pretty certain I'll never talk to this nice man again. But oh, I hope he calls. I know I could call him, but I know that won't happen. I'm too much of a chicken.

When I get back to Gannon, I spend two hours updating Tammie on my experience. I have a new appreciation for the publishing world. I am thrilled to have had the opportunity to travel for Harmon, and I tell her I will gladly do it again. Tammie seems pleased with my work done in Chicago. But she keeps staring at me.

"Anna, is there something you're not telling me?" God, she knows me so well. I didn't want to tell her about Pierce unless he called me when I got home. I don't want to feel like a girl with a crush.

I laugh nervously.

"Tammie, I met an amazing man. Seriously, I think you'd like him. His name is Pierce Seaton, and he works for Gibson Publishers in Des Moines. I had dinner with him every night, and we just hit it off. I don't expect him to call me or anything, but it was the first time I've really had fun in years."

I'm out of breath from gushing this report to Tammie. She is just smiling at me, from ear to ear. She gives me a big hug, and we're both laughing. She knew the time would come, she says. She's seen me coming to terms with my life, and she so badly wants me to find happiness again.

I tell her I'm not sure I'm there yet, but I'm working on it. I am trying very hard to find comfort in the every day things. I appreciate my life, my friendship with her, my faith, my career, and I appreciate the short time I had with my children. I am putting one foot in front of the other every day, and am just working on becoming a whole person again.

I feel like I'm maybe half way there.

89

Two days after the Chicago trade show, Mr. Pierce Seaton calls me at work. It's under the guise of a work question, but we both know better. He finally asks me if I ever get to Des Moines. I tell him once in awhile. He knows that my sister Courtney and my ex-husband live there. He says that if I ever get to Des Moines that he would love to take me out to dinner.

I tell him that would be wonderful. There's kind of that awkward silence, where neither person knows what they're supposed to say next. I don't know if I should invite him to Gannon? But why would he want to come to Gannon? I'm so out of touch with the dating game.

Then Pierce just hurriedly says, "Anna, would you be interested in coming to Des Moines this weekend?"

I laugh out loud, and pray that I didn't offend him. Luckily, he laughs too. We realize we're both out of practice here. I tell him I don't think I have anything on my busy social calendar, and that I would love to come to Des Moines this weekend. We hang up, and I'm so excited! I run into Tammie's office to tell her the news. She's so happy for me. I can't remember the last time that I smiled for this length of time.

90

Two days later, I'm already having second thoughts. What am I thinking? Where am I going to stay? I'm certainly not going to stay at Pierce's house. Will he expect me to? I could call Courtney and see if I can stay at her place. Will he expect me to have sex with him? I've really only spent a couple hours at a time with this man, and now I'm going to spend a whole weekend with him?

I feel guilty for being happy. I go look at my kids' school pictures that are hanging on the family room wall. They've been there for six years. It's still as though time stopped after they died.

Should I move on? What about my kids? I don't know what to do. I call Dr. Hansen and make an appointment for tomorrow during lunch. I need her to talk me through this. I know I'm having a slight panic attack, but this is new territory for me, and I need to be told that it's ok. It's ok for me to feel happy again. It's ok for me to move on with my life. I should not be stuck back in life six years ago. But if I move on, then that means I am leaving my babies behind.

Of course, Dr. Hansen thinks it's great that I have met someone. She encourages me to look at Pierce as a new friend, not necessarily as a potential lover. She tells me to stop over-analyzing everything. To just go with the flow. To let the relationship happen on its own time.

You may end up liking Pierce, and you may not. It's too early to predict what will become of the relationship. But don't doom it before it's taken off. Her words comfort me, provide some solace to me for this new adventure.

Pain is inevitable,
Suffering is optional.

—George Eliot

91

In my dream, I am with Paul and the kids. Most of my dreams have all of us in them. Either I dream of times from the past, or I invent new dreams of us in the future. For example, Connor would be thirteen now, Ryan twelve, and Cassy eleven. So I dream about them at those ages. I dream about them in middle school, with Paul and I in the gymnasium watching the boys play in a basketball game. I dream that we are all at church together, that we go on vacations together, that Ryan broke his arm sliding into home plate, that Cassy had a sleep over for her eleventh birthday. In these dreams the kids look so real. Even though they are older, their faces still look the same.

When I wake up from my dream, I look for Paul next to me in bed. It takes me a few seconds to remember that Paul is gone and the kids are dead. Then the sudden wave of grief hits me hard in the chest. I can't believe I do this over and over again.

You'd think that I'd remember. You'd think that even in my subconscious dream state my mind would tell me the truth. Why do I keep going back in time? Why do I sometimes forget about the accident? I'm getting a little better, but honestly, not a lot. I will wake up, and run to Cassy's room, thinking she's late for school. Only to see her quiet bedroom stare back at me.

I dream that Connor has his first date. He's in the eighth grade now, and he has a crush on Gretchen, just like Tammie and I had hoped all those years ago. He asks his dad and I if we would drive Gretchen and him to the movies this weekend. He is so cute about it, acting as if it's no big deal. Ryan relentlessly teases him and they end up in a wrestling match on the dining room floor.

I dream that Ryan got pneumonia and had a three day hospital stay. I was so scared. He always would get a high fever when he got sick. I dream that I slept in a cot at his bed side for three days, until I knew he was going to be ok. And even though he was twelve, he still needed his mommy there to comfort him. I dream that he still has the whitest hair and the bluest eyes, and that he is a tall, skinny boy.

I dream that Cassy and I are best friends. I dream that we have a super close mother-daughter relationship that is the envy of all mothers and daughters around the world. I dream that we often go on shopping trips together all over the country. We fly to New York, Chicago, LA, and Minneapolis for girl's weekends away. I dream that she looks up to me, and thinks I am a cool mom. Everyone tells me that she is the spitting image of me when I was her age.

Ironically, I don't dream about Paul unless the kids are in my dreams too. I think he just goes with the family picture in my head. He was a part of that family, and that's what my brain remembers. But I can honestly say that Paul is slipping from my memory. And I think I mean that in a good way. Not that I want him to evaporate, but the hurt I used to feel when I thought of Paul has dissolved into just a mere sting.

92

I am forty-seven years old and driving by myself to Des Moines, Iowa, to meet a man I met at a convention. Ick. If I didn't know myself better, I'd think I was desperate.

A few people over the years have honestly suggested that I try internet dating. I was insulted by the insinuation that I needed to date. And even more offended by the assumption that I needed help to meet men. Of course, they would have been correct. But where do some people get off giving free advice?

The truth is, I'm really excited to see Pierce. He called a couple more times this past week, asking me what I wanted to do in Des Moines. He asked if I wanted him to make a hotel reservation for me in Des Moines. I was impressed with that. I told him I would be staying at my sister's house, as she would be out of town. He's taking me out to dinner tonight. And then we'll just go from there. There are so many things to do and see in Des Moines, but neither of us wanted to plan an itinerary. Maybe he'll be sick of me after tonight.

I drive to Courtney's house and am greeted by her. She is headed off to visit a college friend in Kansas City for the weekend. She is tickled that I have a date. Pierce picks me up at Courtney's at seven o'clock and I had forgotten how gorgeous he is.

He is about six foot two, has black, wavy, short hair, and he has wonderful brown eyes. His complexion is flawless. He likes to run, and I think he is in very good shape for a man of fifty. I'm feeling every bit of my young forty-seven tonight.

We have a wonderful time at Bortacelli's, a casual Italian eatery. After dinner we go to a bar that has live music and we just sit and talk for hours. On Saturday, he picks me up at Courtney's and we walk around the four mile trail that Pierce usually jogs every morning. He's kind enough to not make me feel bad for not being a jogger.

It's a cool April day, and you can just believe now in Iowa that summer might come after all. We go to Bruegger's Bagels for brunch, read the papers, and have coffee. He drives me around Des Moines, pointing out different sites. It strikes me that not too long ago I made this same drive around Des Moines and let my husband move here by himself.

It is nice to be with Pierce. There is definitely an attraction between us, yet I feel that he is respectful of our relationship. He hasn't tried to kiss me yet, and I am relieved at that. I feel like we are good friends. That I could tell him anything and he won't judge me for my thoughts. We are comfortable together, and I don't feel like this is a date.

We go to Mass on Saturday evening, and then out to a Mexican restaurant that has the best strawberry margaritas I've ever had. I was getting a little tipsy and laughing at Pierce's stories, when I see Paul walk in. My smile freezes, and my heart stops. I don't know why I am petrified, but I am. I feel like he has caught me in an affair. I have to remind myself that I am not married to Paul anymore.

Paul and Victoria are going to walk right by our table if I don't say something. They aren't looking my way, and I could just let the moment go if I wanted to. Pierce wouldn't know any different either. But at some point, I knew I was going to have to face this. So I reach out and grab Paul's arm as he walks by. He looks down and is definitely surprised to see me.

"Well Anna. What are you doing here?" He appears to be happy to see me.

Victoria turns around and smiles at me as well. I introduce Pierce to Paul and Victoria, and thankfully none of them know each other. I didn't need a soap opera here. I am a bit uncomfortable, but everyone is polite, and I don't explain who Pierce is, really. I just say I am in town visiting him, and that he works for Gibson Publishers. It is a brief moment, as Paul and Victoria's host is waiting to seat them. They hurry off to another room to their table and relief sweeps over me.

"Are you alright?" Pierce asks.

"I'm actually fine, thanks. I didn't expect to see them here. They caught me off guard. But as I've told you, Paul and I truly do have a warm relationship even after the divorce. We've been through a lot together. I wish him all the best."

On Sunday afternoon, when it is time for me to drive back to Gannon, I realize I am sad to say good bye to Pierce. I really enjoyed this weekend. We're sitting on his couch, watching the Bulls play the Orlando Heat. Pierce asks me if he could see me again. I struggle with this conversation. I tell him I really like him and that I, too, had a great weekend. I'm just not sure if I will be good company all the time, I tell him.

"Pierce, I have my good days and my bad days. You've seen me at my best moments. I need you to understand that I'm still pretty messed up with my kids' deaths. I don't know what I want in life anymore. I just take one day at a time. I know I'm scared to death of relationships. I fear putting myself out there again, knowing that I could lose people I love in a heart beat. I'm afraid of relationships. I'm afraid that you will see the real me."

He leans over so slightly and before I know what he's going to do, he kisses me ever so gently on the lips. His soft mouth feels heavenly. I immediately close my eyes and let myself fall into his arms. I was so scared of this, and now I know I only want it. We lay back on his couch, and the kiss is getting deeper and our breathing is getting faster. I haven't felt this way since puberty. I could rip his clothes off right here.

It surprises me when he carefully pulls away from me and stares into my eyes. His breathing is heavy too, and I'm wondering why in the hell he stopped.

"Anna, I've fallen for you. I don't want to scare you off, but I want you to know that I really like being with you. I don't want to rush into anything, and do something we'll both regret tomorrow, but I'm really hoping we can see each other again."

I respect this man. Although I would have had sex with him right here on his couch, I know that wouldn't have been good for our relationship. He definitely has more self-control than I do. I am somewhat disappointed, and somewhat relieved. We hug and I have to stand up so I don't go after him again. He smells so good, and I just want to snuggle into his neck.

On the drive back to Gannon, I find myself smiling for no reason. I'm afraid to say the words out loud, or to even think them. Because it's really too early to know for sure. But the truth is, I think I've fallen in love again.

93

Tammie is so excited for me. She makes me tell her all the details of the weekend with Pierce. I'm trying so very hard not to be giddy like a teenager. But just thinking of Pierce makes me smile and my heart races. I like how he makes me feel. I find myself staring off into space at work, and it seems so bizarre that I am happy. It has been a long time coming.

Work has been going great. Tammie has added to my office responsibilities and she asks me if I'm interested in traveling more when needed. I sign up for a convention in Minneapolis in June and I agree to help with a potential account which will mean traveling to California a few times this summer. The variety is exciting and it has been good for my soul to get the hell out of Gannon.

Pierce and I talk on the phone almost daily. We e-mail or text back and forth a few times a day. Nothing too substantial, but he is my best friend now, and I look forward to our future together. Finally, I feel like life is ok again. I don't want to get too excited, because I know that in a moments notice, things can be taken away from you. But I am finally putting myself out there, as Dr. Hansen has been telling me to do for years.

It has been ten years since my kids died. Ten long, awful years. Every time I think about Connor, Ryan, and Cassy my heart does a flip flop. Tears still spring to my eyes in a moment. I can overhear someone in the office talking about their kid's performance at the basketball game, and I immediately feel pain. It can put me in a downward turn for a week. I will see a blonde girl in the neighborhood and almost call out to her, thinking it is Cassy. My mind plays tricks on me still. I can wake up from a nap and wonder if the kids are playing outside. I beg God to just let me be.

Connor would be eighteen now. He would be in his senior year of high school. He would be playing sports, maybe in the school musical, trying to decide what college to go to next fall. I see him in my mind as a young man. Light brown hair, broad shoulders, his great smile. I have to look up to him to talk to him. I see him holding hands with a young woman, wondering when his love switched from his mom to girls.

Ryan would be seventeen today. He would be a junior in high school, and probably hanging out with his older brother on most days. I like to believe that the boys would have been best friends, having each other's backs when necessary. But I know the reality would have been that some days they would have been the best of buds, and other days they would have despised one another. They had a fairly normal sibling relationship. Good days and bad days. I see Ryan on the football field, the basketball court, the track. He loved to run at a young age. He ran the 400 meter in kindergarten and I couldn't believe that he could make it around the track.

My baby girl, Cassy, would be sweet sixteen if she were still alive. I see her long, golden hair and her long eye lashes. I like to believe that we would have had a close mother-daughter relationship. I think we would have gone on many shopping trips together, had fun lunches and good talks. I think Paul and the boys would have gone on hunting or fishing trips, and Cassy and I would have taken our weekend shopping trips. Some days I get confused on what memories are real, and which ones I have just made up in my mind. That line between reality and fantasy is gray for me some days.

94

Pierce and I finally make love. I thought perhaps I would have forgotten the details, it's been so long. But it all came back to me when the time presented itself. He is an amazing man. I go to visit him almost every weekend in Des Moines. I'm still not quite ready for Gannon to see him in my territory yet. Not that it would matter, but I just need to make sure this relationship isn't a fling before I have the whole town talking about me. I don't need to become the town whore.

Since we're both in the publishing business, we have a lot to talk about with our work. And we understand one another's frustrations. I am still learning the trade, but I know mostly what Pierce talks about when he talks shop to me. And it's so refreshing to complain about coworkers or about a challenge in the office, and then we can just let it go.

He takes me to a different restaurant every Friday night. Then we usually cook in at his house on Saturday evenings. We go to the museums, the art fairs, the down town festivals, and the Science Center. We get tickets to concerts, go to the Iowa State Fair, you name it, we've done it in Des Moines.

We like to exercise together, too, so we usually walk the trail around his neighborhood every morning. I wondered if sex in your fifties would get ugly, but I think our maturity has allowed us to let go of insecurities in the bedroom. It has for me, anyway. Pierce loves me, and I love him. I *respect* him. He treats me like a queen, and for that I am so thankful. He says I deserve to be treated well, and I'm starting to believe him.

I honestly don't think about where the relationship should go from here. I am so content to have Pierce all to myself on the weekends. On the rare weekend that one of us has to travel for work, I miss his companionship. He makes me feel better about myself, and he has brought such joy to my once miserable life. I'm not sure my heart could take it if Pierce walked out of my life. I try not to have those thoughts.

95

I have a renewed sense of self with Pierce in my life. The bottomless pit of grief that used to be my life is now gone. Now I would characterize it as an ache in my heart that will never totally go away. There will always just be a piece of me that is wounded. Until you suffer the losses that I have suffered, I don't think you can comprehend the depth of pain that your heart can endure. But Pierce is my new lease on life.

He has seen me journal for years. I probably have twenty notebooks by now. I write the date on the front of each spiral notebook, the kind that kids use at school. I firmly believe that these notebooks have kept me from totally falling apart over the years. I don't journal daily anymore, but a couple of times a week. Tammie still asks me periodically if I'm ready to publish my work. I tell her I may never be ready.

So tonight I'm writing at Pierce's house, and he asks me if he could read my journal. I bristle at the request. He senses my reaction immediately, and being the good man that he is, he apologizes. He knows that Tammie thinks we should publish the journals, and he knows my thoughts on that topic.

But I trust this man. Why wouldn't I let him into my life and allow him to read my journals? The truth is, I'm afraid he might see how dysfunctional I really am and he will leave me. The truth hurts, and I know.

On a whim, I throw the journal over to him. "Have at it," I say. I get up and go into the kitchen, looking for a bottle of wine. What in the hell have I just done?

I go back into the TV room and Pierce has started reading at the beginning of the notebook. I get bored watching him read, so I go put in a movie in his bedroom. Two hours later, he walks in, with notebook in hand. We stare at one another, and he comes over and kisses me deeply. He drops the notebook, and that is all I remember once his hands begin roaming my body. He is a passionate man, and he turns my knees to jello. His breath is hot, and he is making me wild. I have totally exposed myself to this man, and he still wants me.

Afterwards, we cuddle in bed together. I have to go back to Gannon in the morning.

"Anna, forgive me if it's none of my business. But I think Tammie is right. I've only read one of your many journals, but you have a knack for writing. I think you have a book just waiting to be published."

I drive home the next day thinking about Pierce's confidence in my writing. He hasn't read my earlier journals, the ones that are really painful for me to think about. The journals date back ten years, to the most trying and painful times of my existence. He may not want to read those.

So maybe I should just think about the possibility. What if I were to allow Tammie to publish my story? Then what? What is the worst that could happen? Basically, everyone would know the real me. They would know the most private, awful things about me. The things that I'm too embarrassed to tell anyone, for fear that they would be so disgusted with me. The worst that could happen, I guess, is that people would read the book and think less of me.

But who do I really have to answer to now, anyway? The only people in my life that I remotely care about are Pierce, Tammie, Courtney, and Abby. And I don't think they will shut me out of their lives over my story. And they already know my story. Just not the gory details. Anyone else that might think less of me can go fly a kite.

If Pierce believes in me, then I should believe in me. I'm older and wiser now, and maybe I am ready to share my story. I decide I need to talk it over with Courtney and Abby first, as 'my' story includes them as well. It means that mom and dad's story will be exposed. Are my sisters ok with that? Do they really want our family's dirty laundry exposed to the public?

Courtney and Abby both immediately say go for it. They understand the consequences, and think that it is what it is. I talk to Tammie at work and tell her I'm ready to discuss the possibility of publishing my journals, if she's still interested. She stares at me with a big smile, and gets up to hug me. I caught her off guard with this sudden announcement. Ha—it's tough to pull a fast one on Tammie, and I think I finally did.

I bring in all twenty-two notebooks that I had in my bedroom closet at home. They are all numbered one through twenty-two and have the months, day, and years on them. I have always been very detailed and essentially anal retentive. Tammie asks me which Harmon Publishing editors I would like to review my work. I pick Hannah and Claire, and pray that they won't be weird around me after they've read my life story.

I have one moment two weeks later where I almost back out. The editors are reviewing everything, and Tammie has already told me that the consensus is that it is publishable material. Tammie hasn't read it all herself yet. She claims she wants to wait and have the two other objective editors give their opinions first. Of course, since Tammie is the owner, she can publish anything she chooses. But I know she's a better businesswoman than that. She won't publish something unless it will make her money. She tells me that I'm going to make a lot of money from my story. She thinks it will go over big.

I talk to Dr. Hansen about this. I only see her a couple of times a year now. She's proud of me for finally being able to share my story. She thinks I may need to make weekly appointments with her once the book is published. She says there could be some back lash with memories, feelings, and heart ache. I need to prepare for it, she says. Good God, what have I gotten myself into?

96

Pierce wants me to go on a vacation with him this winter. He says I can pick the location. Anywhere in the world, he doesn't care. I pick St. Lucia in February. I like nothing better than to leave Iowa in February. As I've gotten older, the freezing weather is harder for me to handle. To think about being in the Caribbean in February is a heavenly thought. And the fact that I'm going with the most amazing man in the world just adds to my delirium.

Pierce is such a great companion. He is easy going, flexible, low maintenance and fun. He makes me laugh daily, and for that one characteristic alone, I adore him. I existed without laughter in my life for years before Pierce. He has single handedly turned my desolate life into a blissful existence. Pierce is a romantic and treats me so delicately. I don't know what I did to deserve this man. God definitely knew that I needed help years ago, and He sent Pierce to rescue me.

I should have seen this coming, but I don't. Pierce proposes to me on the trip. I am so surprised! We are at dinner the first evening at St. Lucia. We are at the hotel open air restaurant, watching the sun go down. It is so beautiful here. I could honestly live here all winter.

We are just about to order our second Mai Tais, when Pierce gets up out of his chair and kneels down beside me. I don't have a clue what he is doing at first. Then he pulls a black velvet box out of his suit coat pocket. He has tears in his eyes when he asks me if I'll make him the happiest man in the world.

I immediately cry, of course. He caught me off guard, and I'm impressed with his surprise. He has bought a beautiful, classy diamond ring, and I don't even hesitate in saying yes. I love him and want to be with him forever. We spend the rest of the week talking about our future together.

We know we'll have a quiet, small ceremony in Gannon. He asks me if I want to move to Des Moines to live with him. My heart stops beating for just a moment. I've been here before, and it makes me pause. I can't answer that immediately. That would mean leaving Gannon, my job, and my kids. I don't know. I do know that I want Pierce in my life. I'll have to figure the rest out.

We have a magnificent week in St. Lucia. I just love the Caribbean. We eat lobster, crab, and shrimp. We go snorkeling and boating. We drive our rental convertible around the island, stopping at fun little shops and eateries. The weather is stunning, hot and sunny every day.

We listen to the local live music at night, and dance after a few drinks. I really am having the time of my life. It's only at night, in my dreams, that I struggle. Would Connor, Ryan, and Cassy want me to get married again? I feel as though I am asking for their approval, and I know I don't need it. I feel my happiness and moving on is an act of betrayal to them. I'm not forgetting them, but rather I'm still trying to summon up the courage to live a life without them.

97

When we come back home, everyone in Gannon is so excited for us on our engagement news. At fifty-one, I would have written myself off for new found love. The entire staff at Harmon wants to know the details of my wedding and what I will do after I marry. I have no details to give out. I tell the truth, that Pierce and I haven't gotten that far yet. Only Tammie has the insight to know that I'm overwhelmed and possibly freaking out with all the change going on in my life at the moment.

Pierce is back in Des Moines for the work week, of course. I realize that I am getting a bit tired of this living arrangement. For years now we have had a weekend relationship. It is past time that we live in the same town together. I can't imagine my life without Pierce in it. But I am stressing over how this marriage is going to work out for us. Where will we live? How will we both keep our careers without one of us making a move?

I have Tammie over for dinner a few days after the engagement announcement, and she says, "Out with it. Tell me what's really on your mind. Something's bothering you and I want to know what it is."

I pour out my heart to her. I tell her that I love Pierce with all of my heart, and that I do want to be with him. I don't have a problem marrying him either. It's just that I'm not certain that I can leave Gannon. I don't want to quit my job at Harmon Publishing, and I still feel connected to Gannon. My kids are here and I'm not ready to leave them. Plus, what would I do in Des

Moines? My life is in Gannon. And there's nothing for Pierce to do here. I'm confused.

Tammie understands. She always understands. There are no easy answers to my questions. She tells me there is no rush. We haven't set a wedding date and neither of us is pushing forward too quickly. Just take one day at a time, she tells me. Isn't that what I've been doing for twelve years now? One step in front of the other. We will work it out, I know we will.

98

Harmon Publishing has just produced a new book titled, *The Unspeakable Truth*, by Anna Dennison Dawson. I see it in the local bookstore in Gannon and I feel proud. Everyone is congratulating me and I am still nervous about what will come of it. I have to make some public appearances in Iowa the next few weeks.

I will be at a few Barnes and Nobles signing books, and I will be speaking at schools and town meetings. I have a contract with Harmon Publishing to help promote the book. I just don't want to speak in public. That has never been my thing. I can speak comfortably in front of twenty people, but anything bigger than that and I get too intimidated.

Amazingly, the book sales are going great. I am still in awe that this story is something that interests people. It is the story of my life, and it is sad and tragic. Why would anyone want to read about that? I haven't read the book yet. The editors pulled material from all twenty-two notebooks and put it into one 350 page book. I was supposed to approve the editing process, but I begged Tammie to do it for me.

I trusted her to make the best editorial decisions possible. I knew she would take care of me. I have about thirty copies of the book at home that I can give to family and friends. I'm guessing I'll never give them all away. I don't know thirty people anymore.

I know I should just sit down tonight and read the book. But I know how it ends. I know the pain in the beginning. I know the heartache in the middle. To read it would be for me to relive it all over again. And I do that often enough anyway. I've been told countless times that no one can read the book without crying. I've been told that it touches the hearts of everyone. That I have captured the true meaning of life. What no one seems to understand is that it was never meant to be a *story*. It is my reality. The story is my life. The pain, the drama, the loss, the tragedy, are all mine.

99

Pierce isn't pressuring me, but I know he wonders what in the hell is up with our wedding. I have quit talking about it. I avoid all wedding conversations and am just content to be with him on the weekends. I tell him that I love him and that I want him in my life forever. I know the time will come soon when he deserves an answer.

And that time appears to be this weekend. As I'm driving to Des Moines on this Friday after work, Pierce calls me on my cell phone and tells me he wants us to discuss the wedding this weekend. It has been eight months since he proposed to me. I agree. We need to talk about it. I just don't know what I can tell him yet.

We have *the conversation.* It goes fine. We are not yellers. We respect one another enough to not be mean or call each other names. It's still not easy, though. Pierce wonders if I do truly want to marry him. I tell him the honest truth. I do want to marry him. But I am struggling with leaving Gannon. There. I've said it. He seems surprised.

"Is that all?" He says. "Well, why didn't you say so earlier?"

Pierce tells me that he could probably move to Gannon and work from home, if that is what I wanted. I am shocked. I hadn't thought of that as an option. I assumed he needed to be in Des Moines. But I tell him yes, that would be great if he could work that out. He may need to drive back to Des Moines occasionally, but he would do it for me. He says that there is nothing keeping him in Des Moines. He just really wants to be with me. I am a lucky woman.

He gets it all worked out with Gibson Publishers in Des Moines. With today's technology, they have no problem with him working from Gannon. I feel as though a fifty pound weight has been lifted off my shoulders. But then I begin to worry that Pierce won't like life in Gannon. We haven't spent much time here, and I wonder if he will get bored here and regret it. I pose this scenario to him, but he claims that as long as he is with me, he will be happy anywhere. Have I mentioned that I love this man?

We choose January twenty-fifth to get married. Probably the worst possible weather in Iowa at that time. But the Catholic church in Gannon is open that weekend and it works for Tammie, Courtney, Abby, and Pierce's family to all be here. Tammie helps me pick out a simple, classic white dress for the wedding ceremony. We are keeping it very simple. I don't want any glitz or glamour. I want this to be all about us. It is the second marriage for both of us, and we plan on it being the last marriage for us both.

Although I'm in love and truly beyond happy to be marrying Pierce, my dreams at night have been haunting me. My life has moved on from the accident years ago. But I can't get over the feeling that I'm doing something wrong. A piece of my heart will always belong to Paul and my kids. Am I doing the right thing here?

Two weeks before the wedding, I get my answer. I had been praying to God to please grant me peace. To calm my mind and caress my soul. To give me the strength to move forward. That night, I had a dream that changed my life forever.

My kids have always been prominent in my dreams. They never leave my heart and soul. But in my dream that night, Connor, Ryan, and Cassy come to me. They are eight, seven, and six again. They haven't aged a day since I last saw them, twelve years ago. They run to me and shower me with their hugs and kisses. We have the best time together. They tell me all about their time in heaven with God, how everything is wonderful and I shouldn't worry about them. They tell me they love me so much, and that they watch over me from heaven.

They tell me how proud of me they are for having the courage to publish my story. It is so good to hold them, to kiss their cheeks, and to run my hands through their hair. I can almost swear the next morning that it wasn't a dream. I *felt* them. My hands tingle from their touch. My heart feels their presence.

As they were leaving my dream, they told me that it was ok for me to marry Pierce. They said that they wanted me to be happy, and that they knew Pierce made me happy. I awake in the morning with wet cheeks, and I know immediately what I need to do.

While we are sleeping,
Angels have conversations with our souls.

—Author Unknown

100

I married Pierce with the blessing of my children in my heart. I felt Connor, Ryan, and Cassy with me at the church. I have always believed in angels, but during that wedding ceremony, I knew I had three angels watching over me. And I know, with no uncertainty, that I will see my kids again in heaven.

We decided to get married at our church in Gannon, Sacred Heart. Pierce and I worked hard on our wedding vows, and the young priest who married us, Father Stephen, performed a beautiful ceremony. I feel so at peace now when I'm at Mass, and this matrimonial ceremony was so special for the both of us.

Neither Pierce nor I really believed that we would ever find love and happiness again. I found a simple, white dress at Dillards, and Pierce wore his best suit. We didn't spend money on flowers or decorations, preferring to keep it as simple as possible. I cried when Pierce put my wedding ring on my finger during the ceremony. I could feel his love for me reaching out and enfolding me in his care. I couldn't believe I was so lucky to have found this man.

Pierce and I hosted a small reception at the country club for our families and a few friends after the ceremony. Everyone there was so kind. They were so happy for Pierce and I. Pierce's parents had died years ago, but his brother and sister both flew in from Chicago for the wedding. I felt so much love that weekend. I finally felt at peace again with this life here on earth.

Pierce's family is just as wonderful as he is. His younger brother, Luke, is handsome just like Pierce. It was so obvious they were brothers. I had met Luke a couple of times in the past years, when Pierce took me back to Chicago for family occasions. Luke is a successful stock broker, working down town Chicago. His wife, Sophia has always been friendly and warm and opened her arms to me from the first day that we met years ago.

Luke and Sophia's two college aged sons, Benson and Cameron, even took time off of school to be at our wedding with us. My heart fluttered as I watched these two handsome young men congratulate Pierce and give him hugs. I wondered if Connor and Ryan would have turned out so well. I tried to picture Pierce's brother, Colton, who died at Pierce's hands, here with his family. I'm certain Pierce was thinking the same thing. He has never forgiven himself for his brother's death so long ago.

Pierce's sister, Trinity, is a stunning beauty. Her husband, Harrison, and their daughters, Lily and Mallory, also flew in for the wedding. I'm overcome by all the love I feel. No wonder Pierce is such a compassionate man. His entire family bleeds love from their hearts. You feel it when you talk to them. I so wish I could have met his parents, and told them what a wonderful son they had. I'm certain they would have been so proud of their family.

My sisters are in attendance also. I feel kind of surreal, with all the emotions flowing and the good will pouring out after the ceremony. I drink my first glass of white wine too quickly, and feel my head start to spin. I honestly never, ever imagined I could be happy like this again.

Tammie, Jack, Gretchen, Carli, and Anthony all made it for the big day as well. I tried not to look at Tammie during the ceremony, as my eyes watered and I got a lump in my throat if I even looked her way. She dabbed her eyes throughout the entire ceremony.

At the reception, we have a wonderful dinner of chicken in a wine sauce, potatoes, asparagus, salads, and scrumptious cake for dessert. The alcohol flows all evening, and everyone dances to the band's music until one in the morning. I hated to tell everyone good bye. I was so touched by my family's presence here. I felt like a queen with all of the attention bestowed upon me.

Pierce and I finally thank everyone for coming and we go back to our home. Everyone from out of town is staying at the Highland Hotel in Gannon, and will just get up in the morning and head home. We requested 'no gifts,' but no one seemed to adhere to that request.

Our car is filled with gifts from the reception. I felt guilty just thinking of how much effort and money people put into coming to our wedding. We decided not to go on a honeymoon right after the wedding. We travel so much anyway, and we are both pretty tired after all of the wedding planning. I know we'll go on a few trips this year together, and they will all feel like a honeymoon with Pierce.

The love of family and friends is, indeed, what this whole world is about.

101

After all of the wedding hoopla, we settle into my house in Gannon. I didn't know if Pierce would be comfortable living in my home. I told him the truth, that I probably couldn't ever sell it. I had too many memories from my kids that I couldn't part with yet. Their bedrooms still hadn't changed since the day they died. He has always understood this, and he has never tried to change me. I am so lucky to have found him.

There have been moments when I grieve, knowing that Pierce and I will never get to experience the joy of grandchildren. Pierce was never a parent, and sometimes that does bother him. He is such a loving man, and I know that he would have been a wonderful father.

He is the best husband a wife could ask for. He loves me, takes care of me, and respects me. He knows when I am caught in the past, and when to just give me some time alone. He knows when I need a shoulder to cry on, and when I need to talk. But I think the best attribute of his is his ability to listen. He just listens when I need him to. He doesn't offer suggestions, or give his opinion. He is quiet, and listens to me when I need him to just be there for me.

I continue to go to work every day at Harmon Publishing. We redecorated the study in our home so it works for Pierce's home office. He is thrilled to work from home now, or so he says. He doesn't have the hassles of personnel and annoying people. He is on the phone and computer all day, communicating with Gibson in Des Moines. He travels on average once a month for just a few days. We belong to the fitness center and country club in Gannon and just lead our merry little lives here now.

We go to Des Moines maybe once every couple of months for a weekend. We stay at a hotel and frequent the same places we did when Pierce lived there. He sold his home in Des Moines shortly after he moved to Gannon, so it feels like the ties have been cut from Des Moines for the most part.

At times I do worry that he won't like his new life in Gannon, and that he will up and leave me. But I don't know why I worry about it. Sometimes things just seem too good to be true. I know it's my protective coating, to never assume life is perfect and that it can't change in a heart beat.

It's happened to me before, and I caution myself not to get too confident.

102

I don't know why Pierce and I didn't marry sooner. I love being married to this man! He has completely acclimated to Gannon, and he just fits in here like a well worn glove. He has found a group of men that he plays golf with regularly, he will play a game of racquet ball at the fitness center periodically, and he has gotten involved at Sacred Heart as an usher and lector.

Everyone that meets Pierce adores him. He is modest, witty, charming, and has quite an out going personality. I'm sure people wonder what in the world he saw in me. He has pulled me back into the mainstream community life again.

I feel guilty leaving Pierce at home every morning when I go to Harmon to work. But he swears that it is a relief not to have to go into the office every day. He claims he gets more done now working from home. I just don't ever want Pierce to regret his move to Gannon, or resent me for making him leave Des Moines. I generally come home for lunch to see Pierce, or we meet out somewhere for a quick bite to eat.

We adapt to a nice routine of work during the week, weekend fun time, and we both still enjoy traveling, so we are continually planning our next trip. Thankfully, both of our bosses are quite flexible with our vacation time. They let us have at least four weeks off a year to travel. Tammie has never stopped being overly kind to me, and I am indebted to her forever.

Our married life together is bliss. The years go by quickly, and I just remind myself to live each day to the fullest, and appreciate the moment. Pierce and I don't dwell on events from the past, but rather try really hard to enjoy what we have created together.

Although he has never mentioned it, I know that he sometimes hears me crying at night. I just can't help it. My kids are never far from my mind, and I still, to this day, have wonderful dreams about them. I think I have relived every moment I ever had with Connor, Ryan, and Cassy in my dreams. My heart can be heavy for days at a time, and Pierce knows why. I don't like to talk about it much, and he knows that it's best to just give me some space for a couple of days.

Pierce goes out to the cemetery with me to visit the kids' grave sites. He even started bringing a little hand held clippers to touch up the long grass in the summer. He knows I like it to look good out here. We pray together by the headstones, and I still talk to the kids. I tell them all about our wedding and reception, and I keep them updated as to what Pierce and I are up to. I know they would have loved Pierce. Unfortunately, I can't update them on their dad anymore. Paul and I lost touch years ago, and I really don't know where he and Victoria are anymore. Our lives have marched on.

103

Finally, at the age of sixty, I decide to retire. I have worked for Harmon Publishing for the past eighteen years, and have put away most of my earnings. The money from the sales of my book was a big surprise, and I invested a good portion of that too. Pierce plans to retire next year, when he is sixty-two. We both just feel like it's time. We still have our health, and we want to continue to travel.

We talk about down-sizing to a town home, or something that just isn't so big. But we both know I'll never agree to it. I've lived in this home for thirty years, and I can't imagine being anywhere else. And Pierce has made it his home too. He loves taking care of the yard in the summer, and the back deck is our favorite place to relax and barbeque.

Pierce wants to go on an Alaskan cruise. Neither of us has ever been to Alaska. I want to go to Aruba in the winter. So we do both. We go on the cruise in August, when the whales are supposed to be migrating south. And we pick February to head south to Aruba. I have always needed to have a trip to look forward to. Half the fun of going is the anticipation of the upcoming fun.

The Alaskan experience is breath taking. The country side is more beautiful than I ever imagined. We took a three day land excursion and we were overwhelmed by the natural beauty of Alaska. I wouldn't want to be there in the winter, as I'm not a snow person, really. But I certainly appreciated the landscape.

The winter vacation to Aruba was my typical Caribbean heaven. I love the hot weather in the middle of an Iowa winter. To lie on the beach and at the pool all day every day is not tough for me to do.

Pierce and I both love to read, so we don't need much to entertain us but good books and good weather. We are so compatible, Pierce and I. I think back to when we met on the plane ride from Des Moines to Chicago many years ago. From the first moment we met, we had a connection. It was easy and comfortable. I can't imagine living out the rest of my life with anyone else.

104

Pierce has been done working at Gibson for years now, and we both love retirement. Absolutely adore it. We worried a little that we would be bored. That we would drive each other crazy at home all day long. But that hasn't happened. We are too busy to be bored. In fact, I feel like we're hardly ever home. We volunteer at the Gannon school, at Sacred Heart church, we exercise, we travel, we read, go to movies, go out to eat, take cooking classes, and still have good sex. I don't know if Pierce would say it's good, but at our age, I think any sex is probably good sex.

At seventy, I honestly don't know where the years have gone. My hair would be all gray by now if I didn't color it every five weeks. Vanity makes me hide the gray. Pierce looks stunning with his gray streaks, but I just look old. I struggle to maintain my weight, having gained more love handles than I would like to admit. But all in all, I am at peace with my body at the ripe old age of seventy.

We decide to celebrate twenty years of marriage (can it be twenty years already?) with a trip to Maine in the fall. They say the changing color of the leaves that time of year in New England is amazing. I've been to Maine, but never in the fall. We plan to go to Bar Harbor, see Acadia National Park, maybe go out on a fishing boat, for sure eat a lot of good sea food, and get a taste of the New England way of life. I can't wait. I've had our suitcases open on the bedroom floor for weeks now, throwing something in when I think of it.

We fly out of Des Moines on October third, a beautiful fall day even in Iowa. We get to Bangor, Maine and rent a car. The ride to the resort on the sea side is exhilarating. Pierce and I have discussed purchasing a winter home somewhere warm, but we can't seem to decide on where that should be. We both enjoy traveling to different locales too much, I think. To stay at one place for a few months every winter just isn't us.

We have a glorious week once again. I feel that Pierce and I were made for each other. God really was looking out for me, after all. He brought me the most compassionate man I've ever met. And this man breathed new life back into me when I needed it most.

At dinner that night, Pierce makes a toast to our twenty years together. He holds his wine glass up and is about to clink it against mine, and he just falls over out of his chair. I scream for help. Oh God, please don't take Pierce yet. I couldn't bear it.

Someone at the restaurant calls 911 and an ambulance arrives to get Pierce in minutes. He is lying on the floor, and I can't tell if he is breathing or not. So many kind people run over to help us instantly. But still, Pierce continues to not move. His eyes are closed, and I don't know what to do. I am a blubbery mess. I spilled wine all over my shirt when Pierce collapsed, and now I can't stop crying.

I get into the ambulance with Pierce and the paramedics. It doesn't take us long to get to the hospital. I haven't seen Pierce move yet, and I am so scared. He cannot leave me now. Not on our twentieth anniversary. The medical personnel are so nice. They whisk Pierce off somewhere at the hospital and they take me to a waiting room. Someone checks in on me every half an hour. Finally, they come to get me and say I can go see Pierce now.

I just know that he will be fine when I see him. I bet he forgot to take his blood pressure medicine this morning, that's all. I bet he fainted at the restaurant and he just needs to stay over night for observation. I know everything will be ok. My Pierce will be fine.

In Pierce's room a doctor is waiting for me. A very young woman, this doctor. She hardly looks like she could be out of college. I take Pierce's hand and notice that he is attached to lots of monitors and tubes. I can't stop my tears. He looks so handsome, like he should just open up his eyes at any given moment.

Young Dr. Glenn tells me that my Pierce has suffered a brain hemorrhage. That there was no way to predict it, nor was there any way to prevent it. Sometimes these things just happen. I tell her that Pierce is in great physical condition, that we exercise almost every day. That it is our twentieth wedding anniversary today, and that we are on vacation from Iowa. To please, please help him.

Dr. Glenn walks over to me and takes both of my hands in hers. "I have to be honest with you. Unfortunately, there is a very good chance that your husband may never wake up again. I need you to be strong, and to think about what choices you might need to make here in the next few days."

I am crushed. I sit down in the chair next to the bed, and I let the tears come. I am overcome with sadness, and I feel like this can't possibly be happening to me again. Why does everyone I love get taken away from me? It is not fair.

Dr. Glenn kneels down beside me, and asks me very gently if Pierce had a living will. She says I may need to decide whether or not to keep Pierce alive on the machines. That at this point, he is not showing any brain activity. Tomorrow that could change if the swelling in his brain goes down. But that it doesn't look real hopeful. I hear her, but I don't want to hear her. I look away, and close my eyes.

When I open my eyes, there is just one nurse by Pierce. She tells me that she can have someone take me to my hotel and I can get my things, if I'd like to spend the night here with Pierce. I think that is a great idea. I'm not leaving him here alone.

That night I attempt to sleep on a cot next to Pierce. Dr. Glenn says miracles sometimes happen, but not to count on it in Pierce's case. When a hemorrhage such as Pierce's happens so suddenly, it doesn't leave time for the brain to recover. I hold his hand, and I whisper to him that I love him. He already looks different to me. I don't want him to be in any pain, and the nurse promises me that he is not in pain. She encourages me to talk to him.

I watch the ventilator blow air into Pierce's lungs. I know that if we unplugged the machine, Pierce would not be able to breathe on his own. But how long should I keep the machine connected? What if he miraculously wakes up in two weeks? I've heard of these stories before. But I know that Pierce would not want to live like this. He does have a living will, and he states very clearly in it that he doesn't wish to be kept alive by machines. I have the same wish. It is no way to live. I would rather go be with my Creator.

But that means the end of Pierce, and I can hardly bear that thought. I call his brother Luke and sister Trinity, and we all cry together. I call Tammie, Courtney, and Abby, and no one can believe it. They all offer to fly out to be with me, but I don't want them to. I know what needs to be done. I just never imagined it would end like this for Pierce and I. Our years together were so important to me. Pierce gave me a second chance at life, one that for years I never thought I deserved. I can't believe I'll ever be happy again.

Dr. Glenn is patient with me, and she allows me four days with Pierce. I just need a little time to make sure that he isn't going to wake up on his own. Maybe brain activity will suddenly begin again. Dr. Glenn assures me that he is brain dead. Pierce's brother and sister have both given me their approval at doing what we all know needs to be done. But it is harder than I expected. It is so final, and so very sad.

The time has come, and I can hardly bear it. I am holding Pierce's hand and I watch as the machine is turned off. It takes under a minute for Pierce to die. I can't really even tell when he dies. I know he has been dead, really, since the hemorrhage occurred at the restaurant. But now it is final. My heart is heavy once again. Another funeral, another loss, more pain and heart ache. Will it ever end for me?

105

I talk to Pierce's brother, Luke, back in Chicago. We agree that he should be buried back in Chicago with his family. I fly Pierce's body back to Chicago. His sister, Trinity, greets me at the airport. She and I have always gotten along well. We hug and cry, and we are both still in shock. Pierce was seventy-two, but I swear he didn't look a day over sixty.

I withstand another funeral. I haven't attended a funeral since I buried my children and parents thirty years ago. I just couldn't bear it. Too many memories. The memorial service is beautiful, and my heart feels relieved that Pierce will be near so many loving family members in Chicago. Luke and Trinity are devastated by their brother's death. He was the leader of their family, and Pierce always kept everyone together.

Luke takes me aside after the funeral and tells me that he wants me to know that Pierce had his happiest years of his life with me. Luke says that Pierce told him many times over the past twenty years that I gave him meaning to his life. I am overjoyed to hear this from Luke, but it just makes me cry even more.

I loved Pierce so much. We both found one another when life had dealt us a bad hand. And we were given another try at love, and we did well with it. But Luke's words comfort me, because I do need to be reminded right now that Pierce did love me so very much.

Trinity has the family over to her house after the church service. We share so many good stories of Pierce. It is so sad that the love of my life is gone. I meet many friends and extended family members of Pierce's that I had never met before. Everyone held Pierce up on a pedestal.

We are all taken aback by his sudden departure. We feel bad that we didn't have time to tell him good bye, thank him for so many things, to let him know how much he was appreciated. But we know Pierce, and we know that he already knew all of these things.

I just wander around Trinity's home, wondering what I should do with my life now. I'm alone again. I watch all of the other couples, holding hands, hanging onto one another. They will go home tonight and talk about how horrible they feel for me. I am by myself once again. But this time I am an old lady, and I don't have much to look forward to, I'm afraid.

The flight back to Des Moines, and then my subsequent two hour drive to Gannon is intolerable. My Pierce is not with me, so life has no meaning to me anymore. I left Gannon less than a week before, so excited to be celebrating our twentieth wedding anniversary together. I return a widow.

106

I'd like to be able to say that at the age of seventy and a widow, I lived a full life. That perhaps I retired in Florida to a gated community with lots of activities and new friends. That I traveled the world, and came to terms with my twisted life. Although it would make for an upbeat story, I'm afraid to admit that it's not the way it happened for me.

The truth is that after Pierce died, I became depressed again. Dr. Hansen was no longer in Gannon, having retired years ago and left town. I was referred to a new doctor who gave me new anti-depressants. My physical health was actually in great condition, according to my doctor. It was my mental health that suffered.

After Pierce died, I felt a huge empty hole in my heart. For the past twenty years he was my companion and best friend. We did everything together. From the day I walked back into my house after Pierce's funeral, I knew that I was doomed. Any life that was left in me was whisked away. I felt old, and I truly had no purpose in my life. I was very lonely and I'm embarrassed to admit that once again, I didn't care if I lived or died. There were many days that I begged God to take me. I so badly just wanted to be with the people that left before me.

Tammie had since turned the management of Harmon Publishing over to Gretchen, although she still retained majority ownership. She and Jack were busy with their grandkids, the business, and traveling. I once told Tammie that she had the life that I yearned for. She never endured serious conflict or tragedy during her life time. Her marriage with Jack was stable over all these years. Her career with Harmon Publishing gave her an identity and a purpose to her life.

I did enjoy following Tammie's kids over the years in Gannon. Gretchen went to Iowa State University after high school and excelled in Journalism there. She worked for a few years in Chicago, got married, had two children, and moved back home to work with Tammie. Gretchen was Tammie's protégé, learning everything about the family business that she could to continue it in the Harmon name.

I often looked at Gretchen and wondered if she and Connor would have married, had he lived long enough. A few times over the years Gretchen would mention Connor to me. She had pictures of her childhood friend, and I know that she never forgot him. I loved Gretchen like a daughter, and was so proud of all her accomplishments.

Carli wanted out of Gannon as fast as she could get there. She was always the rebel in the Harmon family, never really satisfied with small town life. After high school she went out to California, much to her parents' dismay. Jack and Tammie worried about Carli all the time. But Carli insisted that she go to UC- Santa Barbara to study art. And she never left California.

I only saw Carli a few times over the past forty years. She came home for holidays every few years. Carli married and divorced a few different times, and I don't know if she ever found what she was looking for. But I will never forget her playing with my children when they were young. Carli had so much fun wherever she went. My kids loved her like a sister.

And Tammie's baby, Anthony, grew up to be a heart breaker. Gosh, he grew up strong and sturdy. I always told Tammie that Anthony could have been a movie star. He had that natural, good looking All-American face to him that the girls could not resist. He went to Iowa State as well, and graduated with a degree in Architecture. Anthony spent time in Europe studying the architecture of the historical periods, fell in love with an Italian woman, and lived most of his life in Florence. It pained Tammie to have him so far away, but she and Jack did go visit Anthony and his family every year.

I loved listening to Tammie's tales of her kids in their adult lives. It did take me a good decade to move past the heart ache of hearing about her kids' lives. But in the end, I couldn't bare to be removed from their lives, too. Whenever I thought of Gretchen, Carli, or Anthony, in my mind my kids should have been right there with them. The pain in my heart never, ever lessened over time for the loss of my babies.

I thought it would, I really did, over time. I was so sadly mistaken.

107

Tammie attempted to get me involved in her social activities in Gannon, but I had no interest. Many of the activities were for couples, and I felt like a third wheel. The card clubs, the ladies' red hat groups, the coffee get-togethers, were all just excuses for the ladies to brag about their kids and grandkids. These conversations left me silent and feeling worse than before I came. So I stopped going altogether.

I did become somewhat of a regional celebrity with my book, *The Unspeakable Truth*. But I was a one-hit wonder. Tammie and Pierce both encouraged me for years to write another story, but I just didn't have one in me. I had never written my journals for a publishing purpose to begin with. They were my private thoughts. That they became public consumption still surprises me when I think about it.

I weathered the storm of shock when people wanted to know if it was all true. I told them it was just a story. That the foundation was based on my life experiences, but that certainly some things had been added or exaggerated to make for better reading. That got me off the hook, and kept people wondering what parts were true and which parts were fictional.

Only Tammie, Pierce, and I knew that unfortunately, it was all the sad truth.

108

So that is the story of my life. I wish it could end as a feel-good story, but unfortunately, that just isn't the case. The past twenty years of my life have been long, boring, and quite frankly, depressing. I have only myself to blame for it, I know. I put no effort into making my last years interesting or exciting.

And so as I lie here on my death bed, waiting for death to arrive, I finally feel good. I am finally anxiously awaiting something. I am excited to be leaving this human existence and going to the next life. For there, I will finally be reunited with my three angels, Connor, Ryan, and Cassy.

I have waited fifty-one years for this. It's all I have ever truly wanted. The best years of my life were when they were alive, and those eight years have kept me going for a long time. I pray that God will allow me entrance into His kingdom. I pray that I haven't fouled up my life so badly that I would be denied access to the only three people that I have ever longed to be with.

The days here at the Charlton Hospice House go by quickly, really. I have nurses in and out of my room quite a few times a day. When I was living at home, I could go for days without coming into human contact. At least here I have people that talk to me. Although they are getting paid to do a job, they seem sincere and do take good care of me. And for that I am grateful.

To wait for death is interesting. It's almost torture, really. Knowing that death will be knocking on your door at any moment allows you time to think about it. For some people, that might be great. Some people might want this time to say their good byes, their apologies, make their amends, whatever. But for others like me, the waiting is just a prolonged death sentence. Hurry up, already.

I've made all of my arrangements. I struggled with what to do with my assets. Courtney died four years ago from breast cancer. That was an awful, awful way to go. And last year Abby died after a sudden heart attack. The only family that I have left are Abby's kids. I am leaving something for each of them. But what is really important to me is to leave something for *my* kids. Since they are not here, I can only leave something in their remembrance. I thought and thought this past year what they would have liked me to do for them.

My attorney will take care of matters after I die. I could have done it yet while I was still alive, but I just didn't want to. I decided to leave most of my assets to the children of Gannon. And any future assets from my book sales will go to the Gannon children.

That may mean money for the pediatric ward at the hospital, or the children's room at the fitness center, or the day care center, or playground. Whatever Gannon feels is needed for their children. I will die knowing that my kids' lives hopefully helped other children in our community.

The Final Chapter

In the middle of the night, my eyes pop open. I hear children's laughter. Who can be here in the middle of the night? I don't see anyone in my room. I close my eyes and again I hear the laughter. I keep my eyes closed this time, and then I see them. My babies! Connor, Ryan, and Cassy are here! They look so beautiful, just as I remembered them when they were eight, seven, and six. They are running, laughing, and I think they are calling my name.

"Kids, kids, I hear you! It's Mommy! I'm right here! Here I am!" I think I'm shouting. I feel my body beginning to get lighter. This is it, I know this is it. I'm dying. Right this very second, my earthly body is leaving me. I'm so excited I can hardly stand it. I'm going to be with my angels.

I hear the nurses come into my room, and I hear the beeping of the monitors next to me. They know I don't want machines to keep me alive. They know I welcome what is happening to me. And they will respect my wishes. They hold my hands and stroke my arms. The love in the room fills me with peace.

I open my eyes again and all I see is my hospital room and the nurses. So I close them again and there are my babies. My heart is filled with joy I can't even begin to explain. This is undoubtedly the happiest moment of my life, and the irony is that it is the final moment of my life. For this, I have waited decades.

My blonde babies run to me, they put their arms around me and I *feel* them. I actually *feel* them in my arms. I touch their hair, their faces, and instead of crying like I always do, I am laughing. I feel no pain, only warmth and love. God has answered my prayers. For this I have waited patiently for years. For this has been my only earthly want, to be with my children forever.

In the hospital room, I literally feel the tingling in my legs, my arms. My head is floating, and I am light as a feather. I feel my lungs take one, final big breath. And then that is it. There is no pain, only joy. There is no more hurt, only pure ecstasy. I follow my kids, and they are running ahead, looking behind them, gesturing for me to follow them. I think they have been waiting for me all these years as well. I go…I go to be with them forever. My wounded soul has finally mended itself.

Sometimes even to live
Is an act of courage.

—*Lucius Annaeus Seneca*

Jill Schafer Godbersen has a Ph.D. in Education from Iowa State University. Jill and her husband, Kent, live in Ida Grove, Iowa, with their three children, Reed, Carson, and Morgan. In addition to her first novel, *The Moment My Life Changed,* she also has children's books available at www.kidsrockbooks.com.

Made in the USA
Monee, IL
06 January 2022

86827323R00207